Samantha
The Women of Valley View

SHARON SROCK

ISBN: 0692410341
ISBN-13: 978-0692410349

THE WOMEN OF VALLEY VIEW SERIES

Callie
Terri
Pam
Samantha
Kate (coming fall 2015)
Karla (coming 2016)

DEDICATION

To Butch and Carol Vansickle.
Carol, you are stronger than you know.
Butch, you left us too soon. Be sure to save us a place.

ACKNOWLEDGMENTS

Thank you. How easily we say the words, how often we take the people we direct them at for granted. I have many people to thank for making Samantha's story a reality. I hope they each feel the love in those two words and the truth in the statement that I would not be writing acknowledgements for a fourth book if not for you. First of all, my Heavenly Father. I hope I found Your words and Your path for Samantha's story. To my husband Larry, our kids, the grands, and the great grands. You continue to make sacrifices and allowances for this crazy thing I've decided to do with my life. Your love and support mean more than I have words to express.

Steve Cash, Captain, Criminal Investigations Bureau, Chickasaw Nation Lighthorse Police. This story required a bit of law enforcement research. Steve's direction and input made my fictional cop seem just a bit more human. Any deviation from "normal" police procedure is totally mine.

Robin Patchen…All of Valley View values your honest red pen and loving insight. Thank you in big red letters!

Kaye Whiteman, Emily Whiteman, Sandy Patten, Teresa Talbott, Wanda Peters, Lynn Beck, Carol Vansickle, Anne Lee, Barbara Elis, Lisa Walker. My prayer partners, my advance readers, my support system…I'm so blessed to have you by my side on this journey. You are my women and I'm planning on keeping you!

Finally a big thank you to the most talented group of writers I know, the men and women of OCFW. Your continued support is beyond price.

CHAPTER ONE

Bobbie giggled as Samantha Evans made another swipe at her daughter's jacket and missed.

Sam rushed up the stairs in the wake of the almost-four-year-old. *How could those little legs move so fast?* Sam paused on the top step to suck air into her lungs. She wasn't out of shape. She climbed the stairs between the main house and her basement apartment a dozen times a day, but rarely at a run.

"Bobbie, don't..." The beep of the alarm as the front door opened told her that the warning came a breath too late. At least her daughter had a jacket on.

Sam hurried across the living room, dodged the large yellow lab racing out the door to join her daughter, and punched in the code to disarm the alarm before it woke the whole house.

She stepped out onto the porch, her arms folded across her chest in defense of the freezing temperatures. Snow from an early winter storm bordered the walk and the street in dirty mounds. Even

1

now, new flakes drifted to the ground, heavy and wet, from low hanging clouds the color of tarnished silver.

Bobbie tipped her face heavenward and opened her mouth in an attempt to catch one of the fresh flakes.

Nostalgia pulled Sam back to her own childhood. Her lips twitched up in a smile. *Iris and I used to do that.*

I guess every kid does. If the snow kept up, Sam would set a big bowl on the porch rail and collect enough to introduce her daughter to snow ice cream after dinner this evening.

A shiver yanked her from the daydream and left her teetering on the precarious line between amusement and parental responsibility.

Bobbie's sneeze shoved her off the fence. "Bobbie Lee Anne Evans, get back inside this house!"

Bobbie turned from her place on the sidewalk, a large, dripping newspaper bundled to her chest. "OK," she answered, obedient now that her mission was accomplished.

Sam ushered the child and the dog into the house, taking a quick step back when the dog gave a mighty shake to dislodge the moisture from her fur. Thankfully the two early morning delinquents hadn't been out long enough to get really wet. She closed the door, and looked down at her daughter's red cheeks and runny nose. She dug a tissue out of her pocket and wiped the chapped little nose.

Bobbie squirmed. "Ow."

"Baby, I'm sorry. I know it's tender." Sam stuffed the used tissue back into her pocket and frowned. "You need to stay inside today. Do you want your cold to get worse?"

Bobbie held up the plastic wrapped newspaper. "G-pa's paper."

The frown turned into a grin. Every day God gave Samantha a new reason to be thankful for her father's return after a ten-year absence. The relationship between granddaughter and grandfather ranked high on that list. "I'm sure G-pa appreciates you going out for his paper, but you need to stay inside for one more day. Do you remember what tomorrow is?"

Bobbie's face tipped up to hers, scrunched in concentration. She swiped at her nose with her sleeve. "Nope."

Sam stooped down to look into her daughter's sapphire-blue eyes. "Tomorrow is the first Saturday in December. We're going to—"

"Pick out our Chrissom tree!" Bobbie bounced in place. The newspaper fell at her feet as she stretched her arms wide. "Jem and I want a biggest one."

"Christmas," Sam corrected, grinning at the mention of her daughter's newest imaginary friend.

"I'm sure G-pa will be happy to fix that for you, but you won't be able to help if you're still so stuffy."

"OK." Bobbie shrugged out of the jacket and held it up to her mother. Without further argument, she retrieved the paper and turned towards the stairs.

Hampered by the bulky roll of newsprint and flanked by the dog, she hoisted her short, chubby legs up the steps to her grandfather's office.

Sam watched her daughter's careful progress and let her heart swell with maternal pride and gratitude. Bobbie was growing into such a beautiful little girl with her blue eyes and dark brown hair. The color of Bobbie's hair matched Sam's, but while Sam's hair was board straight and hung below her shoulders, Bobbie's framed her face in a tangle of natural curls inherited from her father. Louis Cantrell. Samantha shuddered, a sigh of relief coming from the farthest corners of her heart. Thank heavens the curls seemed to be all Bobbie had taken from his gene pool.

Thank You, Father, for blessing me so much. I don't deserve the child or the life You've given me. Thank You so much that Louis Cantrell will never be a part of my child's life.

Louis Cantrell watched the sprawling blue house from his car, which was parked across the street and three doors down. He blew a breath through the weave of his woolen gloves in an attempt to warm his frozen fingers, cursing under his breath when the resulting fog succeeded only in clouding the windows. The weather seemed to conspire against his surveillance in a combination of frigid temperatures and the wet snow coating his windshield. An occasional swipe of the wipers became a necessity, but the heater was a risk he refused to take. A quiet car at the curb could go unnoticed. A car with the engine running, generating clouds of exhaust, not so much.

The sun climbed over the trees, a fuzzy blur of light in the cloudy sky. If there was a God in heaven, warmth would follow. The worn vinyl seat crackled under his weight as he reached for his battered thermos. After a quick shake, he tossed the empty container into the floorboard already layered in unpaid bills and fast food burger wrappers. Just as well. He needed a bathroom, now, and the cold didn't help that either.

He burrowed further into his jacket and allowed his thoughts to wander while the morning dragged on.

4

Five years ago he'd been working in a filthy auto repair shop, a job so beneath him it still brought him shame, when fate finally dealt him a winning hand in the form of Samantha Evans and her kid sister, Iris. Their names brought a greedy smile to his face. Poor little lost girls. Deserted by their father, mother dead, struggling to make it on their own, and way too trusting for their own good. Winning their confidence had been a piece of cake and the money in their two savings accounts the hefty brass ring. But once Samantha told him she was pregnant, his plans to empty both accounts went south, and he'd gone west. He'd cleaned out Samantha's bank account and split for a sunnier climate without a backward glance, putting closed to that chapter of his life.

His fond dream of a high-rolling life in Las Vegas had since become a harsh reality. Thirty thousand dollars didn't go very far in today's world, not if you liked the noise and lights of the casinos. What he'd stolen from Samantha hadn't lasted through the first year. There'd been other cons as the years passed, more bad luck than good. He'd never known when to quit. Now he owed a serious amount of money to some very ugly people. A debt his silver tongue couldn't talk him out of. It was only a matter of time before they came to collect.

Seeing Sam on television with her rich writer daddy a few years ago had been like a big neon sign pointing him back to greener pastures. Knowledge he could put away for a rainy day. Well, it was drizzling, and Louis needed an umbrella. He'd been able to scrape together just enough cash to make the story he wanted to sell sound legit. If this con failed, his life wouldn't be worth the cost of a cup of hot coffee.

The white front door of the house opened. He grabbed a rag from his floorboard and wiped a patch of windshield free of condensation so he could have a better view. His patience was rewarded as a child skipped out of the house and down the two steps to the sidewalk. He squinted through the glass. My daughter? Hard to tell. He searched his heart for any twinge of fatherly feeling or recognition—and came up empty. No big surprise there. Louis had no use for kids, apparently even his own.

He picked up a book from the seat next to him, comparing the child on the sidewalk to the infant in the picture. Didn't really look the same, but knowing his sister's kids, he knew how much the brats could change over time. Kids...he shuddered. Except for the obvious pleasure involved in making them, he just didn't see the point. Why would anyone bring such a long-term complication into her life? Louis had the answer for any woman dumb enough to get herself knocked up. Cryogenics. Freeze the little brats at birth, feed 'em with a tube, educate them subliminally, thaw them out on their twentieth birthday, and send them on their way to fend for themselves. No muss, no fuss.

He watched the kid while grinning at his own clever idea. Today was the first of December. According to the birth certificate he had in his pocket, the one Samantha had so conveniently put his name on, his daughter would celebrate her fourth birthday in just a couple of weeks. Four years...a comfortable buffer against the three-year statute of limitations on any grand larceny charges Samantha might be tempted to pursue.

The child ran to the curb in a red jacket, her dark curls bouncing with each step. She stopped and turned back to the open door, stooping and clapping her hands, her mouth moving in laughter and words he couldn't hear. A huge blonde dog bounded from the house after her. The dog received a hug, and together they continued to the curb to collect the morning newspaper. Dog and child looked up suddenly.

Louis cut his eyes back to the door.

Any trouble identifying his daughter did not extend to recognizing the child's mother, his sweet Samantha. She still wore her dark brown hair in the straight style he remembered, just a little longer. She hugged a baggy sweater around her petite curves. Louis slid lower in the seat. He had fond memories of those curves and her innocent blue eyes. Samantha motioned the child back inside and closed the door.

Louis started his car. He had the right place. After forcing himself to wait a couple of extra minutes to make sure everyone remained tucked inside, he headed back to his cheap hotel room. There were plans to make and a family to reclaim. He hoped they would be as excited to see him as he was to see them.

Sam turned from the stairs and almost knocked her stepmother off her feet. She grabbed Terri by the shoulders and held tight until they both regained their balance. "Mom. I'm sorry. I didn't hear you come up behind me. Are you OK?"

Terri nodded, cringing visibly when the baby she held to her shoulder started to cry. "Oh man, I just got her back to sleep." She rubbed the back of the fussy child. "I've been up all night. Seth had a nightmare about a 'big bue monster,' so no more Aladdin for him for a while. His crying woke up Lilly, and her new teeth kept her up." Terri sighed and shifted the whimpering baby to her other shoulder. "Between my cold, a terrified two-year-old, and a teething one-year-old, I may never sleep again."

"Bless your heart." Sam peered over Terri's shoulder into the living room. "Where's Seth? Did you get him back to sleep?"

"Yes, or rather your dad did. He took him back upstairs a little while ago while I tried to pacify Lilly. I saw your father go into his office a bit ago. He was alone, so I'm guessing he got Seth back to sleep. I was trying to sneak up the stairs to put the baby back to bed so I could catch a nap before they both woke up again."

Sam held out her hands for the dark haired little girl. "Give her to me."

"Thanks." Terri's voice was a hoarse whisper. "But she won't stay with anyone. She even rejected her daddy earlier, and she never does that."

"Yes, but I'm her big sister. Sisters have special powers." Sam plucked the one-year-old from Terri's arms and shooed her away when the baby began to wail. "Go get some rest. She'll be fine as soon as you're out of sight."

Terri held up a hand. "Ah...ah..." She turned her head and sneezed into the sleeve of her robe, then brushed short dark hair from her face as she straightened. Her bloodshot eyes focused on Samantha. "Are you sure? I just need two hours."

Samantha transferred her little sister to her shoulder, rubbing the fretful child's back. "Disappear. I'll give

Lilly a cooking lesson while you catch a nap."

Terri yawned through a second sneeze. "Bless you."

Sam didn't answer. Ignoring the baby's efforts to reach for her mother, Sam took Lilly into the kitchen. She strapped the one-year-old into the highchair and gave her a cup of juice and a cold carrot from the crisper drawer.

Lilly focused militant blue eyes on her sister and swiped both items to the floor. She watched them fall before looking back to Sam with round eyes framed with spiky, wet lashes. Her bottom lip jutted out in a pout and the tiny chin quivered.

Sam sighed. "Those puppy dog eyes don't work on me. You're forgetting that I have one just like you." She retrieved the cup, washed off the carrot, and put both back on the tray, barely catching them before they hit the floor a second time. Hands fisted on her slender hips, Sam faced her baby sister. "Look, squirt, I'm bigger than you, I'm meaner than you, and I'm *way* more stubborn than you."

Lilly glared, hands poised to clear the tray a third time.

"Don't even think about it."

The baby's face lit with a sudden mischievous grin. "Luf Sam."

Battle of wills decided in her favor, Sam ruffled the baby's black curls. "I love you, too. Now let's cook breakfast."

Iris shuffled through the doorway with a loud yawn. "What are you two fighting about now?"

Sam singled out a cookbook with barely a glance for her fifteen-year-old sister. "Fighting implies an equal competition. The brat-ling never had a chance."

Iris pushed away from the doorframe and made her way to the refrigerator, pausing to drop a kiss on the baby's head. "Don't let her bully you, little sister. She's always been bossy." Iris poured a glass of milk, stirred in a healthy squeeze of chocolate syrup, and plopped down in a chair. With her elbow on the table, she placed her chin in her cupped hand and frowned at Sam.

Sam caught her sister's stare, looked down at her feet, and brushed at the hem of her tunic sweater. Finding nothing out of place, she again fisted her hands on her hips and faced Iris. "What?"

"What are you doing up, and dressed up, so early on a snow day? Did you forget about classes being canceled?"

Sam shook her head. "I didn't forget anything. I'm making brunch. We have just enough Thanksgiving turkey left in the freezer for a new quiche recipe I want to try. Patrick's coming over to play guinea pig." Sam turned away and measured flour and butter into a bowl. She bent to the task of combining the two ingredients into a suitable piecrust.

"They're back?"

"Late last night."

"That explains it." Iris made kissy sounds behind Sam's back.

Sam ignored her, frowning at the resistant lump of goo in her bowl. The useless pastry cutter clattered into the sink. There had to be a better way. She dusted the countertop with flour, dumped the dough from the bowl, and began to knead. "Ohhh..." She held up her dough-encrusted fingers. "Iris, come get this ring and rinse it off for me."

Iris joined Sam at the counter, slipped the chunky class ring off Sam's right index finger, and held it under the water. "You're the only girl I know who wears her boyfriend's class ring. It's so out dated."

Samantha glanced at her sister. "Not out dated, old fashioned and romantic."

Iris shrugged. "If you say so. Still, I'm not sure why you wear it if you won't wear it properly."

Sam continued to knead her dough. "I don't wear it *properly* because Patrick and I have an understanding. I won't be officially involved with him until he makes a commitment to Christ. We're both searching for our futures, and I think those futures will intersect down the road, so instead of the promise ring he wanted to buy, I agreed to wear his class ring on my right hand."

Iris shook off the water, slipped the ring onto her own finger, and held her hand up to the light. "What did you say he called it?"

The mound of dough received a satisfied pat. "It's an 'I love you, I'm not seeing anyone else, call it what you want' ring. Right now I'm calling it a friendship ring."

Iris rested her elbows on the counter, her chin on her fisted hands. "Can I borrow your car?"

Sam continued to knead her dough, frowning sideways at her sister. "Why?"

Iris's voice was dreamy. "I'm gonna go cruise the Sonic and see if I can find a hunky guy to run over."

Sam snorted.

"Hey, it worked for you. It could happen twice."

"In the first place, you're too young to drive. In the second place, I didn't run over him, I just tapped his bumper with mine."

"Still..." Iris tilted her head, her bottom lip between her teeth. "Can I ask you a question?"

Sam shrugged as she bent over her dough with a rolling pin.

"Has it been really hard?"

Sam needed no clarification. Her deal with—and feelings for—Patrick Wheeler were common knowledge. She supposed Iris's fifteen-year-old curiosity was common, too.

Still, Sam sighed when she turned to look at her sister. "Iris, sticking with my convictions this year has been the hardest thing I've ever done. As much as I love him, Patrick needs to have a relationship with Christ. He's been faithful to his church attendance over the last year. But I'm going to keep things locked in friendship mode until he makes a decision. I know God is dealing with his heart. I can see it on his face in every service."

Sam straightened from the perfectly shaped pastry crust, washed her hands, and retrieved her ring. She stared at it for a second before slipping it back on her finger. "I want a future with Patrick, but I have to consider Bobbie's future too. She'll benefit more from the Christian father I know Patrick can be, than just the good guy father he wants to be now."

Iris's eyes went round. "Father? He proposed? You won't even let him kiss you."

"Yeah, I know." Her mind flitted back to a single kiss shared on a shadowed porch swing. Even after almost thirteen months, the remembered feel of his lips on hers made her stomach churn with longing. "Trust me, I know. And no, he hasn't asked, but we have talked about it. We both want the same thing, but..."

12

Sam studied her sister's face. "I've made so many mistakes in my life. I just really want to do this right, you know? If I'm going to do that, I have to stick to my guns and trust God to bring things together in His time." She returned to her recipe but gave Iris a hip bump before she continued. "I've got plenty to keep me busy while I wait. God's given me more blessings than I deserve. It's a full time job taking care of what I already have."

"Do you ever worry?"

"About?"

"That maybe Patrick won't change in the way you want him too. I mean, it's been a year. What if he never accepts Jesus into his heart? As much as you say you love him, could you really walk away?"

Sam considered Iris's question in silence for a few seconds. She'd worked so hard to guard their physical relationship, but she had to be honest with herself. Her heart was long gone. What if an emotional involvement was just as bad as a physical one? Her heart pounded wildly at the possibility. "Iris, I don't even want to think about that. Let's just keep praying, OK?"

As if to remind the older girls of her presence, Lilly threw her cup and it clattered on the floor.

Sam began the delicate task of transferring the crust to a pie plate. She spared the baby a quick glance. "Sis, I just sent Terri and her cold back to bed. Since you're up, can you look after Lilly?"

Iris didn't even answer. She held her arms out to the baby. "Let's get out of here before the slave driver puts us to work."

Lilly placed a loud, wet kiss on Iris's cheek. "Luf

Ris."

Iris held her baby sister over her head and gave a quick twirl. "You're a smelly pain in my backside, but I guess I love you, too." She lowered the baby, holding her as far away as possible with stiff arms. "Very smelly...Sam?"

"Not on your life, girlfriend. I'm making breakfast."

"Oh, man." Iris continued to hold Lilly at arm's length. "You knew," she accused.

Samantha sketched an *X* across her heart. "Not a clue, but since she's in your hands, not mine...y'all have fun."

Iris looked from Lilly, to Sam, and back to Lilly with a sigh of resignation. "Come on, kiddo. We'll get your bath while we're at it. I don't think baby powder's gonna cover that up."

CHAPTER TWO

Patrick leaned back in his chair, his eyes fixed on his empty plate. "I would not have believed it possible."

Sam wiped a spot of jelly from the corner of her mouth before smiling at him. "What?"

"I've eaten so much turkey since Thanksgiving, in so many forms. I didn't think these words would come out of my mouth this morning." He motioned to the pie plate in the middle of the table. "May I have another piece of that?"

Steve Evans laughed. "Our Sam's turning into quite a cook. I think she should consider changing her major to culinary arts."

"You planning to foot the bill for two or three years in a fancy French cooking school?" Sam asked.

"If that's what you want," her father answered.

"No," Patrick and Sam answered together. The thought of Sam moving to France boosted Patrick's heart into overdrive. They shouldn't even joke about such things.

Samantha laughed. "No, thanks," she repeated. "I plan to be known far and wide as the cooking social worker. Chocolate-chip cookies will be my calling card, a spatula my tool to right the evils of the world for children everywhere."

"I don't know, Sam. That last batch of cookies you made *really* needed work." Iris forked up her last bite from her plate. "Since we're sort of snowed in, I think you should practice on those later today."

"You ate two dozen out of the last batch," Sam reminded her. "In one day."

"Just sacrificing myself for the good of the fam. Didn't want anyone getting sick."

Sam snorted. "Yeah, you keep telling yourself that, Miss Piggy."

Iris glared across the table. "Last I checked, I weighed ten pounds less than you."

"Not for long."

Terri appeared in the doorway. "Something smells wonderful."

Steve jumped up to pull a chair out for his wife. "You're looking a little better than you did earlier."

"I feel better. I can't believe I actually got two uninterrupted hours. Thanks, Sam."

"My pleasure, Mom."

"*Your* pleasure?" Iris protested. "I'm the one who had to deal with dirty diapers and bath time."

Sam frowned at her sister. "You put Lilly in bed with you, and you both went back to sleep."

"Yes, and she's still sleeping. A job well done."

"Brat."

"Bigger brat."

Terri ignored their bickering and smiled at Patrick.

16

"Did you guys have a good trip?"

"Other than too many snow-clogged roads on the drive home, yes. I always enjoy the opportunity to visit my grandparents in Florida, but it's good to be home." Terri nodded. "Not much better here, as you can see. When did you guys get back?"

"Last night. Mom has to work tomorrow."

"On a Saturday?"

Patrick nodded.

"I suppose anything that keeps her mind occupied is a God send. How's she dealing with the holidays so far?"

The question stung. A year after the fact, his dad's death was still a raw spot in his heart. Patrick shrugged. "She's fine, I guess. She's talking about looking for a full-time job after Christmas. We don't need the money, but I guess she needs to be busy." He reached out to squeeze Sam's hand and sent a wink in Bobbie's direction, eager to change the subject. "Her schedule didn't hurt my feelings. I missed my ladies too much to stay gone any longer."

"G-ma, looky." Bobbie held up a stuffed penguin.

"Oh, wow. He's almost as cute as you are. Where'd he come from?"

Bobbie clutched the animal to her chest. "He's a girl. Patty brought her, and Jem and I love her."

Terri looked at Sam. "Jem?"

Sam shrugged and motioned to the empty chair and cup next to her daughter. "They're studying about angels in her Sunday school class. Emma," she mentioned Bobbie's favorite and now abandoned imaginary friend, "has been replaced. Jem seems to be her personal guardian angel."

Terri winked at Bobbie. "Every girl needs a good angel watching her back."

The sound of the doorbell interrupted their breakfast conversation.

Steve wiped his mouth and pushed back from the table a second time. "I'll get it."

Sam stood as well. "Terri, I bought a wonderful new breakfast tea. It's steeping in the kitchen. Would you like a cup? I'll stir some honey into it for your throat."

Terri frowned. "I don't know, Sam. I've never been a big fan of hot teas."

Sam handed her cup across the table. "My cup's almost empty. Have a taste. If you like it, I'll make us both a fresh cup."

Terri sipped the tea, her eyebrows raised in surprise. "This is really good. I think I'll give it a try, thanks."

Sam nodded and took the cup as her father came back into the room.

"You have a visitor, Sam."

Sam looked up. Recognition slammed against her in a tidal wave of memory. Her smile of welcome became a grimace, the cup in her hand crashed to the table when her fingers went limp with shock.

Louis Cantrell was back.

She stared at the shattered cup, unable to speak, unable to catch her breath, unable to obey the voice in her head that ordered her to run. Fear, surprise, and shock held her paralyzed. She heard her family speaking, but their voices seemed distant beneath the roaring in her ears.

Her body finally shifted into gear. Her hand completed the move to pick up the broken glass, but she couldn't make her fingers grasp a single piece because of the tremors that engulfed her body. She sat hard and closed her eyes.

Images filled her head. His short, curly hair and slate gray eyes that seemed to turn blue when he was excited. The smile she'd fallen in love with...It couldn't be him...it looked like him, but it couldn't be... She took a quick peek. Her eyes clenched against the reality she couldn't, or wouldn't, accept. *It's my imagination playing tricks on me. I was thinking about him earlier and...*

Maybe when she looked again, he'd be gone.

"Sam!"

Sam heard Iris and shook her head. Not yet. She needed just a few more seconds to pretend her life was still normal.

"Samantha!" Her father this time. The urgency in his voice forced her eyes open.

She heard Iris's voice again. "Get him out of here."

Sam focused on her father and reinforced Iris's request. "Please make him leave."

Patrick crouched by her side. He took her hand. "Sam?"

Sam leaned forward and rested her head on his shoulder. Calm, steady Patrick. The man she wanted to spend her life with, a good man, not... "I need to get out of here." When she looked up, she couldn't see for the tears in her eyes. "Bobbie. Where's my baby?"

She swiped at her eyes and glanced around the table. Bobbie sat in her booster seat, arms clutched tightly around her new stuffed penguin. Her lips trembled beneath wide, frightened eyes.

Louis reached out to touch the child's hair.

"No!" Sam jumped to her feet, sending her chair

crashing backwards. She snatched up her daughter, penguin and all. "Don't you dare touch her!" Sam closed her eyes again and felt Patrick's arm encircle her waist.

"Babe?" he questioned again.

"Please," Sam begged. "Get him out of here." Daughter clutched to her chest, she raced from the room.

Patrick flinched as the door separating the kitchen from Sam's basement apartment slammed shut with enough force to rattle the house. *What...or better, who...?* He turned as Samantha's father asked that question aloud.

"Who...?"

Iris provided the answer. "Louis Cantrell." Her voice held a sneer. "You've got some nerve."

"Louis?" The name rocked Patrick back on his feet. He narrowed his eyes. "Bobbie's father, Louis?" Patrick looked at the man who had betrayed the trust of an innocent sixteen-year-old girl. Lied to her, slept with her, stole from her, and abandoned her once she'd told him she was pregnant. His jaw stiffened and drove tension into his neck and shoulders, his hands balled into tight fists at his sides, every protective bone in his body jumped to red alert.

Iris's eyes never left Louis, but she nodded. "Get out."

"You might want to take Iris's advice." Patrick circled the table, closing the distance between him and Louis. "You're not welcome here."

Iris snorted and pulled a cell phone out of her pocket. "Understatement. I'm calling the police."

"That's a great idea." Patrick took a few more steps. "Better call for an ambulance while you're at it."

Louis stepped into Patrick's personal space. "I didn't come here for a fight, but I won't run from one."

Patrick read dismissal in Louis's expression. It infuriated him. He rolled up on the balls of his feet. No way was he backing down from this slimeball. He leaned in. The stench of cheap aftershave assaulted his nostrils and threatened to make his eyes water, but he held his ground. "Good, because I'll be tougher to take advantage of than a defenseless sixteen-year-old girl."

Steve shouldered his way between the younger men. He stood eye-to-eye with Patrick and a shade taller than Louis, and his presence forced both of them to take a couple of steps apart. He ran both hands through his hair, his voice neutral when he finally spoke. "That's more than enough." His gaze moved to Iris. "Put the phone away."

"He..."

"I'll handle it, Iris."

Patrick had never seen Steve angry. Now, as he studied the hard blue eyes and the tight lips behind the older man's calm request, it was easy to see the temper slowly boiling to the surface.

Iris shoved the phone back into her pocket and slumped into her chair. She continued to stare at Louis, her blue eyes twin daggers of disgust.

Terri put an arm around the angry teenager. She whispered something into Iris's ear. Iris shrugged off the attempted comfort of her stepmother in an unusual show of temper.

Steve faced Patrick. "Patrick, I need you to let me deal with this."

The no-nonsense tone of Steve's voice diffused a bit of Patrick's temper and made him remember where he was. He took a single step back, shot a glare in Louis's direction, and met Steve's eyes. "Yes, sir." Steve nodded. "Do me a favor. Go down and check on Sam for me."

Patrick thought of Sam down there, alone and scared. That's exactly where he needed to be. He nodded.

Steve squeezed his shoulder. "Good man. I'll be down in a bit."

Louis's gaze raked across Iris and settled on Samantha's father. *Time for some serious sucking up.* He cleared his throat and took a step back. A low rumble from the corner drew his attention. The big dog he'd seen earlier rested on a fat cushion, eyeing him warily. Louis swallowed and forced his attention back to the older man standing in front of him. "Mr. Evans, I'm sorry. I didn't mean to cause such an uproar." Louis raised his hands in a helpless gesture. "I just need to speak to Samantha for a few minutes. It's really very important." He struggled to force some extra sincerity into his practiced words, depending on his polished façade to get him what he wanted. "I understand Sam's reluctance to speak to me. I understand that you probably don't want me here." He bowed his head. "I can't really blame you. I've made a real mess of things, but I've come to apologize."

Iris snorted again. Louis ignored her. He reached into his pocket and pulled out a bundle of papers. He held them out to Steve. "There's a check in there for ten thousand dollars. I know I owe Sam much more than that. This is just a down payment. I'm here to make things right between us. The other document is a copy of my daughter's birth certificate. It clearly lists me as her father. I want to be a part of her life." He stopped to take a deep breath before adding a mild threat. "I'll take whatever legal steps I need to take to make that happen. Regardless of my past mistakes, she's still my flesh and blood. I don't want her growing up without me."

"Oh, good grief," Iris muttered.

Steve cut his eyes to his younger daughter. "Iris."

Iris held her ground. "Dad, please tell me that you aren't buying any of this. He's a liar, and a thief, and a con artist, and he's not particularly good at any of it. How much skill does it take to swindle a sixteen-year-old?" She motioned to the corner where soft growls continued to come from the dog. "Even Angel knows he's trouble."

Louis dropped his gaze in an outward show of embarrassment. Internally, he looked for a way to *handle* Iris. The know-it-all brat would wreck everything if he didn't find a way into her good graces. *Kid, you better hope I never get the chance to shut you up.* He bit the inside of his cheek until he felt tears sting his eyes. He looked up, hoping the glow was bright enough to be noticed. "Iris, I know you don't have any reason to trust me, but please give me a chance. If I can talk to Samantha, I know I can make her understand. Tell me what I have to do to show you that I've changed."

Iris stood, planted her hands on the table, and leaned forward. "If you think those crocodile tears impress me, think again. I lived through your act once. If I have anything to say about it, I won't live through it again. Neither will Sam." She stopped as childish chatter filtered into the room.

Louis searched for the source, his eyes finally coming to rest on a walkie-talkie device propped on the china cabinet.

The older woman at the table started to rise, but Iris put a hand on her shoulder. "I'll check on them, Mom. You finish your breakfast. I've lost my appetite."

Louis knew her exit won him no points, but he was relieved to see her leave. He focused his attention back on Samantha's father with an exaggerated shrug. "I know I have a lot to make up for. Will you please get Samantha for me?"

Steve Evans met his eyes, finally accepting the papers Louis offered. "I'll take what you've said under consideration, but for now there's nothing you need to say to my daughter, and she obviously has nothing to say to you."

Louis's objections died in his throat when he met the cold steel of Steve Evans's eyes.

"Is there contact information in this paperwork?"

"No, sir, I..."

Steve fished a pen from his pocket and plucked a napkin from the holder in the center of the table. "Write down your phone number and where you're staying. Then you need to leave." Steve hesitated. His next words gave Louis a spark of hope. "I know what it means to want a second chance with your family. I promise someone will contact you."

CHAPTER THREE

Samantha paced, her child clutched to her chest.

How could he...? The question brought a new wave of shudders.

I can't believe this is happening. Louis Cantrell. Here. In her house. Questions of where he'd been and how he'd found them, or why, took a back seat in her mind to *what.* What could he possibly want? The fact that she could have had answers to her questions if she'd stayed upstairs was immaterial.

She bundled Bobbie closer. That slimy excuse of a man would never be allowed to touch her daughter.

Their daughter, a small voice whispered. She shrugged it aside. Surely, he'd given up that right a long time ago.

Bobbie squirmed in her mother's imprisoning arms. "Mama, le'me go."

Sam whispered assurances past her parched throat. "It's OK, baby. I'll take care of you."

"Sam."

She continued to pace the narrow space between the

sofa and the kitchenette of her basement apartment.

"Samantha."

Her step faltered.

Patrick moved towards her, his arms outstretched. "Let me take her for a while. You're squeezing the life out of her."

His words brought the world back into focus. Her grip relaxed. She placed a kiss on the dark curls of her daughter's head. "Sorry, baby." Sam stopped pacing to lower herself to the sofa, but she still clung to her daughter.

Bobbie took advantage of her mother's relaxed grip and snuggled the penguin to her chest. She leaned back to look into her mother's face. "Mama, was that a bad man?"

Sam closed her eyes and pulled her daughter back into her arms. How could...*should*...she answer that question? "Don't worry about him. He's just someone...someone I used to know. He surprised me, is all. I'm sorry I scared you."

Patrick sat beside her and gently pried Sam's arms loose. He scooted Bobbie onto his lap and tickled her belly with the stuffed penguin. "Did you give it a name?"

"Frosty."

He tickled her again. "Frosty is a snowman, goofy girl."

Her sing-song laughter filled the air. "Frosty the penguin ..."

The interaction between Bobbie and Patrick brought a fresh tremble to Sam's lips. *This is what I want for you, baby.* Her gaze strayed back to the door at the top of the stairs. Her heartbeat thudded loudly in her ears. *Not that!*

Patrick planted a kiss on Bobbie's forehead. "I need you to take Frosty to your room for a while so I can talk to your mommy."

"A grown-up talk?"

Patrick chuckled. "You're a little bit big for your britches this morning. Yes, a grown-up talk."

Bobbie scrambled out of his lap, stopping to pat Sam's knee. "Jem says not to be scared."

"Really?"

Bobbie nodded, her earnest blue eyes fixed on her mother's face.

"Tell Jem I said thanks."

"OK." Bobbie raced for her bedroom, chattering to Frosty and Jem. The door slammed shut and immediately cracked back open. "Sorry." The door closed with a soft click the second time.

Sam sat back in the cushions, limp with the aftereffects of nervous adrenaline. Her eyes drifted closed on a deep breath as her heart rate slowed to its normal rhythm. She opened her eyes to stare at the ceiling and caught a glimpse of Patrick's concerned expression in her peripheral vision.

He took her hand. "I'm still here."

She hadn't realized how cold her hands were until he held one in his warm grip. She turned and melted against him. When his arms came around her, she snuggled into his embrace and wept.

Chick Malone checked his watch as Louis strode down the front steps of the house. The elapsed time and the slumped shoulders did not spell a successful start to their endeavor. Well, Chick corrected, *Louis's* endeavor, since Louis had no idea he was being watched. But Chick had as much at stake in the outcome of this con as Louis did.

I've got a real bad feeling about this. The thought of failure made his leg throb. He rubbed the damaged muscle and delivered a whispered pep talk to himself. "Relax, man. It's too early in the game to be thinking about failure. Remember, if the kid can't get the job done, you can. There won't be any need to try and explain a second botched job to the boss. Take a deep breath. Everything's cool."

Patience, Chick reminded himself. *But not too much.* He was here to safeguard the boss's investment and to keep Cantrell focused on the goal. He'd give the kid a couple of days to work out a plan. If he failed, well, Chick was an expert at persuasion.

Satisfied for the time being, he turned the key in the van's ignition. The uncooperative vehicle sputtered to life while Louis fumbled for his keys a few yards away. *No need to hang around being all obvious.* He knew where Louis was staying, and now he had the address for the skirt and her kid. He pulled the van from the curb, unconcerned about Louis seeing him. They'd never met, and the plain white van provided a great neutral cover. If he left now, the kid wouldn't get spooked.

Chick turned the corner, watching in the rearview mirror until Louis disappeared from sight. He followed his advice and pulled in a deep breath, exhaling slowly. Time to explore his surroundings and find some lunch.

"Shh, babe. It'll be all right." When his words of comfort failed to stem the tears, Patrick gave up on words and simply held on. *I love her so much.*

The idea no longer gave him pause. Love at first sight was a cliché he'd never put any stock in. He gained a controlling interest in the idea, however, the moment Samantha Evans backed her Mustang into his truck in the Sonic parking lot. The second her blue eyes met his, round with shock and concern, every other woman faded into the background. Their yearlong battle over faith—Samantha's Christian beliefs versus his lack thereof—had done little to deter his feelings.

He knew she prayed for him. She knew he loved her. She'd refused a promise ring, choosing to wear his class ring instead. They dated each other exclusively. They shared time with each other's families. He loved her daughter with his whole heart. He'd haul her to the courthouse tomorrow if he could, but Sam refused to take their relationship to the next level until Patrick made room in his heart for a God he wasn't sure he believed in.

The death of his stepfather twelve months earlier had driven that wedge of unbelief a little deeper. Despite his faithful church attendance over the last year—the product of a promise made to Dave Sisko—he still struggled with the concept of being *saved*.

Sam stirred in his arms, and Patrick snapped back to the present. He dropped a kiss on the crown of her head. "Better now?"

Sam nodded against his shoulder.

"Can you talk to me?"

Her sigh trembled in the air between them. Sam shifted and glanced at Bobbie's bedroom door, her answer the barest whisper. "Bobbie's father."

Patrick nodded. "I got that much."

He took a few seconds to arrange what he knew of

Samantha's history in his head. Iris and Samantha's father, Steve Evans, had bailed on his family thirteen years ago, choosing a drug habit over his responsibilities as a father and husband. Ten years later, their mother, Lee Anne, had died in an auto accident. Sixteen years old, afraid of being separated from her little sister, Samantha had taken on the responsibility of making a home for both of them. She'd been an easy target for a con man like Louis Cantrell. Samantha had given her trust to the wrong person. She'd paid for that mistake in both cash and blood. Abandoned again, inheritance stolen, a baby on the way.

Patrick had no defense against the loathing that shuddered through him. A man who took advantage of a woman—a teenager—wasn't a man, in his book. If Terri and her friends hadn't come along to help the girls when they had, they wouldn't be sitting here today.

"How...?"

Sam shook her head. "I don't know."

They both looked up when a knock came from the kitchen side of the apartment door. Patrick's heart ached at the look of fear that flashed in Sam's eyes.

"Who is it?" she asked.

"It's me." Steve's voice filtered through the closed door.

Sam sat straight, wiping her eyes with the sleeve of her sweater. "Come on down."

Steve pushed the door open and came down the stairs, a grim expression etched on his face. "Sweetheart, tell me what I can do to help."

Sam shook her head. "Is he gone?"

"For now."

"For now?"

Steve sat in a chair that faced the sofa. He clasped his hands, rested his elbows on his knees, and leaned forward. "Just for now, I'm afraid. He wants to talk to you, and you're going to have to oblige him." He hesitated for a moment. "He wants to see his daughter."

"Not in this lifetime."

Steve lifted a shoulder. "He said he wants to be a part of her life."

Samantha snorted. "He's got no interest in Bobbie. The only thing Louis Cantrell is concerned about is how much trouble he can cause."

Steve pursed his lips. "Maybe so." He laid a stack of folded paperwork on the small coffee table separating him from his daughter. "He left these for you."

Sam made no move to pick up the documents. She looked from the papers to her father.

He answered her unspoken question. "A check for ten thousand dollars and a copy of Bobbie's birth certificate. The check is a down payment on repaying what he stole from you. The birth certificate names him as Bobbie's father. He threatened legal action if you deny him his rights."

Sam leaned forward, her blue eyes fixed defiantly on her father's face. She picked up the papers and ripped them in half with a quick motion. She stacked the pieces in her hand and tore them in quarters for good measure. They fluttered to the floor from her open hands. "No."

"Samantha, you need to at least listen to what he has to say."

Sam pushed to her feet. "No. Not just no, but over-my-dead-body *no!*" The last word bordered on panic.

Patrick reached for her, but Samantha brushed him aside. He ran his fingers through his hair, more than a little frustrated. Not at her refusal of his comfort, but at the knowledge that there was so little he could do to make this situation better.

She faced her father, hands on her hips. "*You* need to listen. He can't come here after four years and lay claim to the daughter that I've raised without his help. It doesn't work that way. He lied to me. He stole from me. *He* walked out on *me*...and his child. As far as I'm concerned, there are some things that don't deserve a second chance."

Steve's face lost some of its color at her vehement words. He sat back with an indrawn breath, his head bowed over his clasped hands.

Sam stopped her rant, rushed around the coffee table, climbed into her father's lap, and buried her head in his shoulder.

"Daddy, I'm so sorry. I didn't mean you. I wasn't thinking about you." Her next words were barely audible. "I'm scared."

Steve tightened his arms around his daughter. "It's all right. You didn't hurt my feelings. You just made me realize how alike Louis and I are." He tilted her face up to his. "You gave me that second chance, baby. You and your sister. The life we've made since you allowed me back in, it means the world to me. Is it possible he's looking for the same thing?"

Patrick listened to the conversation with guarded interest. Steve couldn't be suggesting that Sam allow that lowlife back into her life...into Bobbie's. Yes, Sam needed to talk to him but the thought of anything more than that tightened his chest.

Sam struggled to her feet, her voice a little calmer when she spoke again. "Stop it! I don't believe that, and I don't trust him. I would never compare you to him. Louis will never be a quarter of the man you are." Sam's words restored the breath to Patrick's lungs. She motioned to the torn pieces of paper on the floor. She directed her next comment to Patrick.

"You're a lawyer. Can he do this?"

Patrick shook his head. "I'm a law student with two years to go." He pulled his hands down the length of his face. "Family law isn't my field of study. But, if it makes a difference, I agree with your father. You're going to have to talk to him."

When Samantha started to object, he interrupted her. "Babe, I don't like it any more than you do. But if you don't know what the man wants, how can you fight him?"

Sam objected anyway. "I don't need to talk to him to fight him. He stole money from me. He was a twenty-three-year-old man who slept with a sixteen-year-old girl. I know for a fact that both of those things are against the law. He wasn't around for me to press charges against four years ago, but I don't have a problem pursuing it now."

Patrick stopped her. "It's not gonna be that easy. I'm not qualified to answer your specific questions, but I can promise you there are all sorts of legal ins and outs that are going to come into play here. I think you should listen to your dad. Talk to Louis and find out what he wants. I'll go with you. In fact, I insist on going with you."

Samantha came around to the sofa, stood on her tiptoes, and kissed Patrick's cheek. "I may take you up on that, but not just yet." She disappeared into her bedroom, returning a few seconds later with her cell phone. She sat on the edge of the sofa and began scrolling through numbers in her directory.

Patrick sat beside her "Who are you calling?"

"Someone who can answer my questions. I refuse to go into this battle empty handed." She waited for the phone to be picked up on the other end.

"Pam, its Samantha. Is Harrison in his office today?"

Samantha sat on her sofa dressed in hunter green leggings and a long striped sweater. She had her legs folded up underneath her, a Bible open in her lap, and a fingernail—gnawed down to the quick—in the corner of her mouth. A glance at her watch told her she had an hour until their appointment with Harrison. Patrick would be back in about thirty minutes. He and her father were both going with her to the lawyer's office.

Sam worried the fingernail a little more, jerking it out of her mouth when she drew blood. She watched it bleed for a second or two then stuck it back in her mouth. Her attention returned to the open Bible and the verse of the Psalm she'd just read:

I have set the Lord always before me: because he is at my right hand, I shall not be moved.

She closed her eyes, her whispered prayer loud in the quiet room. "Oh, Jesus, what do I do? I've never felt like this before. I thought I was done with bad things. I know how childish that sounds, but You've made my life so much better than I deserve over the last couple of years. You've spoiled me. I've forgotten how to deal with adversity."

She stared at the wall with unfocused eyes, allowing the full impact of that truth to absorb. Life had been nearly perfect since Callie and her friends brought their father back into their lives. Even better this last year with Patrick sharing most of it. She'd begun to believe in the dream of happily-ever-after. She'd thought, until this morning, that she had a handle on her future. *Did I get it all wrong?*

Her prayer resumed on a sigh. "Please go with us today. Help me remember that You are at my right hand. That You'll never forsake me. That I can do all things through Your strength. Mostly that You love me, and that nothing comes to me without first going through Your hands."

Samantha felt the cushion beside her shift. She opened her eyes. Bobbie, fresh from a nap and dragging the stuffed penguin by the ends of its blue scarf, climbed to sit next to her. The almost four-year-old patted her mother's open Bible. "Read to us, Mommy."

Sam put an arm around her daughter and read the Sixteenth Psalm aloud. The words caused fresh tears to run down her cheeks.

Preserve me, O God: for in thee do I put my trust. O my soul, thou hast said unto the Lord, thou art my lord.

She looked up from the page to find her daughter's worried blue gaze locked on her face, a small frown embedded between her eyes. Bobbie reached up and ran a finger through the fresh tears.

"Mommy?"

Sam closed the Bible and gave Bobbie a quick squeeze. "I'm OK. Why don't we practice your memory verse instead?"

Bobbie clapped her hands. "He will order His angels to p'tect you." The room echoed with her delighted enthusiasm. "Jem and I like that verse."

Sam managed a smile. "You do?"

"Yep. Jem says that's his job. To p'tect me." Bobbie tilted her head. "What's p'tect mean?"

Sam smoothed black, curly hair away from Bobbie's face and kissed the tip of her nose. "Protect, baby. It means to take care of you." She stared down into the blue eyes, so much like her own. *I'll never let anything hurt you.* "That's my job, too."

They both looked up as the door at the top of the stairs creaked open.

Terri peeked through the opening. "Seth is having a snack. Is there anyone down here who'd like to join him?"

Sam closed her eyes as Bobbie scrambled off the sofa and pounded up the steps.

I'm scared, Father, not for myself, but for my child. Please take that fear away and help me replace it with the wisdom I need to fight this battle.

CHAPTER FOUR

Samantha followed Harrison's secretary down the short hallway to the lawyer's private office. Her hands were clammy with sweat, and she wiped them on her pant legs.

The secretary seated Samantha, Patrick, and her dad in front of the lawyer's desk. "Mr. Lake is on the phone in the other office. He'll be with you shortly." She retreated, closing the door behind her with a soft click.

Sam immediately got up to pace. Nervous energy and anxiety fueled her restless need for motion. She walked back and forth, one hand on her hip, the other slipped beneath her long hair to knead neck muscles knotted tight with tension. *It'll be OK. I was too young and stupid to see Louis for what he was five years ago, but I'm neither of those things this time. I'll...*

Harrison opened the door and stepped inside, pausing on the way to his desk. He held his arms open, and Sam walked into the comfort he offered. Harrison Lake, Attorney-at-Law, more honorary uncle than

37

friend, enveloped her in a comforting hug.

"We'll fix this." He released her and led her back to her chair. "Steve, Patrick. Quite a turn of events this morning. Tell me what happened."

Samantha held Patrick's hand while Steve recounted the morning's conversation with Louis Cantrell. "He was very polite. I told him that I needed some time to talk to Sam. He left the check for ten thousand dollars, a copy of Bobbie's birth certificate, and his phone number and said he'd wait to hear from us."

Harrison nodded. "You believe him?"

Steve shrugged. "I don't know what to believe. He seemed sincere. But, I'll have to defer my opinion to Sam's experience. She's the only one with any firsthand dealings with the man. It's certainly an easy matter to verify the validity of the check. As far as the birth certificate, Bobbie's paternity hasn't ever been a question. It's not the fact that he has it, it's how he intends to use it."

Harrison nodded. "Let me see the documents."

Steve and Patrick looked at Sam. Samantha opened her purse and pulled out a handful of ragged paper. She leaned forward and laid them on the green desk blotter in front of Harrison.

At Harrison's raised eyebrows, Sam sat back and crossed her arms. "I don't want his money, and I don't care what he wants where Bobbie is concerned."

Harrison raked the torn papers together and dropped them into his trashcan. "What do you want, Samantha?"

"I want him arrested. Today."

The lawyer sat back with a nod. "Tell me why."

Samantha fought to keep her jaw from dropping in

disbelief. "You know..."

"Humor me," he requested. "Pretend I don't know the story. Tell me your side of it. You can give me the abridged version."

Sam shook her head but complied with his request. Her clipped, toneless words echoed in her ears as she described the nightmare she and Iris had lived through. "After Mom died in the accident and we found out that our foster father was a letch, we took Mom's insurance money out of the bank, bought a car, and ran away. We rented an apartment, paid a whole year's rent up front, put the rest of the insurance money in the bank, and settled in to wait for my eighteenth birthday."

She closed her eyes against the painful memories. "When the car began to act up, I took it to a garage for repairs. Louis was the mechanic who worked on it. He took advantage of me, physically. When I told him I was pregnant, he vanished, along with the money from my savings account. Thirty thousand dollars." She leaned forward. "I want him in arrested."

Harrison leaned back and folded his hands on the desk. Sam watched his gaze track from one of them to the other. He took a deep breath.

"Samantha, before I begin, I want you to know that I'm on your side, but I can't lie to you. Arresting Louis Cantrell isn't going to happen."

Samantha surged to her feet. "What? But he—"

"Sit down. I'll do my best to explain."

She looked at her father and then cut her eyes to Patrick. "You knew?"

Patrick shrugged. "I suspected." He reclaimed her hand. "Sit down and let Harrison explain the laws to you."

Sam jerked her hand away and stared at Harrison. "How can he not go to jail? I was sixteen. He was twenty-three. He got me pregnant and stole thirty thousand dollars from me."

Harrison steepled his hands on his desk. "Let's deal with the physical part of your complaint first. Did he threaten you? Did he force you? Was he in any sort of position of authority over you? Father, teacher, boss, coach, or pastor?"

Samantha frowned and shook her head.

The lawyer raised his hands. "Then the physical aspect of your relationship was unfortunate, but not illegal. The legal age of consent in Oklahoma is sixteen. It's scary, but a sixteen-year-old girl in this state can choose to engage in sexual activity if she wants. Age difference does factor into it, but a sixteen-year-old and a twenty-three-year old, four years after the fact..." Harrison shrugged. "He wouldn't even get a slap on the wrist."

Sam swallowed around a lump in her throat. "The money?"

Harrison shook his head. "Grand larceny carries a three year statute of limitations in this state. He's home free on that one as well."

"Well that's just great." Sam pushed up from her chair again, her jaw clenched so tight she had to make a physical effort to loosen it before she could continue. "Everything he did to me, everything Iris and I suffered because of him, and he gets off scot-free. I can't believe this!"

"I'm sorry, Sam. The legal system doesn't always seem fair, but it's all we have to work with. We can order a paternity test and sue him for child support—"

Samantha cut him off, eyes narrowed. "I don't need a test to know who Bobbie's father is."

"Take a breath, sweetheart. That's not what I meant. The court will need a test to justify a child support claim."

She motioned to the trashcan next to Harrison's desk and the shredded papers inside. "If I wanted his money, I wouldn't have torn up his check." Sam stopped behind her chair, leaned forward, and braced herself against its leather back. "Can we at least take steps to keep him away from Bobbie?"

Harrison's tone was solemn. "He has a right to see his daughter, Sam. We can use his past actions against him to stall, and we can request limited and supervised visitation, but he will get visitation rights. It's just a matter of time."

Sam closed her eyes as her last line of defense melted at her feet. She walked to the door in a daze. "Thanks for being honest, Harrison." She opened the door, her next comment a mere whisper. "I guess you really do reap what you sow." She walked out, allowing the door to close softly behind her.

Patrick stood to follow her.

Steve stopped him. "Let her have some time, Patrick. She's got a lot to digest." Sam's father turned to Harrison. "What's our next step?"

Harrison shook his head. "That depends on what he wants. Unfortunately, Sam's going to have to talk to Mr. Cantrell before we can know where to go from here. My immediate suggestion? Take your own advice and let her have some space. Samantha's one of the most level-headed young women I know. If you'll give her time to think this through, I think she'll make good choices once she gets over the initial shock."

He turned his attention to Patrick. "I'm going to give you some fatherly advice about women. Stick close and hang tight. Sam's going to have to work through this. Don't take anything she says too much to heart over the next few days. Be there for her, but don't push. I know how much you want to protect her, but this is her battle. She's the general. You guys"— Harrison motioned to include Steve—"are the support troops for this engagement."

Steve and Patrick both stood and shook hands with Harrison over his desk.

"Thanks for meeting with us on such short notice," Steve said.

"More than my pleasure. Let Samantha know that I'm here for her anytime she needs me. Have her call me once she speaks to Mr. Cantrell. We'll work out a strategy once we know what he's after."

Both men stepped through to the reception area. It was empty.

"She took off," Patrick said.

"Sam likes to walk when she's troubled," Steve told him. "She has her cell phone. She'll be fine."

Patrick ran his hands through his hair. The same Florida sun that had given him a winter tan had baked his scalp right through his blond hair. His scalp itched as it peeled. "I don't like this, Steve. It stinks in more ways than one."

"Agreed." Steve clapped the younger man on the back. "Let's go back to the house so you can pick up your truck. If Sam's not home in an hour or two, I'll track her down."

Patrick rode back to the Evans home in silence, trying to take his cues from Sam's father without much success. *I should be with her.* The snow had stopped and the sun had come out. For now, the fickle winter temperature hovered around the fifty degree mark. She'd worn a light jacket for their visit to Harrison's office. One that would be of little use to her if she stayed out too long. The early December weather would bottom out again once the sun started to set.

"We should look for her."

"Not just yet. She needs to work this out for herself. I speak from experience. You can trust her, but you can't rush her." Steve pulled the car into the driveway. "Do you want to come in and wait for her?"

Patrick shook his head. "No. I've got my own thinking to do." He looked at his watch. It was just after two. "Call me if she's not home by five. It'll be getting dark by then."

"Will do."

Patrick raised his hand in farewell before climbing into his truck and starting the noisy diesel engine. He drove aimlessly for several miles. He stopped at the Sonic for a soda and then found himself, unintentionally, in front of the gym that squatted behind Valley View Church. The parking lot was empty except for Sisko's truck.

Dave Sisko, just "Sisko" to most everyone, was the youth pastor of Valley View Church. He'd been working with Patrick over the last year, trying hard to show him the value of having a personal relationship with God. At the sight of the truck, the events of the long day settled into a hard lump in the pit of Patrick's gut. "Let's just see what religious platitudes Sisko can spread over this situation." He slammed out of his vehicle and headed into the gym.

The main area of the cavernous building was empty and dark, but loud music pounded from the kitchen. Patrick stepped through the swinging doors just as Sisko, his back to the room, straightened from the large deep freeze.

Sisko made some notes on a clipboard and bent to peer back into the depths of the appliance.

Patrick cleared his throat loudly.

Sisko turned, his blond hair hanging in his face, the corners of his blue eyes crinkled in smile lines. He reached to toggle off the CD player. "Hey, Patrick. I didn't expect to see you today. When did you get back to town?"

"Last night."

"Wow, quick trip." He studied Patrick with a grin. "The Florida sun agreed with you. You got a tan while you were gone. Hope you guys had a great time."

"It was OK."

"Good. You can tell me about it while I work." He motioned to the open freezer. "I'm doing an inventory for the New Year's lock-in supplies. Halloween pretty much wiped us out." He offered the clipboard to Patrick. "Grab a pen. You can write while I count."

Patrick refused the clipboard, folding his hands behind his back. "That's not why I'm here."

Dave Sisko pulled himself up to his full five foot eight. His smile of welcome changed to concern. "OK. What's up?"

Patrick opened his mouth then snapped it shut. He had Sisko's full attention, but he didn't know where or how to start. He shoved his hands into the pockets of his jeans and stared at the floor for a few seconds. When he finally looked up, he knew there was a frown growing on his face.

"Sam's a Christian, right?"

Sisko crossed his arms and nodded.

"God loves her?"

Sisko nodded again.

"Do you and God talk?"

He nodded a third time. "Yeah, Patrick, it's called prayer. What's up with you?"

Patrick didn't bother with an answer. "You two need to get your stories straight."

The youth pastor held up his hands. "Whoa, bud. You need to take a deep breath and a giant step back. What's your problem this afternoon?"

"My problem? I'll tell you. I am sick to death about hearing how much God loves us, how God takes care of us because we're His children. I *hear* it, but all I *see* is indifference on His part. My dad died, Alan died. Both unanswered prayers. Now He's letting Sam's life get jacked up." He crossed his arms and met Sisko's gaze with a stony stare. "I gotta tell you, I'm not feeling a lot of love. If this is fatherly love, I don't need a father, here or in your precious heaven."

Sisko's eyes widened. "Patrick, I can tell you're upset about something and spoiling for a fight, but you need to check some of that attitude. Now, what happened to Sam?"

Patrick took a deep breath, shoved his hands back in his pockets, and spilled the whole ugly story. He began with breakfast and ended with their visit to the lawyer's office. When he finished, he scrubbed at his face with both hands. "So, Sam's off somewhere, by herself, trying to come to terms with what Harrison told her. I don't know where she is, and even if I did I don't know how to help her." He glanced at his watch. "If I haven't heard from her or Steve in the next thirty minutes, I'm gonna start driving around to see if I can find her."

Patrick was only a little calmer when he circled back to his original theme. "How can a God that's supposed to love us let stuff like this happen?"

Samantha walked and searched for answers to her questions. Not about God's love for her—she believed in that completely—but about the way life cycled around and what she was going to do next. Her parting words to Harrison echoed in her ears. She knew she was forgiven. But a murderer might get saved in prison and sit on death row, pardoned by God but not the public, dealing with the consequences of his past life until his punishment ran its course. *Is this a consequence or a punishment for the life I lived? How do I tell the difference?*

She stumbled on an uneven crack in the sidewalk. The winter light was fading along with the sun's warmth. Her arms folded across her chest as she hugged the jacket a little tighter around her. It was time to pull the plug on the pity party and get home to her daughter. Samantha dug her phone out of her pocket and turned it on. There were a dozen missed calls from Patrick. As she erased them one-by-one, a niggle of joy bloomed in her heart. Saved or not, Sam was grateful for his steady presence in her life. *I probably don't deserve to be loved by someone so wonderful.* The prayer that came on the heels of that thought was more than a year old and automatic. *Jesus, please touch Patrick's heart.* She tapped in her father's number.

"Sam. I was about to send out the hounds." Her father's voice sounded anxious.

"Sorry." She looked at the sign on the corner. "I'm at Washington and Elm. Can you come pick me up?"

CHAPTER FIVE

Patrick's question hung in the air. Sisko frowned down at the clipboard, leaving Patrick to fume in the heavy silence. "Can't answer that one, can you? Know why? 'Cause there isn't an answer. It's all smoke and mirrors designed to make us poor, simple humans feel better. Truth be told..." He pursed his lips and shook his head. "We're on our own."

Sisko pinched the bridge of his nose between two fingers before running his hand down the length of his face. "You can't really believe that. Is that all you've gotten from the time we've spent together over the last year?"

Patrick stopped to boost himself up onto the counter. He waited until Sisko took a similar position across from him. "I'm sorry I barged in here and vented all over you. I knew we needed to have this conversation, and I guess now's as good a time as any." He paused and inhaled a fortifying breath. "I don't want to lose your friendship, but I have to be honest with you. Sam's problems aside, I still don't get the point of this whole church thing."

"Patrick..."

He held up his hand. "Let me finish. You asked me to give you a year to show me a side of God I'd missed. I've watched you this year. I don't think I've ever seen anyone more dedicated to what they believe. There isn't a thing wrong with what you're doing and what you're working for. It makes a huge difference in the lives of the kids here, and in the community. They're better people because of the things you're teaching them. My mom taught me the same things, and I'm a balanced person because of it."

Sisko tilted his head. "I'm confused. You don't believe it, which means you think it's a lie. But because it's the same lie you were taught, it's OK with you if I continue to teach it?"

Patrick rested a hand over his heart. "I don't think it's all a lie. I believe in God. I'm not an atheist or anything. But I don't believe in a God who watches over each and every one of us every second of every day. I don't believe in a God who cares about our daily aches and pains and problems. I think He's much too busy keeping billions of planets in orbit to worry about what color socks I choose in the morning." His glance went to Sisko's bare feet stuffed into worn athletic shoes. "Or whether we wear socks at all. God gave us a brain, and I think He expects us to use it to get through this life the best we can. Beyond that..." Patrick shrugged. "The jury is still out on the 'beyond that' part."

Sisko scooted off the counter, his face etched in a confused frown. "Let me get this straight," he said.

"You believe there's a God who made us, but not one who watches over us?"

"Pretty much. If I had to argue God's existence in front of a jury, I could do that without trying. But arguing for a God who takes an active interest in our daily lives?" Patrick shook his head. "I'd lose that case in a heartbeat. There's just—"

The ringing of Sisko's cell phone interrupted the conversation. He continued to stare at Patrick while he reached for it. He diverted his gaze long enough to look at the screen and held up a hand. "Hold that thought. It's Lisa." He connected the call. "Hey, babe."

Patrick watched as every bit of color drained from his friend's face. Whatever he was hearing on that phone was not good news. Patrick pushed himself from the counter.

"What...? Is everyone OK? Call...of course you did. I'm on my way." Sisko jammed his phone into one pocket and fished his keys from another. His hands were shaking so badly the keys fell to the floor.

"Dave?"

The youth pastor bent down to retrieve his keys. They clattered against each other in his trembling fingers. "I have to go." He fumbled a key off the ring and tossed it to Patrick. "Lock up for me."

Patrick snatched the key from the air and stared after Sisko as he sprinted for the door. "What's wrong?"

"My house is on fire."

Patrick, immobilized by shock, watched Sisko sprint from the room.

His house...? Questions roiled in Patrick's mind. Look for Sam? Follow Sisko? Who needed him the most? He shook himself loose of the stupor and rushed to turn off lights and lock doors. His earlier question to Sisko took precedence over all the others. In all of this, where was the God Sisko and Sam followed so faithfully?

Samantha closed her eyes and allowed the hot water of the shower to wash away the dirt and grime of the fire while it soothed a weariness that went all the way to her soul. Her heart ached for Dave and Lisa Sisko. Everyone was safe, but their house was a total loss. She couldn't even comprehend the work that lay ahead of her best friend and her husband.

She took a deep breath of the steamy air and wrinkled her nose in disgust. The bitter odor of burnt wood and wet ash lingered in her nose and clung to her skin. She lathered body and hair with her favorite mango scented bath products. Her clothes would never come clean.

The call about the fire had come on the heels of her father's arrival to pick her up. They'd rushed to the Sisko home to see if there was anything they could do. They'd arrived to find the house engulfed in flames, and three frightened, teary children being comforted by parents just as tearful. Sam closed her eyes at the memory and shut off the water. To lose everything, three weeks before Christmas. Wrapped in a towel, Sam searched her dresser drawers for her comfortable, fuzzy PJs. She needed to be cocooned in something warm and familiar this evening.

Having declined an invitation to eat upstairs with the family, she busied herself in the apartment's little kitchen, making a late dinner for her daughter. She wanted some time alone. A few minutes to put things in perspective. The happenings of the day had shaken her foundation and proved to her how quickly things could change from happiness to despair. *That's a lesson I should be familiar with by now.* Her mind shifted from Lisa and Dave's issues to her own past—and a possible future with Louis in it. Sam shook her head, wishing she could focus on someone else's problems for a little while. *Major fail.*

Sam's eyes tracked to the napkin stuck to the refrigerator with a bright red magnet in the shape of the letter L. Dad left it there this morning. She sighed at the irony of his choice of magnet. L for Louis or loser? Either way, somewhere through this long day, she'd come to the conclusion that she would have to call him. Her fingers massaged her temples. And she would. *Just not when I'm too tired to think straight.*

She placed grilled cheese sandwiches and cups of tomato soup on the table. Cups for Bobbie's benefit. It was easier, and much neater, for her daughter to sip the soup than spoon it. The soup received a garnish of tiny croutons and a pinch of bright green basil. The orange, tan, and green made an appetizing color combination that she hoped would appeal to her daughter. The scent of toasted bread and melted cheese certainly had her own stomach growling in hunger. Samantha wanted nothing more than to huddle down here in the security of her basement apartment, snuggle up with her little girl, and enjoy some quiet before tucking Bobbie in for the night. Then she'd have some time to think.

She went to Bobbie's bedroom door and found her daughter sprawled on the floor with crayons and a drawing tablet. As Sam stood in the doorway, the first genuine smile since breakfast tugged at her lips. The new penguin had a piece of paper and a crayon in front of him as well. The scene served as an unnecessary reminder that Bobbie loved Patrick almost as much as Sam did. *Father, please help me sort this out, for her good as well as mine.* "Dinner's ready, baby."

"K, Mama." Bobbie ripped the page from her tablet and brought it with her to the door. "Here."

Sam crouched and took the picture. If she turned it sideways and squinted with one eye, she could just make out the shape of a face. "That's very pretty, baby. What is it?"

Bobbie reached up with both hands and touched the sides of her mother's mouth. She pushed up gently. "Mama's smile. Jem says you shouldn't be so sad. He's watching you too. See?" Bobbie pointed at the other side of the picture.

That portion of the drawing looked like a stick with wings, with JEM, printed in oversized letters beneath it. Sam smiled for real and pulled her daughter into her arms. "How can I be sad when I'm having dinner with my favorite little person?" She put Bobbie in her booster seat and took a chair across the table.

Bobbie followed her mother's lead, bowing her head over her plate. She reached a pudgy hand across the table and linked her fingers with Sam's before offering up a mealtime prayer. "Jesus, bless our food. Amen."

"Amen." Hoping to inspire Bobbie's appetite, Samantha picked up her sandwich and took a healthy bite. "We both need to eat a good dinner and get a good night's sleep. Tomorrow is a big day."

As anticipated, Bobbie followed suit, chewing a bite of her sandwich and slurping her soup. She swallowed.

"Is Chrissom tomorrow?"

Bobbie's continued trouble in pronouncing Christmas made Samantha smile.

"No, but I'll show you how to count on the calendar after we eat. We're leaving early in the morning to pick out a tree. Everyone can help decorate it once we get it home."

Bobbie bounced in her seat, innocent excitement shining in her eyes. "But not Seth or Lilly. They're both babies. I'm a big girl."

"Too big for your britches, most days." She reached across the small table with a napkin and wiped soup from the corner of Bobbie's mouth. "You're right about Lilly, but I'm sure G-pa and G-ma will have something Seth can do. It wouldn't be fair to leave him out, would it?"

Bobbie shook her head, dark curls whipping from side to side. Seth was obviously forgotten in the face of more important concerns. "Can we have one for down here too?"

"A tree?" Sam looked around the apartment. There was plenty of room and it would be nice for Bobbie and her to form some traditions of their own. *I can fix a small dinner for Patrick tomorrow night while we decorate.* She smiled as the thought of the homey evening took a bit of the sting out of Louis's unexpected presence. "How does a little girl like you come up with such great ideas? We'll have to find some time to go shopping for our own decorations."

"I want pink and purple!" Her daughter's expression turned earnest. "Santa's coming. Have I been very good?"

"Absolutely the best little girl in the whole wide

world."

"Yay!"

"Have you thought about what you want Santa to bring you?"

Bobbie nodded vigorously. "I want a bike, and new books, and a baby that talks."

"Those are cool ideas. We'll have to make a list and see if we can find Santa at the mall."

"Oh boy!" Her daughter's excitement gave way to silence as she focused on her dinner. Before she could finish she dropped the crust of her sandwich and rubbed at her drooping eyes.

Samantha pushed her own plate aside and stood to retrieve a damp paper towel, returning to clean her daughter's face and hands. The chair legs screeched on the vinyl floor when Sam pulled it away from the table. "Scoot. Get your pajamas on and brush your teeth. Call me when you're ready for your story. It's bedtime for very good girls."

With Bobbie's teeth and hair brushed, story read, prayers said and child—and penguin—tucked in for the night, Sam drew the comforting quiet of the apartment around her like a sweater still warm from the dryer. On the other side of the door at the top of her stairs, there was a fire blazing in the fireplace, companionship, and conversation. She tilted her head and listened. Sounds filtered in from the house above. The sound of feet, the murmur of unintelligible voices. Sounds so common she normally didn't even hear them. Tonight they held no appeal. Sam cleaned the small kitchen, gleaning comfort from the routine chore.

She loaded the last dish in the portable dishwasher and ran a towel over the countertop. When she heard the door at the top of the stairs creak open, she knew who it was without looking.

Iris descended the steps two at a time.

Sam put a finger to her lips. "Shh. I just got Bobbie down."

Iris nodded, continuing on a straight line for the cookie jar. She opened the cabinet and pulled down a couple of plates and cups.

Sam leaned against the counter, watching while Iris assembled their snack. "Do you think Mom had any idea?"

Iris put the cookies and milk on the table. "About...?"

Sam nodded at the table. "She always cushioned bad news or took the sting out of a bad day with cookies and milk. I wonder if she had any clue we'd still be doing it years later."

Iris shrugged and took a seat. "I don't know, but it works." The look she directed at Sam contained a gentle rebuke. "I can't believe you stayed gone all day."

Sam sank into her own chair. "I needed time, sis. You know I think better on the move. Then we heard about the fire..." She picked up the chocolate sandwich cookie, twisted it apart, and licked out the creamy center. Not many of her college friends would choose a fifteen-year-old to confide in, sister or not. But then none of her college friends had endured what she and her sister had. The bond between them ran deep.

Iris studied her from across the table. "It's horrible about Dave and Lisa's house, but it's just stuff." She boiled it down to the basics that only those who'd lost everything could understand. "As long as they have each other, they'll be fine."

Iris's words would've sounded harsh to a bystander. All Samantha heard was hard won assurance born out of experience. Experience she could identify with.

Iris pushed ahead. "So, what are you going to do? I heard Dad telling Terri that you couldn't press charges against Louis. I don't get it, but I guess Harrison knows what he's talking about. I say you ignore him like the pond scum he is, and he'll eventually go away."

Sam looked away. "I don't know what I'm going to do. I can't just pretend he isn't here. There's more to consider than my own feelings." She answered Iris's frown with a heavy sigh. "Think about how you felt growing up without Dad. Is that what you want for Bobbie?"

"No, but..."

Sam held up her hand. "Do you remember right after Mom died? You suggested we look for Dad. I vetoed that idea." She closed her eyes. "We would have been so much better off if I hadn't. Louis Cantrell isn't the father I want for my child, but my wants don't change the facts. I can't afford to make a wrong decision a second time." Sam bowed her head over her plate. "In the whole reaping and sowing scheme of things, maybe this is happening because I made the wrong choices before."

Iris sat back, crossed her arms, and frowned at her older sister. "That's just about the dumbest thing I ever heard you say."

Sam shrugged, not the least bit wounded by her sister's candor, but suddenly weary from the extreme emotions of the day. She glanced at the kitchen clock. Had it really been less than twelve hours since Louis walked back into her life?

A deep yawn overtook her. The effort to stifle it made her eyes water and her nose run. She grabbed a napkin, blotted moisture from her eyes, and swiped at her nose. "I don't have any answers for either of us right now." She held up a hand to interrupt when Iris started to speak. "I know you love me, sis, and I know you're only trying to help. But this is something I have to figure out on my own."

CHAPTER SIX

Patrick rolled over and glanced at the clock. Seven AM. He grabbed his phone. The world was falling apart for two people he cared about, and after a sleepless night, he needed an update. Sisko was an early riser, so he'd start there. The connection clicked open before it rang a second time.

"Morning." Sisko's voice was rough.

"Hey, man. Did I wake you?"

"Nope. I gave up trying to sleep hours ago. I've been reading my Bible and praying for a couple of hours."

Patrick rolled his eyes and propped himself up against the headboard. "Man, I am so sorry. Have they figured out what caused it? Is there anything I can do for you guys?"

A sigh rumbled in Patrick's ear from the other end of the connection. "Help? Not really. Cause? The fire marshal said they'd be investigating over the next few days. According to him, Christmas trees, space heaters, and fireplaces are the three big causes for house fires this time of year. We didn't own any space heaters, but the tree was up and Lisa had a fire burning in the fireplace."

Patrick heard a yawn.

"Sorry. Anyway, we'll just have to wait and see. I keep telling myself that my family is safe. That's the most important thing. The rest is just stuff."

Patrick shook his head. He'd been a guest at the Sisko home many times. The stuff Sisko referred to included a number of irreplaceable items, among them, a collection of ministry reference books handed down to Sisko by his preacher grandfather, full of the elder man's handwritten notes. He could only guess at the fate of the porcelain bells Lisa had collected since she was a child, not to mention baby pictures and things stored on computers.

Sisko's next words shook Patrick out of his reverie.

"I guess what it boils down to is that some days you're the pigeon, and some days you're the statue."

"This isn't funny, Dave—"

"You'll notice I'm not laughing." A sigh rumbled in Patrick's ear. "Sorry, my reserves are running on caffeine and grit right now. We'll be OK. I don't understand what God has in store for me and my family, but I know He has a plan."

Silence stretched between the two men for a few seconds. "How can you say that after—?"

"Patrick, I know you don't understand where I'm coming from, but being a Christian doesn't exempt you from bad things. Daniel, Moses, Job...they all had trials to overcome. They all stayed on the path God mapped out for them. They all came out stronger on the other side. I have to trust that we will too. That's why they call it faith. Look, I appreciate you checking on us, but I have to run. The insurance adjuster wants to meet me at the house first thing this morning."

"You'll call me if you need anything?"

"Absolutely, but I think we're good for now. Mitch and Karla got their RV out of storage and brought it over for us. It's ours for the duration."

Patrick disconnected the call. He stayed in bed for a few minutes longer, deep in thought. He'd grown up with all those Bible stories, too. What did Sisko see that he was missing? For him, those stories seemed to be something to learn from, a matter of experience and faith.

Patrick's spin was something completely different. When he read or heard about David and Goliath, Daniel and the lions, Jonah and the whale (seriously?) all he got was an old fairy tale where things had turned out fine, and the story had been twisted into some...God-orchestrated lesson.

He swung his feet to the floor. The whole thing drove frustration into his heart and soured his mood. He didn't get it. He'd certainly never seen it.

Sam bunched her jacket tighter around her shoulders then bent to double check Bobbie's coat zipper as well. The temperature was so much colder than last year at this time. Her memory drifted to the mild days last November. Saturdays spent racing go-carts and taking walks with Patrick. Not this year. She shrugged, Oklahoma weather tended to be fickle.

They meandered through the rows of evergreens in an old-fashioned tree farm. Acres of Christmas trees in various sizes, just waiting to be selected, cut, and taken home, where they would become the focal point of the house for the next few weeks. Sam studied some of the smaller offerings, looking for the perfect addition to the corner she'd cleaned out for that purpose.

The air was heavy with the scents of pine and smoke, the ground carpeted in snow and shed pine needles. It was a lovely place. She forced yesterday's concerns to the back of her mind. There seemed to be an unspoken agreement to focus on the here and now for today. There would be plenty of time to help the Siskos, and more than enough time to deal with Louis, after their family outing. It might be escapism, but it worked for now.

She looked back when she heard a cough behind her. Terri and her cold were along for the ride this morning. She pushed Seth and Lilly in their big double stroller. Sam's father walked beside them, one arm around Terri's shoulders, the other hand balancing a saw across his shoulder.

Sam smiled at the picture of contentment they made. These were the things her father had missed and Terri had always dreamed of having. Seth was old enough this year to enjoy Christmas and all the trappings. She knew her parents weren't about to let him miss a single second of fun. Samantha doubted the two-year-old boy's interest in today's tree shopping. His curiosity would reach its peak when all the pretty gifts went under the tree. Lilly's interest would focus on the shiny balls and lights. Sam laughed to herself. Keeping her independent little brother and her rambunctious baby sister away from the tree for the next three weeks would be a battle of wills for everyone in the house.

Patrick took her gloved hand in his.

She smiled and returned the pressure he applied to her fingers. *I love you.* Her heart warmed with the knowledge that those feelings were returned. He'd been at their door bright and early this morning, an active participant in every aspect of Bobbie's Christmas. He loved her, and he loved her daughter. He wanted the three of them to be a family someday. Sam wanted that too, now more than ever.

"Mommy, my nose."

Sam glanced down and tugged Bobbie off the path, allowing the rest of the family to move ahead. She fished a tissue from her pocket and held it gently against the chapped little nose. "Blow."

Bobbie's forceful exhale rattled into the tissue.

"Honk, honk. You sound like a goose," Patrick teased.

Bobbie convulsed into giggles, which escalated to squeals of excitement as Patrick swooped her up and tossed her over his shoulder.

He left Bobbie dangling and held out his free hand to Sam. Together the trio returned to the path. They walked, and Samantha allowed herself to indulge in a small fantasy. Patrick, Bobbie, and her, a family, shopping for their own tree to sit in a corner of their own house.

Patrick raised her hand and brushed a kiss over her gloved fingers, igniting a prayer from the deepest part of her heart. *This, Father, just this.*

Their eyes met over their gloved hands. *Why is his expression so drawn this morning?* She studied him from under her lashes as they hurried to catch up with the rest of the family. There was something going on behind his eyes. Nothing she could put her finger on, but it went deeper than just concern about everything that happened yesterday. Her daily prayer for Patrick whispered up from her heart. *Jesus, please make Yourself real to him.*

Worry niggled, threatening to steal the joy from the day. *How can I expect to help him when I don't know how to help myself?* She sighed. A restless night spent tossing and turning hadn't yielded any solutions to her problems. Even though the thought chilled her more than the morning air, she'd accepted the need for a face-to-face meeting with Louis and a conversation she couldn't imagine having.

Sam forced those thoughts aside. For now, with Patrick and Bobbie at her side, she had everything a woman could want. Was it wrong to pretend, for a little while, that they were a family?

Metal barrels with carefully banked fires inside occupied strategic locations throughout the tree farm. The fires smoldered along the path. They passed one as a family of four stopped for a few seconds to warm their hands and feet. Teenaged kids who seemed to make an effort to look like they didn't care about the tree. Sam suspected differently. *Who could be indifferent to the promise of Christmas?*

Vendors dressed in festive costumes were already set up, their wares consisting of overpriced cups of hot chocolate, coffee, and apple cider, all intended to heat up places the warmth from the fires couldn't reach.

When thirty minutes of looking hadn't produced a tree that met everyone's standards, they gathered around one of the smoking drums and sipped drinks from foam cups decorated with holiday designs.

Iris stomped her tennis-shoe-clad feet. "My toes are numb."

Sam glanced from the tennis shoes covering Iris's feet to the fur-lined boots on her own. "Mine are nice and toasty."

Iris narrowed her eyes at her sister. "Yeah. Well, when we get home, I'm going through your closet. I know you borrowed my boots last year and didn't return them."

"Mine are brown, yours are black."

"Exactly." Iris placed her hands on her hips. "You got those new black leggings for Christmas last year and asked to borrow my boots. I haven't seen them since. I'll just bet they're stuffed in a dark corner of that department store you call a closet."

Steve tossed his cup into the trash and stepped between his daughters. He looked at Iris. "When we get home, look out in the garage next to the sleds. When I unboxed the outside decorations last week, I think I saw your boots, sitting right where you left them to dry *ten months ago.*"

Iris inched a little closer to the warmth of the barrel. "Why didn't you tell me?"

"I didn't know you couldn't find them," he answered. "So stop nagging your sister."

Sam grinned and stuck her tongue out at Iris. "Told you I didn't have them."

Iris watched her sister over the rim of her cup. "Cow," she muttered.

"Brat," Sam retaliated.

Steve put an arm around both of his daughters. "Girls. Christmas time. Peace on earth, good will to men and all that." He motioned to the stroller. "You're setting a bad example for your siblings."

Iris looked around her father. "Lilly couldn't care less, and Seth's asleep."

"Pretend he's awake." He tilted his head in Sam's direction. "You sound like you're feeling better this morning."

"Hmm..." She stopped to make sure Bobbie wasn't listening. Her daughter stood a few feet away, carrying on an animated conversation with an elf. "Not better, just resigned. I'm not thrilled with the idea, but I've accepted that I have to face Louis. I don't know that I can ever trust him, but if he's sincere in looking for forgiveness..." Her shoulders lifted in a small shrug. "I'm obligated to forgive him."

Patrick stared at her over his cup. "Excuse me? Forgive him?"

Sam raised her hands. "What choice do I have?"

He tossed his cup into the fire and grabbed Sam's hand. "Excuse us just a minute." He pulled her to the side.

He dropped her hand and faced her with his hands fisted on his hips. "What, exactly, are you thinking?"

"That I have to see him. I thought we agreed on that."

"Beyond that?"

Sam gazed up at Patrick with a puzzled frown. "I'm not sure yet. I don't like it, but I have to consider the fact that he's Bobbie's father and keeping them apart might be a mistake."

Patrick rubbed his gloved hands over his face. "What happened to you between yesterday and today? I thought you didn't want anything to do with him."

"I still don't, but the Bible says I owe him forgiveness because I've been forgiven. As for the role he'll play in Bobbie's life, I'm praying about it."

"The Bible says?" He paced away a couple of steps. "The Bible says," he repeated when he faced her again. "I can't believe it. You and Sisko really need to find your way out of your rose-colored religious fantasy world and join the rest of us in reality. Life is not fair. Not everything that happens is for a *deeper purpose*. You guys need to accept the fact that life bites sometimes, and no one really cares all that much."

Sam frowned. "Don't drag Dave and Lisa into this. What's wrong with you?"

Patrick waved her question away. "You're going to let that slimeball have a place in your life?"

"I didn't say that."

"Yeah, you did." Patrick stared at her, his eyes narrowed to slits. "You still have feelings for him, don't you?"

Samantha took a step back. "Do you hear yourself? Are you crazy? How in the world did my words get so twisted between my mouth and your ears?"

"There's no other logical reason for your abrupt about-face since yesterday."

"I'm not trying to be logical. I'm trying to be a Christian in a difficult situation. I'm trying to trust God to show me what's best for all of us. I'm trying to be a good example to my daughter and my *unsaved boyfriend*." Samantha delivered those last words through clenched teeth.

Patrick snorted. "That's the sorriest excuse I've ever heard in my life."

His words stung. Sam looked at the ground.

"Patrick, please don't do this."

"What am *I* doing?"

She looked up. A single tear escaped her eyes. "You know I love you. But I warned you a long time ago that if the day ever came that I had to choose between you and my faith, you'd lose. Don't make me choose, Patrick."

"Your faith is about to get you into a lot of trouble."

"I'm sorry you feel that way. I have to do what I think is right."

"So this is where it ends, huh? I'm not good enough for you because I can't believe what you believe."

Sam faced Patrick, toe to toe. A head shorter but she mirrored his hands-on-hips posture. "Patrick, you're overreacting. I never said anything about ending things between us or taking Louis back into my life..."

Patrick made an impatient gesture with his hand. "Your actions are speaking loud enough. I'm out of here. Good luck with this whole thing." He took a step away, then turned back, hand outstretched.

"What?"

"My ring."

Samantha hid her hand behind her back. "I don't think so."

"You don't think so?"

"That's right. You're going to come to your senses in a day or two and realize how much of a jerk you're being." She held up her hand, wiggling the ring in his face. "When you do, this will be one less thing you'll have to apologize for."

Patrick turned away without an answer. He stalked to his truck, slammed the door, gunned the engine to life, and drove away.

Samantha watched him go, her breathing harsh. Clouds of steam hovered over her head. Her throat ached from the deep gulps of cold air. Her heart ached more. Their first fight. She turned back to find her family staring at her. She tugged her leather jacket back into place and headed towards the next section of trees.

Sam took the saw from her father as she passed. "Come on, let's find our tree." She hefted the saw. "I need to get physical with something."

The tree was up in the main part of the house. The lights twinkled in a rapid succession of red, green, and blue. There were even a few wrapped presents underneath it already. Terri believed that a Christmas tree needed gifts under it to be completely decorated.

Sam sat in her apartment, staring at the little tree Bobbie had picked out. The sounds of her family filtered through the closed door. Bobbie was upstairs having hot chocolate and cookies with Grandma and Grandpa. She'd be down here shortly, anxious to start on their tree.

Just the two of us. Nice, but not the picture she'd envisioned. Sam curled up on the sofa, phone in hand, preparing to make the hardest phone call of her life.

She punched in the numbers and prayed when it started to ring. "Jesus, please show me what I'm supposed to do."

"Hello."

"It's Samantha."

"Oh, thank God, baby, thank God. I've been waiting for the phone to ring."

Sam held the phone away and looked at it with a frown. *Baby? Who's he kidding?* She took a deep breath.

SHARON SROCK

"What do you want, Louis?"

She heard a matching sigh from the other end of the phone. "I know you must hate me. I don't blame you, but I really can explain. Everything I did, I did for you and our baby. I..."

Sam snorted rudely. "Wait, wait," she interrupted him. "You lied to me, you got me pregnant, you stole from me, and left me to have your child, alone. And you did this all for me? How can I ever thank you?"

"I know how crazy I must sound. But if you'd let me explain, I know I can make you understand."

"Louis, just get to the point. You wanted to talk to me. I'm listening."

"I need to see you in person. I want to see my daughter."

"Anything you have to say to me, you can say over the phone. If, or when, I decide to allow *my* child into this, it's going to be on my terms, not yours."

"Sam, please."

She was surprised to hear what sounded like real desperation in his voice. "Look, I'll meet you someplace public to talk if that's what you want. But it's just going to be me. Bobbie will not be a part of this until I know what you what. I won't have you disrupting her life."

"Can we meet tonight?"

Sam shook her head. "No. It's late. And before you ask, tomorrow is church and family time. I'm not changing that. Monday after my morning classes is the earliest I can get free."

"Two days? Sam, I need..."

"Take it or leave it."

His sigh came through the line a second time. "Fine.

70

Where and when?"

"There's a coffee shop on Main Street. Ground Zero. I'll see you there at two on Monday afternoon."

"All right. I'll see you then. Sam, I'm sorry—"

"Save it for Monday, Louis." She disconnected the call without waiting for a response, dropping the phone on the cushions like a hot rock. She stared at it for several seconds before going up to retrieve her daughter. They had a tree to decorate and Samantha planned to do everything in her power to make the evening a pleasant memory for both of them.

The phone on the scarred nightstand rang again almost before he released it. Louis yanked it back up. "Sam?"

"You better be sick or dyin'."

"What...? Who is this?"

"My name's not important, bucko. Let's just say I'm an associate of Mr. Carson's. A very curious associate."

Louis felt a clammy sweat pop out on the back of his neck. "Curious about what?"

"Curious about why you've been hibernating in that room all day when there's work to do. Work that ain't getting done while you watch TV and suck down beer."

The sweat tricked down his back. Did these people have ears in his room? "Relax, I just arranged a meeting for Monday."

"That's two days from now. Do I need to come over there and light a fire under you?"

"You need to stay out of my business and let me work."

"As long as you owe the boss money, it ain't just *your* business. The boss is getting impatient."

"Impatient? I've only been in town forty-eight hours."

"You promised him results when you borrowed the additional fifteen thousand. The boss don't take bein' lied to."

Louis took a deep breath. He'd love to tell this thug, and his boss, where they could go, but he wanted to be alive to keep Monday's appointment. "Listen, I'm working on it. I've seen her. We're gonna talk on Monday. I can't just show up and start making demands. I need the time to convince her that I can be trusted."

This was met with loud, barking laughter from the other end of the phone. "Good luck with that, ace. We'll talk again tomorrow."

"But I'm not seeing her till—" Louis heard a beep, realized he was talking to dead air, and hung up the phone. He sat on the edge of the broken-down mattress and cradled his head in his hands. "Oh man."

CHAPTER SEVEN

Sunday morning at Valley View Church combined a continental breakfast of donuts and pastries with camaraderie for those who wished to arrive early enough to partake. Men hung out in clumps, drinking coffee and sharing stories. The fellowship hall rang with their rowdy laughter. Women visited with friends they hadn't seen in a week while corralling kids and breaking their diets to enjoy the sweet treats.

Samantha settled Bobbie into a chair. "Sit right here. I'll go get your honey bun."

Bobbie bounced and pointed. "Nana Kate, Nana Kate."

Sam followed the excited four-year-old's pointing finger and saw Patrick's mother, Kate Archer, coming in from the cold.

"I want to sit with Nana Kate."

Sam pulled the chair away from the table. "Go ahead. I'll bring your breakfast over there."

"Yay!" Bobbie raced across the room, darting

around people like a bunny in the forest dodges tree trunks. Kate looked up at the toddler's squeal, stooped, and rocked back on her heels as Bobbie launched herself into her outstretched arms. Sam met Kate's eyes from across the room. Kate inclined her head toward some empty chairs at the far end of one of the tables. Sam nodded in response and turned to collect breakfast for the three of them. It did not escape her notice that Kate was alone this morning. Patrick was MIA. The prayer came automatically. *Jesus, touch his heart.* The small shrug following her prayer was new. *I'm sorry he's upset, but I have to do what's best for my daughter. I can't tell him what I'm doing, 'til God tells me what I'm doing.* She bent her head over the loaded breakfast tray. *Father, please tell me what to do.*

Sam crossed to her daughter just in time to hear the tail end of the conversation.

"...and his scarf matches his shoes."

She sat the tray on the corner of the table with a smile for the older woman. "I'm so glad you guys are home. Do I need to tell you that the penguin was a huge success? If he wasn't *sleeping* out in the car, we'd have four for breakfast."

Kate's green eyes twinkled. "Those Build-A-Pal stores are amazing. Every animal God created plus baby dolls. Patrick was pretty sure Bobbie's collection didn't include a penguin. I'm glad he was right."

Sam laid a honey bun on a napkin, placed a foam cup of milk beside it, and addressed her daughter. "Eat your breakfast, sweetheart. Sunday school starts in a few minutes." She pulled her own chair out, sat, and unwrapped a frosted cherry pastry. "Speaking of Patrick..."

"Sulking in his room like a five-year-old." Kate reached across the table and rubbed Samantha's arm. "Are you OK? I hope you don't mind, but he told me about..." Her eyes cut to Bobbie, the rest of her comment sufficiently vague. "...your friend."

Sam shrugged. "It's been an interesting couple of days." She too, glanced at Bobbie from beneath lowered lashes. The child was enjoying her breakfast, oblivious to the grown-up talk around her. Bobbie broke off a few pieces of the honey bun, placed them on a napkin at the empty space beside her, and chattered to Jem. Sam shook her head and returned her attention to Kate. "I'm sorry. I know I've hurt—"

"Shh. No need to go there. I'm his mother, remember? I've seen him sulk before." Kate's long blonde hair shifted on her shoulders as she shook her head. "I've been blessed to love two good men." She paused to clear her throat. "But Chad Wheeler, God love him, was a black belt sulker. Patrick's just like his father in that regard, although how he can act like a man he can't remember is beyond me." She pinched off a bite of her glazed donut and chased it with a sip of her coffee. "I know you'll do the right thing. Whether he's acting like it or not, Patrick knows that, too."

Sam propped her elbows on the table and rested her chin on her knuckles. "I wish I shared your confidence."

Chick Monroe wheeled his white-panel van around the corner and away from Valley View Church. He glanced in his rearview mirror and caught the silhouette of the large white cross dominating the landscape in front of the building. He shuddered, chilled by old memories.

"But, Pop..."

"No buts. Get out to the shed, boy. Someone left that gate open, and now my prize bull is dog food."

"Glenn..."

"You'd push the blame off on your bother to save your own backside? I'm ashamed to call you my grandson. Glenn's a good boy, called to preach. He denied it, and I got no cause not to believe him. That leaves you, and you've been nothing but trouble since you came to live here."

PopPop pulled the razor strop from the nail beside the back door. "Get on...I don't understand why you can't be more like your big bother. I swear I'm gonna put the fear of God in you, even if it kills you."

Chick closed his eyes on the memory of the beating purchased with his brother's neglect and lies. But he couldn't forget the words that fell with each swing of PopPop's arm.

"The good book says that a person's heart is full of foolishness, but the rod will drive it out.

"You're on your way to hell, boy, and I mean to put you on a different path here and now.

"How do you expect God to use you like he's using your brother when every word out of your mouth is a lie?

"You're never gonna amount to anything in this world if you don't get some religion under that thick hide."

Chick drove, relieved when the cross disappeared from view. He had no need of religion, hypocrites, or Bible-quoting do-gooders who lied to your face. He'd left home that night, and he'd been on his own ever since. A ragged breath filled the van, and he forced the memories back under a layer of indifference. He didn't need them, didn't need his family, and certainly didn't need a God who would leave a fifteen-year-old boy broken and huddled on a sawdust floor for a crime he hadn't committed. *Where had God been that night?* It was all just so much religious mumbo jumbo.

Chick turned his mind back to business. His gut clenched. *I've got a bad feeling about this whole operation.* Yesterday's surveillance had amounted to squat. Louis never left his hotel room, and the kid's attitude infuriated Chick, forcing him to reveal his presence sooner than he'd planned. He remembered the tremor in the younger man's voice during their brief conversation last night. *Talk about the fear of God.*

Yes, he had to give Louis Low Life a chance to work, but Chick was here because Mr. Carson trusted him to make sure Louis got the work done. Chick chewed on the toothpick hanging from the side of his mouth. He'd give the kid a few days to come up to snuff, but he'd be ready to step in at the first sign of failure.

He angled the van into a narrow parking space in front of a hole-in-the-wall diner. The van died the instant he took it out of gear. *Worthless piece of trash!*

Hopeful for a decent breakfast, he climbed out of the van, swearing when the oversized door connected with the car beside his.

Chick determined, anew, not to screw up this assignment. He wanted his company car back. He hated driving this hulking, contrary, under powered...thing. He limped to the door of the restaurant, favoring his left leg. Having the Charger taken away from him was the least of his punishments for his last mistake. He slid into the booth and rubbed at the dull ache in his thigh, an ever-present reminder that Mr. Carson didn't do well with failure or excuses. Chick would not be on the receiving end of his wrath a second time.

Controlled chaos. Mostly controlled, anyway. The transition from Sunday school classes to worship service in Valley View's large sanctuary was a crazy jumble of folks. A couple hundred adults shuffled through the halls, older kids raced for the gym, younger ones wailed from behind the closed doors of the nursery.

At least Bobbie didn't cry anymore. She enjoyed the playtime and the Bible stories. Sam paused at the door to the toddler area. Half a dozen three- and four-year-olds sat around an elevated video screen.

"I've got one more for you," Sam said.

The attendant hurried over to unlock the bottom half of the split door. "And there's Miss Bobbie. Grab a seat, sweetheart. We have a new video this morning." She smiled at Samantha. "We're still learning about guardian angels."

Bobbie jumped up and down. Her memory verse spewed forth in excitement. "He will order His angels to... protect you."

The worker clapped her hands in praise. "Very good!"

Sam bent to kiss the top of her daughter's head before ushering her through the doorway. "She practiced that verse all week. She's become fascinated with angels this last month."

"That's normal. No kid, especially the girls, can resist stories of beautiful winged creatures. It's the stuff of fairy tales, only better."

Samantha nodded, loitered just long enough to watch her daughter take a seat, and then headed into the sanctuary. She scanned the crowded pews. Benton and Callie Stillman sat next to the center aisle five rows from the front on the right side of the building. Karla and Mitchell Black, six rows back, next to the aisle along the far wall, Pam and Harrison Lake in the middle of the pew, four rows ahead of them. She found Mom and Dad on the far side of the building. She'd sit with them this morning, since Patrick was playing hooky.

Conversation buzzed around her as fellow worshipers found seats in the crowded auditorium. Bits and snips reached her ears. Questions about the fire, ideas about help and how to offer it. She looked for Dave and Lisa, eager for news from the source, wanting to reassure herself that they were OK. Her shoulders sagged a bit when she didn't see them. *Of course they aren't here.*

Sam settled into her seat, anxious for Pastor to come to the front. He'd have news and a plan of action for the help her friends needed right now. She hadn't been a member of Valley View Church for very long, but she remembered how the members of the congregation had rallied to help two abandoned, struggling girls. Yeah, struggling because of Louis Cantrell. With more than a little effort, she pushed those thoughts aside. It wasn't denial. Her problems with Louis would not be resolved today. No reason to allow tomorrow's worries to steal today's joy. Besides, help for Dave and Lisa took priority this morning.

Instead of the praise and worship team, Pastor

Gordon mounted the two steps to the platform and faced the congregation from the pulpit. The bustle and whispering died immediately.

"I know our hearts are heavy for our youth pastor and his family today. I spoke with Dave and Lisa this morning. They're tired and dealing with the twins' nightmares, but otherwise they're fine. I want to thank Mitch and Karla Black for their quick response in providing their fifth wheel as temporary lodging. Many of you offered your homes, but I know the Siskos will be more comfortable in their own space. The initial finding from the fire marshal points towards a problem with their chimney. It's a tragedy for them and a reminder for all of us with fireplaces to have them checked out before we use them."

He paused and pulled a folded check from the breast pocket of his suit. "I know you guys came prepared to give. Let's get the ushers up here for a special love offering. Let's bless the socks off the Siskos."

Patrick prowled around the empty house, lonely and restless. His mom was peeved with him because he'd chosen to stay home today. Yesterday's harsh words with Sam still rang in his mind. Missing church today would not win him any points on that front. He shrugged, feeling at odds with the world. He rolled his eyes. *Heck, if both of my dads really are looking down on me from heaven, I've probably put a frown on their faces, too.*

At least Sisko wasn't mad at him. That thought brought Patrick up against the brick wall of helplessness. As much as he'd like to help his friend, there wasn't a lot he could do this morning.

He jumped when his sock-clad foot came down on one of Merlin's chew toys, sending a loud squeak into the quiet room. The black cocker spaniel raised his head from the doggy bed in the corner of the living room and wagged his tail. Patrick gave the rubber hot dog a half-hearted kick, sending the dog into frenzied barking as he chased the toy, cornered it, retrieved it, and delivered it back to Patrick's feet. The dog sat and stared up with large, soulful eyes. Patrick stooped and scratched a favored spot behind the dog's left ear. "I'm not in the mood to play right now."

The one-year-old pup flopped down on his belly with an almost human sigh, doggy reproach shining in his black eyes.

Patrick stood and mentally added the dog to the upset-with-Patrick list. *Why can't anyone see this situation from my point of view?* He wanted to be Samantha's husband and Bobbie's father. Louis Cantrell's return threatened that goal. A tiny voice of reason reminded him that there was more than Louis standing between him and his plans. Sam had made it clear that there would be no future for them until he came around to her religious beliefs. A position his mother agreed with. His sigh bounced around the room with Merlin's. He frowned at the dog. "And speaking of my mother...what's up with your mistress?"

Merlin's head tilted to one side, and his brows ticked up in question.

Patrick continued aloud. "I want Mom to love Sam and Bobbie. She does, but does she have to take their side in our first argument? What sort of loyalty is that? She's my mother." He glanced at Merlin. "I love Sam, and I want to protect her from this sleazeball. You're a guy. You'd protect your woman from harm, wouldn't you?"

The stubby black tail wagged in response.

Patrick paused in the doorway, leaned his head on the casing, and groaned. "A dog. I'm asking a dog for advice on my love life."

Sam reclaimed her seat as the ushers exited, and the praise team yielded the platform to the pastor. Brother Gordon reclaimed his place at the pulpit. Verses for the text of his sermon flashed on the screen behind the old minister. She thumbed through her Bible, looking for Philippians 3:13.

"It's so good to see everyone out to worship with us this morning. While we're waiting for a report on our offering, let's go ahead and turn to our text." The elderly pastor removed his glasses and gave them a quick polish with a handkerchief. "Our verses today might not be familiar to a lot of you, but this morning we're going to talk about the hazards of living in the past and how to avoid it."

The pastor settled his glasses back on his face. "I've been in the ministry for more years than some of you are old. The most common thing I hear from the unsaved is how bad they've been. They ask me how God could possibly offer them forgiveness after the horrible things they've done. I tell them that's stinkin' thinkin'." He paused as the congregation chuckled. "I want us to look at the apostle Paul and King David this morning. I don't think any of the people I've ever talked to were murderers. Paul and David both were. Paul directly and David by proxy."

Sam bookmarked Philippians and continued to the

next reference on the screen, II Samuel, chapter twelve. She scanned the words as the preacher warmed to his subject. A series of words snagged her attention. "...the child also that is born unto thee shall surely die." She focused on the words, the sound of Brother Gordon's voice lost under the sudden pounding of her pulse in her ears. A shiver crawled up her spine.

God took the baby for the sin of the parents?

Her tender heart kicked in, and tears sprang to her eyes in sympathy for bereaved parents long dead. She couldn't imagine the guilt of losing her child because she'd been in the wrong. The very thought made her itch to hold Bobbie close. Her feet twitched with the urge to check on her baby. She drew in a deep breath and forced her shoulders to relax. *I'm being silly.* Bobbie was safe in the nursery. This whole thing with Louis was making her paranoid. She'd dedicated Bobbie to the Lord. Sam rested in the fact that He watched over her baby, even when she couldn't.

CHAPTER EIGHT

Samantha dunked her biscotti into her cocoa-flavored latte. Her nose wrinkled. The combination of flavors wasn't as comforting as cookies and milk, but it would have to do for now.

Louis was late. If he hoped to impress her with some new-and-improved version of himself, he was off to a miserable start. Over the door, a clock in the shape of a grinning coffee mug dominated the room. When the hands marked the top of the hour, the vents around each number emitted a coffee scented steam. *Cute in a tacky sort of way.* The two o'clock show had come and gone fifteen minutes earlier.

She kept watch out the door, her fingers drumming an impatient beat on the tabletop.

And there he was.

Sam tried to swallow and couldn't. The sight of Louis—and the knowledge that she had no choice but to deal with him—had her teeth clenched so tightly her ears ached with the pressure. *Father, please give me wisdom.*

Louis stopped just outside the door, using the reflective glass as a mirror.

Samantha watched him smooth his hair and straighten his shirt. She dug deep for a neutral expression, silently coaching herself on the necessity of having a Christian attitude. Hard to do with her heart threatening to pound out of her chest. It would be a waste of time to go on the defensive before hearing what he had to say, but she did not intend to be taken advantage of a second time.

Oh, Patrick, I wish you were here.

Louis pushed through the door, and Sam shelved all of that. She had to focus, had to figure out what he wanted.

He pulled out the chair. "Sorry, I'm late. I had a job interview at one, and it ran a little long." The smile he pointed in her direction was brilliant. "It went great. I think they might hire me."

His tone indicated that he expected her to be happy with this news. She let it go and consumed another bite of soggy biscotti.

Louis leaned forward, arms braced on the table, hands clasped. "Would you like that?"

Samantha studied him over the rim of her cup, still struggling for detachment. "Louis, what you do or don't do with your life ceased to matter to me several years ago. I'm here because you asked to speak to me. You shouldn't read anything into it that isn't there." She set the cup on the table. "What do you want?"

Louis returned her scrutiny. She wasn't going to cut him any slack. *Not the naïve kid I left behind.* He had one chance at this. One shot to appeal to her sympathies.

He reached across the table, intending to take her hand. She slid it out of his reach. He put on his most earnest expression. It had served him well in the past.

"Sweetheart, I owe you such an apology."

Sam shook her head. "Funny how you weren't so worried about your apology back when I could still have your sorry butt thrown in jail. Get to the point."

Louis conceded the point with a shrug. "I won't bother to deny that my visit is well timed, but it really is just a coincidence. If you'll let me explain, we can get down to the business of putting our little family back together."

Samantha propped an elbow on the table and buried her face in her hand. Blue eyes stared at him from between splayed fingers.

Her cynical pose stiffened his back and his jaw. He rehearsed his story in his head for a final time. *Calm and steady now.* If he couldn't win her confidence or at least her sympathy, he'd be worse than stuck.

He'd be dead.

Louis sat back, prepared to weave a story that was as much lie as truth.

"They were coming for me, Sam. I had to leave when I did or risk putting you and our child in danger. It broke my heart, but I couldn't stay and take a chance with your safety."

"They?"

"Money men for my bookie." Louis didn't have to try for the glow of tears. His current situation was enough to put tears of fear in any man's eyes. "I have a gambling problem, Sam. My counselor, back home in Nevada—"

Samantha held up a manicured finger. "Nevada?"

Louis nodded.

"A gambling problem?"

"I know now that it's a sickness, I—"

"You stole thirty thousand dollars from me and moved to Nevada, the casino capital of America, to *escape* a gambling problem?"

"Sam, I know how it sounds. I'm not doing a very good job of explaining, but you'll understand if you'll let me finish."

"Sure." Sam looked around and caught the eye of a young man clearing a nearby table. She crooked a finger in his direction. "Excuse me."

He hurried to her side. "May I help you with something?"

"Do you guys serve popcorn here?"

He shook his head. "'Fraid not. Is there something else I can get for you?"

Sam waved him away with a smile. "No thanks." She sat back in her seat, crossed her arms, and stared at Louis.

"Popcorn?"

"Yeah. It's my favorite snack with a good tearjerker. I'll try to muddle through without it, though." She made a motion with her hand. "Go ahead."

Louis's façade of patience slipped a bit. *That wise mouth of yours will be the second thing to go, just behind the kid.* "I'm glad this amuses you."

"Sorry. Please, continue."

"Anyway, I was already deep in debt to some really bad people when I met you. I shouldn't have involved you and Iris in my problems, but...Sam, you just took my breath away." He stopped, waiting for some sort of reaction.

When Sam remained silent, he pressed ahead. "I'd never met anyone like you. Beautiful, sweet...and innocent. The fact that you needed me...trusted me...you made me feel ten feet tall." He reached for her hand again, and once more Sam evaded his grasp. "You have to believe me. I never would have hurt you if I'd had a choice."

Louis sighed. Nothing in her unblinking, stony gaze indicated she was buying his story. He decided to lay all of his fictional cards on the table, rushing through the details he'd practiced so meticulously.

"These men came to the garage looking for me, just a few days after you told me about the baby. I owed their boss fifty grand, and they wanted money now. They gave me five days to come up with half of what I owed. They had a picture of you and Iris, they knew I'd moved in with you, and they threatened to hurt both of you if I didn't come through." He met her eyes, striving for sincerity. "I didn't know what to do. I knew they meant it, and I was terrified for you and the baby. I know it was wrong of me to take your money and leave without any explanation, but I figured if I gave them thirty and just disappeared, they'd leave you and Iris alone. I couldn't tell you what was happening or where I was going. If they came to you and you didn't know anything, they wouldn't have any reason to bother you."

He twisted a napkin into a knot as he talked. "I went to Nevada because I have an uncle there who owns a garage. You have to believe me, I haven't been near a casino since I left. I've been working and going to therapy and saving every penny I could.

"I tried to call you once I knew the baby was here, I

swear I did. I wanted to send you some money, but you guys were gone. When I saw you on TV three years ago with your dad, I couldn't believe it. You looked so happy...and my little girl...Sam, she's beautiful, just like you. I—"

A vibration from the cell phone in his pocket derailed his thoughts. He ignored it. It could only be one person. *Buzz...buzz...buzz*...He took a quick swallow of water and pushed his explanation home. *Buzz...buzz...buzz...* "I kept working and saving, and just as soon as I could get away, I came back for you. You must hate me. I don't blame you." *Buzz...buzz...buzz*..."But, can you please give me a chance to prove to you that I've changed?" *Buzz...buzz...buzz*..."I want to be a part of my little girl's life." *Buzz...buzz...buzz*...Why hadn't he left the stupid thing in the car?

Louis pushed back from the table. *Idiot thug was going to drive him crazy.* "I'll call you." He bolted through the door, ducked around the corner of the building, and yanked the vibrating cell phone out of his pocket. A quick check of the display confirmed his suspicions. And why hadn't he taken the time to program the voice mail? Carson's goon had his nerves tied up in knots— that's why. And the results were rookie mistakes. He connected the call, his frustration overriding his common sense. "What?"

"Did you talk to her?"

"Seems like you'd know that if you were following me."

"I'm here to keep you focused, Nancy. If I have to stick close enough to wipe your keister, you won't like it very much. Now answer my question."

"I was trying—"

"Trying don't get the job done, bud. There won't be much left of your skinny hide if I have to take a hundred grand out of it."

Louis swallowed at the threat. "I told you I'll get the money, and I will. Your boss knew, when he loaned me that last fifteen, that this would take some time. We agreed that it would need to be a long-term investment. So leave me alone and let me work!"

"Listen, smart guy. Don't give me attitude. The boss didn't mention no long-term investment to me. He sent me out here to look out for his interests. That's my job, and that's what I'm gonna do. You're playin' in the big leagues now, so suck it up, quit whining, and get it done. Don't expect no kid gloves from me, 'cause I left 'em at home."

Louis rubbed his brow. How could anyone be so stupid? "I don't want kid gloves. I just want what Carson and I agreed on. Call him if you don't believe me."

"Can't call him. He's out of the country on more important business than a small fry like you. He left strict orders not to be disturbed. It's just you and me, jerk face, and if you don't want me takin' this thing into my own hands, I better see some results real soon."

Louis started to answer, but the silence of a dead connection left him sputtering before he got a single word out of his mouth. He tapped the useless phone against his forehead. How could anyone be so...Louis lowered his hand and stared at the phone. What did he mean by taking things into his own hands?

Sam picked at biscotti crumbs on her napkin. When

Louis had run from the coffee shop, he'd left Sam more confused than before their meeting. His story had been so...strange. Rushed in places, practiced in others, and there at the last, almost as if he was making it up as he went along. Why would he do that? None of this made any sense.

A gambling problem? Crooks? Threats against her and Iris? *Is there a single word in all that I can believe?* As far as she was concerned, their meeting had been a waste of her afternoon. She was no closer to understanding the reason for his return now than she'd been on Friday.

She heard hissing and looked up. The coffee mug over the door was steaming three o'clock. Sam wadded up her napkin, stuffed it inside her empty cup, and tossed everything in the trash on her way out the door.

Sam drove home, picking through Louis's story, trying to find a single tidbit of useful information hidden among the blarney he was so good at spinning. Nothing. *I did it for you.* Her snort of disbelieving laughter filled the Mustang. If it weren't so ludicrous, it'd be funny.

Her hand hovered over the phone lying in the passenger seat. She needed to let Patrick know that the meeting was over. Memory jerked her hand back to the wheel. Patrick wasn't speaking to her right now.

With nothing useful to dissect in her conversation with Louis, her mind went back to her fight with Patrick. *"You still have feelings for him."* Did he really think that? Did he really think she could ever pick Louis over him? Her knuckles went white on the steering wheel at the very thought.

Father, why did you make men so contrary? Patrick and I

have been dating for a year. He has to know my heart. I mean, I've told him often enough how I feel. Bobbie loves him. He's the only father I see in her future. We're both just waiting for him to make a place in his heart for You. Can You work a little harder on that, please?

And Louis? I still need to know what he wants. I need to know what You want.

Her cell phone chimed with an incoming text message as she pulled into the drive. She shifted the car into park and thumbed open the message. Lisa Sisko's number flashed onto the screen.

Can U come by?

She typed in a quick "yes," put the phone away, and shifted the car into reverse. Bobbie could stay at the day care center a little longer. A talk with Lisa sounded perfect just about now.

CHAPTER NINE

Louis hit redial for the fifth time. He had to get some control over this situation, some room to work. *I don't know who this goon is, but...*

"What?"

Finally. "We need to talk."

"Yeah, so talk."

Louis paced his small hotel room. "I want a meeting."

"This ain't about what you want. It's about what the boss wants. He wants results. He wants a return on his investment. He wants his money."

"I've only been in town four days." Louis's voice rose with each syllable. He clamped his lips together and struggled for some composure. "Look, I have three months. I promised Mr. Carson a status report every thirty days. A con like this takes delicate planning. I can't just—"

"I'm tired of hearing about what you can't do. Why do you gotta be such a Nancy boy? You've talked to the skirt at least twice, and you're still empty handed. This kid is your daughter, right?"

Louis rubbed his forehead. *Why did hired muscle always come without a brain?* "Yes."

"The grandfather has money, right?"

"Yes."

"This money is what you need to settle up with Mr. Carson, right?"

Louis rolled his head on his shoulders, trying to relive the tension suddenly knotting his muscles. "Yes, but—"

"*No buts!*"

Louis jerked the phone from his ear at the outburst.

"Look, Nancy, it's a simple equation. You plus the kid equals Grandpa's money. Grandpa's money equals a happy Mr. Carson. You need to focus on that."

Louis tried again. "I have a contract..."

Laughter flooded the room from the phone. "Oh, Nancy, you're killing me. A contract? You think there's a piece of paper anywhere to tie this scam to Mr. Carson? The only thing tying you to the boss is me. There's only two things you need to know about me. I ain't a patient guy, and I'm watching."

The phone went dead in Louis's hand. No amount of redial got the goon back on the line. Louis tossed the phone onto the scarred chest of drawers, sank to the bed with his head in his hands, and tried to force his brain to come up with a plan.

The fifth wheel that was temporary home to the Sisko family was parked next to Valley View's gym. Sam stopped next to Lisa's minivan, bunched her coat around her shoulders, and picked her way around frozen patches of asphalt to the front door. The temperature was climbing, the thermometer on the Mustang's dash read a balmy thirty-five degrees, but it was going to have to get a lot warmer to melt the mounds of ice and gray snow scraped and piled along the roads and around parking lots.

Her breath fogged around her. As much as she needed to go home to sort through her conversation with Louis, she needed her best friend more. There had to be something in what Louis had said to give her a clue about his real intentions. Maybe Lisa could help her find it. Sam's shoulders slumped. *And that's just about the most selfish thought in the world.*

She climbed the four metal steps to the front door of the travel trailer and knocked. It wasn't hard to imagine a family of five taking a leisurely vacation in one of these, but living in one for an extended period of time?

A muffled "come in" filtered through the door. Sam pushed through and found herself reevaluating her initial estimation. The door opened into a spacious living area with two recliners and a couch. A flat screen TV hung on the right hand wall for optimum viewing. To her left lay a compact kitchen area. A large picture window on the opposite wall allowed the meager winter sunshine access to the room and was fronted with a table and chairs. Just beyond the kitchen, two steps led up to a closed door.

Lisa placed freshly washed cups into a compact dish drainer and turned. She wiped her hands on a towel and allowed her dark brown eyes to roam the space. "What do you think?"

"I think it's the Taj Mahal of camping trailers. It's

bigger than the apartment Iris and I shared before Dad came back, and way bigger on the inside than it looks on the outside."

Lisa nodded. "The slide outs make all the difference." She nodded to the closed door. "There's a bathroom up there, complete with shower and a bedroom with a queen-sized bed. The couch folds out into a second queen."

Sam took it all in. "Quite a set up. Lucky for you guys Mitch and Karla had this thing sitting in a storage lot."

Lisa smiled.

Just a little too brightly?

"Well, the insurance would have paid for an apartment. But this isn't much smaller, and staying here allows us to put that money towards a new house."

Sam caught the barest hesitation in her best friend's voice. "That sounds like a plan but, how are you, really?"

A rare look of sadness washed across Lisa's face. Sam rushed forward and gathered her friend into her arms. Lisa accepted the embrace for a few seconds before she stepped back. She took a deep breath, straightened her back, and blotted her eyes with the dish towel.

"We're fine." Lisa turned back to the sink. "We're...we'll be fine."

Samantha allowed the moment to pass, accepting the rawness of the loss and Lisa's desire not to dwell on it. She changed the subject. "Where are the kids?"

"Terri sent your dad over to pick them up." Lisa opened a miniature refrigerator. "You want something to drink?" She continued when Sam nodded. "It's too cold to let them play outside, and there isn't much room to play here, so Terri, being Terri, said they could run off some of their excess energy at the day care for a couple of hours every afternoon. She's such a sweetheart." Lisa handed a can of soda to Sam and motioned to the couch. "I'm surprised she didn't mention it to you."

Sam accepted the sweating can and sat beside her friend. "She might have. I've been a little preoccupied lately."

"Dave told me about some trouble you had over the weekend."

"How...?"

"He talked to Patrick Friday afternoon."

Sam nodded. *Of course, he'd go to Sisko.* "I'm glad Dave was there for him. I'm afraid I wasn't much good for anyone on Friday, and now..." Sam sighed and stared at the can in her hands. This whole thing just made her feel *old*. "I haven't talked to him in a couple of days."

Lisa placed her hand on Sam's arm. "Is there anything we can do to help?"

Sam took a sip and licked the fizz from her upper lip. Previous thoughts of soliciting Lisa's advice mixed with the reminder of her friend's sad but determined expression. "I appreciate the offer, and there's even a selfish part of me that planned to take advantage of you when I got your text. But you have enough on your plate just now."

Lisa sat back and crossed her arms. "It's not *taking advantage* if I offer. Now dish. Give me something useful to focus on. What can I do?"

Sam slumped in her seat, rested the can on her knee,

and traced lines through the moisture. Maybe listening to her problems would be therapy for Lisa. "For Patrick and me? Not much. It'll iron itself out." *I hope.* "As for the other...I just came from a meeting with Bobbie's father. I'm still not sure what's going on or what he wants. He's making noises about wanting to be a part of Bobbie's life, about wanting us to be a family." She shook her head. "Me, make a family with him? I don't think so. How he could even think that is beyond my understanding. The breath she exhaled carried frustration with it. "Then he ran out of the coffee shop like his shoes were on fire."

"Did he have anything to say about where he'd been?"

"Oh yeah." She gave her friend Louis's fantastic tale of self-sacrifice and protection. Her shoulders lifted in a shrug when she finished. "If even part of what he said is true—"

"Do you think he's telling the truth?"

Sam's unladylike snort echoed in the small space. "No! But I'm honest enough to admit that that's a knee-jerk response."

Lisa's expression grew thoughtful. "Samantha, I have two questions for you. What do you want out of all of this? More importantly, what do you think God wants out of this? Because I promise you there's a reason why this is happening now."

Sam threaded her fingers through her hair. She raised her head and stared into Lisa's eyes, unafraid to lay her heart bare before her friend. "Me? Bottom line? I want to spend my life with Patrick. Bobbie and I both love him so much. But I don't want Bobbie to grow up with the same hurt Iris and I grew up with.

Knowing...thinking...that her father didn't love her enough to stick around. If I allow Louis into her life, I can probably kiss Patrick goodbye. If I shut Louis out, and he's legit, how can I answer my daughter's questions later?" She took a deep drink of her soda. "My heart says run, my head says listen, and the rest of me worries about being wrong."

She blew her bangs out of her face with a discouraged breath. "I don't know what God wants. I'm asking, but I'm not getting a lot of answers yet. I thought a life with Patrick was where God was taking me, but..." She trailed off, unable to make sense of it in her own mind, much less in words. "There's no middle ground here, no way to compromise."

She allowed her conversation with Louis to run through her mind again. Her stomach clenched even as her heart fluttered with anxiety. There were no neon signs to point out the path she should take. All she had was a mind-numbing assurance that her life would never be the same, regardless of her decision. Her breath came out in a long exhale. "Anyway, two problems, no answers, prayers appreciated."

Patrick looked up from his plate when his cell phone clattered to the table beside his untouched dinner. His mother stood across the table from him, arms folded across her chest, her face shrouded in a no-nonsense expression he hadn't seen since the fourth night he'd broken curfew the week he turned seventeen. The memory of that punishment still had the power to make him cringe.

He smiled up at his mom in what he hoped was a convincing manner. "Dinner's great!"

"And you'd know that how?" His mom nodded at the phone. "Call the girl."

Patrick ducked his head, stubbornness stirring in his heart. *I'm a grown man.* He forked up a bite of his spaghetti. "Maybe later."

His mom pulled out a chair and sat across from him. "Patrick, look at me." When his eyes met hers, she grinned. "You look about ten-years-old with that pout on your face."

He shrugged and forked up another bite. "I don't want to talk about it, OK?"

"What do you want? You moped in your room all day Saturday. You skipped church yesterday. And here you are on Monday evening, still sulking." She tilted her head, blonde brows climbing over green eyes. "Do you love Samantha?"

"My feelings are irrelevant since Louis Cantrell—"

"I'm not asking about Louis. I'm asking about you."

Patrick's shoulders slumped. "Yeah."

She nodded to the phone. "Then call the girl. Tell her. *Fight* for her. I know you're confused and a little hurt by what you *think* is going on. But you've left Sam to deal with this emotional nightmare on her own. How do you think she's feeling?" A few beats of silence passed while Patrick mulled her question. "I want you to consider something. If you don't stand up for her now, what happens next time?"

Patrick met his mother's solemn green eyes. "What next time?"

"Life is fickle, sweetheart. There's always going to be a storm to weather. Do you want Samantha to know that she can depend on you, or do you want her to look back on this and know she had to deal with it without you by her side?"

He picked up the phone and twisted it in his hands. "Well, she didn't actually *say* she wanted Louis back in her life."

A muffled ring tone sounded from the kitchen. His mom scooted back from the table and prepared to find her own phone. "I don't imagine she did. If I had to choose, I'd choose you."

Patrick pushed his dinner aside. He wasn't hungry, and his action brought Merlin "the leftover king" to full alert at his feet. Patrick stared down at the dog, missing Sam and Bobbie with an ache greater than hunger. In the last twelve months, he couldn't remember a time when he'd gone two days without at least talking to them. Merlin's whine brought his mind back to the present. The dog sat up and placed his paws on Patrick's leg.

"I wish you really were a wizard. I could use some crystal ball help just about now." He looked up as his mom came back into the room. The sight of tears filming her eyes brought him to attention. "Mom?"

"I'm OK." She sniffed. "That was Harrison. He has Alan's estate details all worked out. He'd like to see both of us in his office tomorrow."

"Me, too? Did he say why?" Patrick lifted a hand and hurried to explain. "I mean, I don't mind going with you, but for him to ask me to come seems a little odd."

She shook her head. "He didn't say, but I'm sure he has a good reason. Can you come with me after your classes?"

"Absolutely." Alan had been gone for more than a year. It broke Patrick's heart to see the pain of his death fresh on his mother's face. "I'll be home by three. I can skip a class if we need to be there earlier."

"Three's fine."

Patrick stood and picked up his dirty dishes. He pulled them close when his mom held out her hands for them. "I was going to help you clean up," he said.

"No, I need some time alone and something to keep my hands busy while I think." She juggled the plates into a neat stack. "I'll do this. You go call Sam."

He picked up the phone and swallowed. Sam's final words from their argument on Saturday came back to haunt him. *"You're going to come to your senses in a day or two and realize how much of a jerk you're being."* Yep, she was right. Being wrong stank like week old garbage. His mom paused in the doorway, a meaningful stare aimed in his direction.

"I'm working on it."

CHAPTER TEN

Sam zoned out of the conversation, too much on her mind to be an active participant. *I should have stayed home.* Her mind worried the twin problems of Louis and Patrick, refusing every command to let it rest. She shifted in her chair, stuck, with no reprieve in sight. If she hadn't ridden to Callie's house with Terri this evening, she would have excused herself and gone home.

She caught herself smashing a piece of pumpkin cheesecake into a pile of orange mush with her fork. She laid the utensil aside, took a sip of her soda, and tried to tune back into what Karla was saying.

"I can't believe my baby is home for good." Karla's green eyes sparkled this evening, excitement erasing years from her face. "I can't get over how good Nicolas looked."

Kate smiled and forked up a bite of her dessert. "My first husband served. I know from experience, the Air Force does keep them fit."

"I can't wait to see him." Callie propped her chin in her hand and tilted her blonde head in thought. "It's been...four...five years since he was home last? I know you're thrilled at his decision to come home to Garfield for good."

Karla sat back. "It's a total God thing. For there to be an opening for a detective in the police department, Ida's house still sitting empty, even the weekend security job he snagged at Party Palace. So many little things just fell into place."

Pam stirred creamer into her coffee. "Party Palace?" She shuddered. "I've seen those poor security guards. Trapped in that cavernous room, surrounded by all that deafening noise all day." She shook her head. "Not even for money."

"You and me both." Karla shrugged. "And he doesn't need the money. He told me it's a way to reconnect with the community." Her expression turned thoughtful. "As far as I'm concerned, that's a step in the right direction. Nicolas was always such an outgoing young man. Mitch and I have never been able to get him to tell us what happened during that first tour overseas. But whatever it was, he closed himself off from everyone. He spent the last twenty years moving from assignment to assignment. We were lucky if we saw him every couple of years or so." Her gaze tracked around the table. "I know you guys have prayed with me over the years, but he's home now. It's time he got his life back on track, with God and his family."

Callie laid her hand on her friend's arm. "We're not gonna stop praying for him. God didn't bring your Nicolas through twenty plus years of dangerous deployments for nothing. He must have a plan for his life."

Karla nodded. "I hope that plan includes a wife. It's hard to see the other three settled with their own families and Nicolas still alone. Now that he's retired..."

Pam steepled her fingers under her chin, shrugging back her shoulder length brown hair. Samantha caught the innocent tone in her voice when she spoke. "How old is Nicolas now?"

"Forty-two," Karla answered.

Samantha ducked her head and hid a smile as Pam's coffee brown eyes cut to Kate.

"Forty-two and never married. Maybe—"

Kate intercepted the look. She shook her head, blonde hair flaring around her face. "No."

Pam tilted her head. "No what? I just think—"

"Just no." Kate motioned to Terri. "I've heard about how you guys work. Silent prayers, innocent gatherings, pretended non-involvement. And look at her. Married three years with two babies—"

"And happier than I've ever been in my life," Terri interrupted.

Kate nodded. "And I'm happy too. I've buried two husbands. I am the original example of unlucky in love. I don't believe in third times the charm, wouldn't open my heart up to the risk if I did." She picked up her coffee. "I have a son"—she smiled across the table at Sam—"and the hope of a daughter and a granddaughter in my future. That's enough for any woman."

Samantha pushed her dessert plate to the center of the table. "Yeah, well. That's not much of a hope if Patrick doesn't pull his head out of his shorts and start seeing what's right in front of his face."

Kate sat forward. "He didn't call you?"

The image of her cell phone, abandoned on her nightstand, flitted behind her eyes. *Shoot!* "I haven't talked to him since Saturday morning."

Kate patted her arm. "You will."

Sam's heart fluttered behind her ribs. She missed him so much. The crack in her voice was unexpected and unavoidable. "Thanks, Kate."

Callie moved her own plate aside and leaned forward on crossed arms. "Lover's spat?"

"I wish that's all it was."

"That doesn't sound good," Karla said. "What's up?"

Sam looked from Terri, to Kate, to Pam. "You guys didn't tell them?"

Terri and Kate both shook their heads. "You're a grown woman, sweetheart," Terri said. "It's your story to share, or not."

Pam shrugged. "You called the house as a client. All I know is what you told me over the phone. Beyond telling me to keep you in prayer, Harrison hasn't told me anything about your conversation, and he won't, not unless there's a case filed and research that needs to be done."

Karla leaned forward next to Callie. "I don't like the sound of this."

Sam closed her eyes, overcome by the love enfolding her from around the table. How did someone with no one end up with so many people to love her? Pam Lake, Callie Stillman, Kate Archer, Karla Black, and her stepmom, *Mom*, she corrected, Terri Evans. A legal researcher, a medical practice manager, a woman's shelter volunteer, a retired government worker, and a day care owner. From the outside looking in, such ordinary women, but there was such wisdom and faith in this circle. Together they presented an awesome combination of experience, age, years of Christian living, study, and teaching. Each with the Christian families she dreamed of having. Samantha drew a jagged breath and dumped the whole story on the shoulders that waited to help her bear the load.

Her hand shook as she mopped tears from her face with a crumpled paper towel. "I'm so confused and scared."

"He's an idiot to come to your house like that," Pam said. "You must have been in total shock. Was Harrison able to help? How soon will the charges be filed?"

Sam's chuckle bordered on sarcasm. "There are no criminal charges in Louis Cantrell's future."

Pam sat back in obvious surprise. She combed dark hair from her forehead with her fingers, brown eyes puzzled. "Why...?"

Sam watched drops of moisture trace rivulets down the side of her glass. They reminded her of tears. She shoved the maudlin thought aside and shook her head. "No charges." She shrugged and tossed her long hair over her shoulder and away from her face. "You know, I'd have never even tried to press charges if he'd stayed out of my life and Bobbie's. But once he turned up on my doorstep, I just knew I had him. What I have is exactly zero."

"How can you have zero? You were just a baby..." Karla trailed off.

"I guess there's a big difference in how the law was

applied forty years ago and how it works now. According to Harrison, sixteen is the legal age of consent in this state." She pushed back from the table, standing to pace and talk it out for herself and everyone else.

"I might have been a very naïve sixteen-year-old, but I was old enough to make my own decisions. The law's on his side on that one." She shrugged as she paced. "He never forced me. I thought I loved him. I'd have felt funny about pursuing a rape charge, but I'd have done it to protect my daughter." She stopped pacing, faced the table, and spread her empty hands. "Nothing."

"He stole from you," Callie reminded her.

"Yes he did, and as strange as it might sound, I'm angrier about that than my loss of innocence. The innocence was mine to give, and right or wrong, he gave me Bobbie." She shrugged. "How can I be angry about that? But the money? That's different. Mom left that life insurance policy to take care of Iris and me. I can't forget what we went through when the money was gone."

"Well, there you have it, sweetheart," Kate said. "Go get him."

"Not possible." Samantha explained what Harrison had told her as Pam nodded her agreement. "There's a three year statute of limitations on grand larceny. He wins again. I've got a cynical little voice in my head that tells me he knew he was home clear before he stepped into the house Friday morning."

"I'd listen to that little voice if I were you," Kate told her.

Sam returned to the table. "Oh, I plan to. But I just

feel so helpless. He's caught me with my defenses down again. I don't know where to go from here." She picked up her watered down soda and took a long swallow to cool her throat. "It's feels like I'm being punished. I guess I deserve it, but it hurts."

The women looked at each other, frowns gathering between five sets of eyes.

"What?" Sam asked.

"Sometimes," Pam began, "the past comes back to bite you."

Callie nodded, her voice cautious when she spoke. "Sweetheart, you're not questioning your forgiveness, are you?"

"Oh no, Callie, not ever. I know God forgave me. But I'm smart enough to know that forgiveness doesn't mean I get off as free as Louis seems to be." She twisted Patrick's ring on her finger, searching for words to make them understand. "Forgiven or not, I still have to deal with the consequences of what I did."

Callie's voice transitioned from concerned friend to teacher. "Yes, you do, but the bad things that happen in our lives aren't always consequences or punishment. Sometimes, bad things happen to make us grow, or to test our faith, to see if we've learned enough to stand strong. But regardless of the source or the reason, God never lets us face these things alone. Psalms 34:19 says that the righteous face many afflictions but the Lord will always come to the rescue. That's a Callie paraphrase, not a quote, but the intent remains the same." She reached across the table and stilled Sam's nervous hands, waiting until Sam looked up before she continued.

"Daniel and Joseph were good people who were in

the wrong place at the right time. Job...well, as much as he thought he'd been abandoned, he never really was. Now's the time for you to learn from those examples. You aren't facing this alone, either."

Sam nodded and stared at the circle of women through a haze of tears. Her voice was hoarse with the effort to keep them in check. "I'm scared, guys. I don't know what Louis wants. I don't want Bobbie to be hurt by my decisions or his actions." She held out her hands to her friends. "Will you pray with me?"

The six women held hands in silent prayer for a few seconds.

Karla finally voiced what they were all feeling. "Father, we need peace and strength and protection. Grant Sam the wisdom to see where You're leading her. You never leave our side. You never leave us to fight alone. Calm her fears where Bobbie is concerned. Lord, there is no situation too big for You. None of this has taken You by surprise. Your word says that our steps are ordered by You. Let Sam rest in that truth."

Sam retrieved the napkin from under her glass and wiped her streaming eyes. For the first time in days, she felt a measure of peace. Could answers be far behind?

Terri stood and tugged Sam to her feet. "Go get our coats, hon. We need to head home."

Callie raised a hand. "Sam, do you have time to stay and help me clean up. I'll run you home once we're done."

Samantha sent the older woman a puzzled look. It was obvious Callie wanted a few minutes alone with her. Heaviness settled in Sam's chest. What could Callie possibly have to say that she couldn't say in front of the others?

"Sure."

The other women took the hint, carried their plates and cups to the kitchen, and said a hasty goodbye.

Callie moved around her kitchen, wiping counters and rinsing dishes. She restocked the little drawer under her coffee maker with fresh Kcups in preparation for the next morning. She tossed a dry towel to Samantha.

"Take that bottle of spray cleaner and wipe down the table for me."

Sam did as she was asked. When she returned to the kitchen, she leaned against the counter, crossed her arms at her waist, and shook her head. "We both know that you didn't need me to help clean. It'll take you longer to drive me home that if you'd just straightened the kitchen up on your own. What gives?"

She watched as Callie's hands stilled and her eyes closed. Her lips moved in a few silent words. *Prayer? For me? Oh, this can't be good.*

Callie shifted to mirror Sam's pose. She leaned forward and tucked a stray strand of Sam's long brown hair behind her ear. Her hand slid from there to cup Sam's chin. "You've become such a beautiful Christian young lady in the last three years. Do you have any idea how much I love you and how proud I am of you?"

"I do know that. I love you, too. Now what's got you mumbling prayers and stalling?"

"We need to have a conversation about Patrick."

Sam shrugged. "Not a lot to say. We had a fight. But we love each other, and it'll work itself out."

"What if it doesn't?" Callie bit her lip. "What if it's not meant to?"

Samantha's stomach clenched at Callie words. "What do you mean?"

Callie turned back to the soapy water in her sink and rinsed a few more plates. Her words came slowly. "We've...I've...watched you and Patrick over the last year. You're an adult and he's a good boy, you make a lovely couple and it's easy to see how much he loves you and Bobbie. None of us want to meddle, but after what you said tonight, I've changed my mind."

"About Patrick being a good boy or my being an adult?"

Callie gave a halfhearted chuckle. "About the meddling. We're concerned about you."

Sam's face heated. *Did she think...*"Callie, we haven't...I mean...we're keeping our promise to each other. We haven't been intimate."

"I'm not concerned about the physical part of your relationship, it's the emotional part that concerns me." She turned again and held Sam's gaze with her own. "I told you a year ago to be Patrick's friend but to guard your heart. That's probably the best advice I could've ever given you. I was a Christian when Benton and I married, but he wasn't. He was a lot like Patrick. A good boy that I thought I could change. We were married for almost twenty-five years before he accepted Christ into his life." She reached across the space and twined her fingers with Sam's.

"I was wrong to think that I could change him, only God can change a heart. And as much as I loved him, as supportive as he was, those were tough years. Every week that I went to church by myself was a heartbreak. That's not what I want for you."

Callie pulled her into a hug. "You're just like my own daughter, and I want good things for you. Just promise me that you'll use part of this time to consider things. We all love Patrick, but God might be trying to redirect your future."

Sam laid her head on the older woman's shoulder. Try as she might, she couldn't see her life without Patrick. Had she allowed her heart to overrule her good sense?

It rang, and it rang, and it rang. When Samantha's voice mail picked up for the seventh time in the last ninety minutes, Louis poked the disconnect button with a vicious jab. He drew his arm back to throw the thing against the faded beige of the hotel wall. The fleeting thought of spending part of his dwindling finances to replace it had him turning at the last second and pitching the thing, full force, into the covers of the unmade bed. The cloud of expletives that followed its flight was impressive, even by his standards. He rolled his shoulders. It felt good to let go for a second. Presenting a polished, repentant façade to the world was hard work.

Louis stomped around the room, sweeping flat surfaces free of everything not bolted down, kicking at anything unlucky enough to lie in his path. He clenched his hands together and imagined them around the throat of Carson's thug.

He paused in the middle of the mess he'd created, chest heaving with harsh breaths and spent energy. "I blew it." *No, that stupid goon blew it for me, and that's exactly what I'm telling Carson if this thing falls through.*

Slumping down on the side of the bed, he took a few deep breaths and gave himself a muttered pep talk. "It'll be OK. You just need to focus." He closed his eyes and thought aloud, listing options and approaches.

"Sam isn't the submissive, needy girl she was five years ago. Demands didn't work, and sweet talk had failed..." His aggravated sigh filled the room. "Well, I don't know if sweet talk would have worked because the goon..." The pulse throbbing in his temples accelerated. "Forget the goon and focus. What comes next? You've faced stubborn marks before." Louis sat up. *Presents.* Nothing went to the heart of a female, even a half pint one, faster than a nice, shiny doodad. He frowned. *Doodad's meant money.* He cursed the thug again.

CHAPTER ELEVEN

Sam pulled her Mustang through the Starbucks drive-thru on the way to class Tuesday morning, thankful that caffeine civilization had finally come to Garfield. *Well, not really to Garfield.* Just conveniently on the interstate between her home and the university twenty miles north of Garfield. The line of waiting cars stretched ten deep around the building. That was fine. She'd allowed plenty of time for this important detour. *Might as well put the time to good use.*

She pulled out her smartphone and did a quick check of her email, deleting a message from someone claiming to be an Algerian lawyer holding a multi-million dollar inheritance with her name on it. *Where do these people come from? If your gonna scam someone, learning the language seems like a logical first step.* Next up, two messages from blogs she followed. Those went into a file for an uninterrupted reading after Bobbie went to bed tonight. There were a couple of emails from members of her study group and her bank statement was ready for viewing. Nothing earth shattering.

Messages cleared, she glanced at the time and entered a familiar phone number. There wasn't a smidgen of sleep in Lisa's voice when her best friend picked up on the other end.

"You're out early."

"I'm making up a class I missed when Bobbie was sick early last week." Sam eased her foot off the brake and inched forward a car length closer to the caffeine boost her morning needed. The white van behind her did the same. "We missed you at Bible study last night."

"I planned to be there, but Pastor Gordon stopped by with a check for us."

Sam heard a hint of suppressed emotion in Lisa's voice.

"I'm blown away by the generosity and love—"

"You shouldn't be. You guys mean a lot to Valley View."

"I won't ever doubt that again, but...wow! I mean Dave and I have given in dozens of love offerings over the years. It never crossed our minds that we'd ever be on the receiving end, you know? It's a very humbling experience. The insurance company will send money for living expenses and stuff soon, but in the meantime, this is such a blessing. Dave and I took the kids shopping after Pastor left. We all needed clothes, and their coats needed replacing, and, well, toys are a necessity at this age. The twins each picked out a new truck and they got teddy bears to sleep with, and Alex found a doll. No nightmares last night, thank goodness."

"Oh, bless their hearts. I'm glad to hear they're

adjusting. It's the kids I called about. I know Terri arranged for some playtime for them through the week, but are you free Saturday?"

Two more customers received their orders and pulled their cars through the line.

"I can't think of anything," Lisa said. "What do you have in mind?"

"Between the weather and her cold, Bobbie's feeling a little cooped up. I'm taking her to Party Palace to take advantage of some indoor playtime. If you guys want to join us, I'll spring for pizza."

"What a great idea, but you don't have to buy our lunch."

"Are you trying to cheat me out of a blessing?"

"No..."

Two cars peeled out of the line without ordering, obviously not willing to wait. *Wimps!* "Then I'm buying lunch. Meet us out there at eleven. The kids can run their little heads off and stuff up on pizza while we have a nice long visit." One car remained between her and a mocha latte. "Hey, I gotta go. It's almost my turn to order."

"Where are you?"

"Starbucks."

"Oh... I think I really hate you." A chuckle filtered through the speaker. "Eat a scone for me. We'll see you Saturday at eleven."

Samantha tucked the phone away and grinned. If she hurried, she had time to backtrack for an additional errand. After she got her order, Sam retraced the five miles back to Garfield.

She reached the gym parking lot and pulled close to the trailer. She set a tall mocha latte and a tightly wrapped strawberry scone on the step of the RV and pounded on the door. The second she heard footsteps, she jumped back in her car and sped away. Her cell phone rang sixty seconds later. Sam ignored it, confident that she'd played a major role in getting Lisa's day off to a fine and properly caffeinated start.

Patrick laid the dog-eared magazine aside and stood as Harrison strode into the waiting room. The lawyer squeezed his shoulder before taking his mom's outstretched hand in both of his.

"Kate, I'm glad you two could make it in on such short notice."

"It's going to be a relief to finally have it finished." She paused, and Patrick saw her smile go tight with grief. "It's hard to believe Alan's only been gone a year. It seems much longer."

Harrison nodded and motioned down the short hall. "Let's continue this in my office." He ushered them through the door and waved his hand at the visitors' chairs arranged in front of his desk. "Have a seat. Can Stephanie get either of you something to drink?"

Patrick shook his head as his mom sat. Their mutual "No, thanks," mingled in the air as Harrison circled behind his desk to take his seat.

"All right, let's get started." The lawyer turned his attention to the open folder resting in the center of his desk. He studied the papers for a few seconds before lifting his head and focusing on Kate. "I don't know what you're expecting to hear, but I think you are going to be pleasantly surprised. Alan was a shrewd businessman."

Kate nodded. "He worked with people and their

finances every day. He knew the importance of planning."

Harrison continued to flip through the pages of the folder. "New home in your name. Business interests properly liquidated and the funds all in order. Life insurance policy up to date. I've never handled an estate so well prepared. He didn't leave a lot for me to do."

Kate offered a sad smile. "Alan knew his time was limited. He wanted to make sure I was taken care of."

The office was silent as Harrison continued to read, jotting an occasional note on a yellow legal pad.

He looked up and pushed his reading glasses to the top of his head. "I'd say he succeeded." He leaned forward on his elbows. "Kate, you are about to be a wealthy woman."

"I'm sorry?"

"You guys retained me as the personal representative for Alan's estate. I've been working on several issues since he died. I haven't said anything to you about most of it for two reasons. I knew you were adequately provided for in the short term, and I'd made promises to Alan. He made some final arrangements that weren't to be discussed until now, since it was impossible to determine a bottom line before everything sorted itself out."

His mother reached across the small space that separated their chairs, and Patrick took her hand. Her fingers were ice cold in his grip.

"What are you telling me, Harrison?"

"That Alan had one of the best business heads I've ever seen. He had a financial interest in several small businesses, a private stock portfolio, and a substantial inheritance from a grandparent that didn't reach maturity till his forty-fifth birthday."

"I knew about the inheritance," Kate said. "He got a quarter of the annuity on his twenty-fifth birthday, a quarter on his thirty-fifth birthday, and would have received the balance at age forty-five."

Harrison nodded and stretched across his desk to hand Kate a sheet of paper. Patrick released his mother's hand, watching a small frown gather between her eyes as she read the paper. Patrick looked back and forth between the two older adults.

"Twenty thousand dollars?" she asked.

"A month, for the foreseeable future."

"What?" The single word came out as a strangled croak.

Harrison sat back and crossed his arms over his chest. "I've cleared all the investments, paid all the taxes, and worked with Alan's personal accountant to re-invest the proceeds according to Alan's final instructions. Your portion amounts to a paycheck in the amount of twenty thousand dollars on the first day of each month."

"I can't...I mean...Are you joking?"

"Kate, I don't get paid to joke."

She stood and circled the room twice before coming to a rest behind Patrick's chair. He felt her hands on his shoulders, the tremor in her fingers transmitted through the thick weave of his heavy sweater. She cleared her throat.

"I'd like to reallocate some of those funds."

"As in..."

"Twenty thousand a month is obscene, Harrison. The house is paid for. I don't have that many monthly expenses. Some of that money needs to go to the kids."

"You can be the doting mother and stepmother all you want, but the kids, all three of them, are handsomely provided for as well."

His mother reclaimed her seat, and as she did, Patrick tried to decipher the look on her face. He failed.

Her breath shuddered as she leaned forward. "Explain *handsomely provided for*."

"Three trust funds. One million each, dispersed much as Alan's was. One quarter at age twenty-one, one quarter at age thirty, and the balance at age forty."

The lawyer turned to Patrick. "This is why I asked you to come today. Since you're past your twenty-first birthday, the first installment of your inheritance will be forthcoming just as soon as deposit arrangements can be made."

Patrick sat back with a hard swallow. *Two hundred and fifty thousand dollars?* The continuing chatter between his mom and the lawyer got lost in the implications of Harrison's words. That kind of money could open a lot of doors for a law student looking to take on a ready-made family. The first of those doors swung open with a loud creak, knocking the image of Louis Cantrell back several feet.

Thanks, Dad!

He glanced at his watch, suddenly anxious to be gone. His plans to drop off his mother and head straight to Samantha's took a backseat to an unexpected errand.

Patrick. Samantha's heart raced at the tap on the door at the top of the stairs. Excitement, pure and simple, sent her up the steps, double time, and caused her hand to tremble on the knob. -*Four days!* Even though Sam had plenty of checks and balances built into her relationship with Patrick, a necessity until he accepted Christ into his heart, he was still her first real boyfriend, and this had been their first real fight. With no experience to measure the last few days against, they might as well have been weeks. She took a calming breath and muttered the same prayer she'd prayed every day for the last year, the same prayer that seemed to go unheard and continued to go unanswered. "Jesus, please touch Patrick's heart."

She pulled the door open, expecting tentative words of apology and a hug. The tornado of passion that swept through the open door stole her breath as well as her resolve. Samantha found herself wrapped in Patrick's strong arms almost before the door closed behind him. The length of his body held hers captive against the wall of the stairwell as his lips rained kisses across her face.

Her surprised gasp was swallowed whole as his mouth took hers in a kiss that tested the limits of her control. She fisted her hands against the front of his shirt and teetered on the edge of reason. Patrick lifted his mouth, his breath harsh, his heart thudding hard against hers.

"Baby, I'm so sorry."

His mouth descended, cutting off her response. Samantha lost herself in the kisses she'd denied both of them for a year. She wanted time to freeze right here. Here, where nothing existed except the two of them. No school, no family, no fight, no Louis, no religious duty...From somewhere in her soul a small voice finally made itself heard. *Wait!*

Sam turned her head to the side. Patrick's lips simply moved to her neck, tracing frenzied kisses across the sensitive skin. "Patrick?"

Some note of surprise or uncertainty in her voice must have registered. Patrick stilled. He lifted his head and took a step back. His hands cupped her face, forcing her eyes to meet his.

"Sam, I love you so much."

"I love you too. I—" A trembling finger across her lips halted her response.

"This has been the longest four days of my life. I never want us to fight again." He buried his hands in her hair. "I never want to be without you again." He lowered his lips to hers. This time his kiss was soft and tender, soothing instead of ravaging. Restrained feelings and denied passion pounded at Sam like surf on a rocky beach. She had no defense against this. He straightened, his harsh breath meeting hers, and held her gaze with his.

"Marry me."

CHAPTER TWELVE

Patrick watched the desire on Sam's face give way to shock before finally fading into confusion.

"Have you lost your mind?"

Patrick grabbed her hand and led her down the stairs. "Not exactly the answer I was looking for." He sat on the sofa and pulled her down beside him. "Where's the munchkin?"

"Upstairs with Seth. Mom and Dad are helping them make ornaments." She shook her hand free of his and crossed her arms. "Don't try to change the subject."

"Not changing the subject. I have some things to tell you, and I need your undivided attention." The small box in his pants' pocket provided a continuous pressure on his thigh. His stomach turned somersaults, and every sweat gland in his body shifted into overdrive under Sam's heated stare. "Samantha, I want...I mean, I need..." His mouth dried up like the Sahara. *OK, Wheeler, where's all those fancy words you spent the last two hours rehearsing?* "Man!" Patrick scrambled to his feet, dug the small box from his pocket, and shoved it into Sam's hands.

Her indrawn breath filled the room. "Patrick?"

"Just open it, OK?"

Samantha's gaze shifted to the box. She turned it in her hands, obviously trying to determine top from bottom. Once she found the small silver latch, the lid flipped open to reveal the square-cut emerald nestled inside. The tiny diamonds surrounding the brilliant green stone caught the reflection of the overhead light and cast prisms around the room. She touched the stone with fingers that shook before she looked up. "It's beautiful."

Patrick sat back down beside her and took the box from her trembling hands. "Let's try it on."

"I—"

He pulled her hand into his. "Humor me for just a second." He slipped the ring on her left ring finger. Their breath mingled in a joint gasp at the ring's perfect fit. With her hand in his, the dam holding back his words finally broke.

"The ring belonged to my father's mother. Mom wore it for a long time. It's been biding time in a safe deposit box until I could find the person I wanted to share my life with." He stopped to lace his fingers with hers, knowing his heart lay bare at her feet. The pounding in his chest eased when he saw his feelings mirrored in her eyes. "I found her a year ago in a crowded Sonic parking lot."

Sam's eyes darted to the ring and back to his face.

"Patrick, we still—"

"I know what you're going to say. We're still in

school. We don't have jobs. How would we support ourselves? Where would we live? Those aren't issues anymore." At her puzzled expression, he rushed to explain the meeting with Harrison and the inheritance coming his way. "I can provide for you in a way I never expected. If I found a part-time job, we could make the money stretch until I'm out of school. More important than that, if we're married, I can protect you. This whole thing with Louis...it's made me realize how vulnerable you and Bobbie are. As long as I'm just the boyfriend in the background, he has the upper hand."

He paused, covered their linked hands with his free one, and slipped to a knee in front of the sofa.

"Samantha, I love you." He kissed her fingers. "Marry me. Make me the happiest guy in the world. I promise, on my life, I'll do everything I can to be the father Bobbie needs and the husband you deserve."

Sam stared into Patrick's eyes. Heaviness bloomed in her chest and became a physical pain. How could the happiest day of her life be the worst day of her life? She bit her lip to keep it from trembling, but she couldn't stop the tears as easily.

"Do you have any idea...?" She tried to swallow around the lump in her throat. "Do you know how much I love you?"

"I hope so."

The silent plea in his words crushed her soul. "Oh, Patrick." Sam pulled her hand free, the weight of the emerald and all it represented heavy on her hand and in her heart. She stood and paced. When she turned, Patrick was still kneeling by the couch, watching her with a hooded expression.

What am I supposed to say to him, Father? Her mouth opened as words formed but thoughts fled. Was there any way to make no sound like maybe? She combed the fingers of her left hand through her hair, flinching when the ring tangled in the long strands.

She pulled in a deep breath, walked back to the sofa, and held out her hand. "Patrick, there is absolutely nothing in this world that would make me happier, but—"

"Sam." Patrick scrambled to his feet and wrapped her in an energetic hug.

"But...no." The words were so lightly whispered, Sam wasn't sure he'd heard her. When his arms went slack, she knew he had.

He released her and stepped back. Disappointment and anger occupied his face in equal measure. "Do I even need to ask why?"

Sam shook her head.

"It's the whole church thing, isn't it?"

"My relationship with Christ isn't a *thing*. It's who I am." She reached out to him, shrugging when he ignored her hand. "I love you, and I'm honored that you love me. But how long would you love me if I denied the salvation that makes me lovable?"

"I'm not asking you to deny anything." Patrick's voice was harsh. "I'm not saying you can't be a Christian if you marry me. Just because I don't believe what you believe doesn't mean that I'm going to turn into some...some control freak who won't let you think for yourself. Go to church all you want. Raise our family on the seat beside you." He shrugged. "I have friends there, too. I'll probably go with you most of the time."

Every week that I went to church by myself was a heartbreak.

Patrick took a deep breath, his struggle for calm evident in tight lips and furrowed brow. He sat and patted the cushion beside him. "Come sit down so we can talk instead of arguing."

She took her seat and he turned to face her. "I know how important your beliefs are to you. I'm sorry if I made them sound trivial. That's not what I intended to do. But there are more important things to consider right now than religion."

He held out his hand and smiled when Sam laced her fingers with his. "I want to take care of you and Bobbie. I love you, and I want to protect you. I'll admit that my need to take care of you is putting romance in the back seat right now. This whole thing with Louis has me spooked. We still don't know why he's here, why he's suddenly making noises about seeing Bobbie."

Sam lifted her eyes when he tugged on her hand.

"Which one of us do you want in her life?"

She shook her head. "You still don't get it, do you? Even if I married you tonight, who I want in Bobbie's life might not be an either-or situation. I don't know why Louis is here, and as much as I'd like to pretend he has no part in my daughter's life, he is her father. The fact is, marrying you is not the solution to my problems. The fact is, whether you acknowledge it or not, God is the only answer to any of this." Sam untangled her fingers from his and bowed her head over her hands. She twisted the emerald ring as tears fell to her lap. "The fact is, nothing is more important to me than God's will for my life and Bobbie's. It's not about *going to church*. It's not about *religion*. It's about having Christ as the foundation of our marriage. It's about being on the same page while we raise our family." She raised her face to his. "It's about relationships. Yours and mine. Two halves making a whole." She slipped the ring off her finger. Its absence tore a hole in her heart. "The fact is, no matter how much I love you..." She placed the ring in his hand and closed his fingers around it. "I can't accept this until you understand that."

She watched through tears as Patrick stared at his fisted hand. "I never really believed you'd say no."

"I don't want it to be no. What I want it to be is *not now*, but maybe later. Can't we just leave it at that for now?"

"Whatever." Patrick seemed to move in slow motion. He retrieved the small black box, shoved the ring inside, and stuffed it back into his pocket. He stood and held out his hand. His mouth hardened as Sam looked up at him. He nodded to her right hand. "I need that one too."

"But—"

"No buts. Both or neither."

Samantha eased the chunky class ring off her finger. The hole in her heart ripped wider with every centimeter the ring moved. She held it for a second before dropping it in Patrick's outstretched hand.

Patrick spun on his heel, crossed the room, and took the stairs to the kitchen two at a time. He didn't slam the door, but its closing echoed in the empty room as Sam toppled onto the sofa and wept.

The windy Oklahoma weather whistled past the door of Louis's cheap room. He shivered as fingers of cold air crept under the door, crossed the threadbare carpet, and nipped at his bare ankles just like the blue heeler puppies his grandpa used to raise.

The memory did not bring a smile to his face. He had no more use for dogs than he did for kids. Take, take, take. Time, money...your very soul if you allowed yourself to get attached. There was no explaining why a rational person would let himself fall into such a trap. Life on his own, make or break, sink or swim, living or dying—Louis grimaced at that thought—was good enough for him. He rose and covered the gap beneath the door with a towel. The place was ancient, an old motel made into pay-by-the-week micro apartments. He'd lived in worse. This would do until he could squirm his way back into Sam's good graces.

Louis returned his attention to the items spread out on the small table. Receipts, mostly. The only way he could talk Mr. Carson into loaning him the additional fifteen grand had been a promise of strict record keeping. The big guy wasn't taking any chances on Louis gambling away any of this money. It chafed, a lot, to be kept on such a short leash. The hoops he'd had to jump through to get the money and the watchdog sent along to follow his every movement made him nervous. Obviously his bookie didn't trust him. The con man looked up into the age-frosted mirror of the old dresser. He flashed his best smile. *What's not to trust?*

He bent to his task, bottom lip clenched between his teeth while he totaled the pile of cash register tickets, bank stubs, and receipts with painstaking accuracy in a small notebook. Ten thousand dollars for Sam. Various travel, lodging, and living expenses. The room was his for a month, but he needed to find some part-time work to supplement his dwindling supply of cash. He picked up the receipts from today's shopping and rolled his eyes. Another hundred of his precious dollars down the drain, and for what?

He didn't mind the bracelet so much. When Samantha finally came around to his version of reality, he'd consider the pawnshop treasure money well spent. The memory of her soft curves under his hungry hands and lips, and the anticipation of a repeat performance, almost made the money worth it.

It was the other gift that made him grind his teeth. Are parents crazy? Who paid forty-five dollars for a hunk of plastic with fake hair? Louis spared a glance for the brightly wrapped gift leaning against the wall next to the door. *And five extra dollars to have it wrapped.* A doll for his *daughter.* His mind stumbled over the word. *A necessary part of the plan.* He couldn't get to *Daddy's* money without winning Sam. Wouldn't win Sam by ignoring the kid. And, with Mr. Carson's muscle breathing down his back, demanding results, he had to kick this plan into motion tonight.

He finished his accounting session, shoved the bulk of his remaining cash between the worn mattress and box springs, and folded two one-hundred-dollar bills into his wallet. The big bills made him feel important. Nothing could beat the big spender rush that went along with making some poor schmuck at a convenience store break a hundred for a cup of coffee. His fun would be short lived, though, if he couldn't convince Samantha to give him another chance.

Louis sighed and tried to prep himself for the evening to come. Dropping in unannounced could be dicey, but he counted on the gifts to pave the way to his first face-to-face meeting with his daughter. What did fathers do with kids? Maybe he could talk Samantha into dinner. That seemed safe enough, and McDonald's would be a reasonable and thrifty idea. The suggestion of the enclosed playground might win him some *daddy* points. Once the kid was busy, he'd be free to begin work on Sam.

With a plan in mind, Louis changed into a clean shirt, slipped on socks and shoes, slapped on some dollar store aftershave, and raced through the howling wind to the car. Fifteen minutes later, he pulled the rattletrap vehicle to a halt in front of Samantha's house and grabbed the two packages from the seat beside him. He narrowed his eyes at the blue pickup truck taking up a good portion of the drive. The same truck had been here on Friday morning. He figured it belonged to the blond kid with the smart mouth. His words and actions pegged him as Sam's boyfriend. Well, loverboy's time was limited. The A-team had arrived.

Louis bounded up the porch steps, prepared to knock. The door flew open before his hand ever connected with the wood, and he found himself face-to-face with loverboy. The men stared at each other for several seconds. Louis sneered. Patrick groaned. And before Louis could anticipate the move, the younger man's fist connected with Louis's jaw. The gifts fell from his limp arms. The last thing Louis remembered was his slow motion slide to the wooden planks of the porch.

CHAPTER THIRTEEN

The door at the head of the stairs crashed open against the opposite wall. "Sam, you better get up here," Iris called out.

Sam raised her head from the tear-drenched sofa cushion. *Why can't people just leave me alone?* The sound of raised voices and crying children sliced through her pity party. *Bobbie.* She rolled to her feet. "I'm coming, sis. What's wrong with Bobbie?"

Iris stood in the doorway, blocking her progress, a smirk on her face. "Bobbie's fine. Mom took all the kids up to her bedroom."

"Then what...?"

"Your new boyfriend just punched your old boyfriend in the face. I've never seen Dad so mad. Louis better be glad he's unconscious."

"Oh good grief." Sam shouldered around her younger sister, rushed to the living room, and out the open front door.

Her father stood on the porch, hands on his hips,

eyes riveted on a set of taillights disappearing into the dark. The acrid smell of burnt rubber lingered in the frigid night air.

She dismissed Patrick and focused on Louis, spread-eagle on the porch. Angel stood next to him sniffing at his extremities. The dog's tongue snaked out and licked his exposed cheek. Even in the dim illumination of the single light bulb, Sam could see the thin trickle of blood from his split lip and a bruise blooming on his chin. *Why do guys have to use their fists for everything?* She shooed the dog away, stooped, and shook Louis's shoulder. "Get up, Louis."

Her father joined her next to their fallen visitor. "He's out."

"What happened?"

"I'm not sure. Terri and I were bringing Seth and Bobbie into the kitchen for a snack when Patrick came barreling up the stairs. Bobbie went chasing after him, trying to show him the ornament she just finished. He didn't even acknowledge her, just yanked the door open to leave. The next thing I know, Bobbie's howling and Patrick's crouched over Louis, rubbing his fist, and grinning."

The prone body on the porch groaned, and Louis rolled to his side. His eyes were closed. He was still out.

Her father continued his explanation. "I pulled them apart and tried to get Patrick to talk to me. He shrugged me off. I was in the middle of letting him know I didn't appreciate him causing a scene in front of the babies. He just stomped out to his truck and peeled out of the drive." He met Samantha's eyes. "I've never seen him act like that. What did he mean by 'You're welcome to her'?"

"He said that to you?"

Steve motioned to Louis. "He told Louis that right before I separated them." Sam sent a glance in the direction Patrick had taken. Anger replaced misery. "Stubborn, pigheaded, idiotic..."

Louis began to stir. Sam kept her hand on his arm as he sat up and blinked.

"Are you OK?"

Louis worked his jaw back and forth and used tentative fingers to explore his chin. "That little punk punched me in the face. I'm gonna..." His eyes met Sam's for just an instant before they fluttered closed again. His body went limp and Sam clutched his arm to keep him from hitting the porch a second time.

"Louis?"

She looked at her father. "Help me get him in the house before we all freeze to death." Together, Sam and her father pulled Louis to his feet. They supported him between them, his body dead weight on their shoulders. Sam put one arm around his waist and slapped the uninjured side of his face with her free hand. "Wake up, Louis." When that failed to gain a reaction, she smacked him a little harder. "Louis—"

Louis grabbed her hand. "Hey..." He paused and looked around. "What happened?"

Sam shifted to position herself more firmly under his arm. "Can you walk?"

"Yeah." He tightened his arm around her shoulder. His bruised face split into a leering grin. "But this is really nice."

Sam narrowed her eyes and nodded toward the open door. "Just walk." Once they were in the house, Sam backed him up to the sofa. "Sit."

Freed of his weight, her dad closed the door and leaned against it.

She took a step away and crossed her arms at her waist. "Which part of 'you're not welcome here' did you not understand?"

"Samantha, sweetheart, I had to see you. I made such a mess out of our meeting the other day. I brought..." He stopped and looked around the room. "I had a gift for my daughter."

"It's probably out on the porch." Steve pulled the door open.

"Thank you, Mr. Evans. There were two."

"Angel, what are you...?" Steve came back in a few seconds later with the gifts. The bow on the larger of the two gifts was shredded and covered in drool. He placed them on the sofa next to Louis with a shrug.

"Thank you, sir."

"Umm-hmm." Sam's dad stood in the middle of room, hands on his hips, obviously waiting for some sort of explanation.

Sam faced her father. "Can you leave us alone for a few minutes?"

He put his hands on both of her shoulders. His eyes searched her face. "You sure?"

She nodded. "Just keep Bobbie upstairs for me for a little bit longer, OK?"

Her dad squeezed her shoulders, treated Louis to a silent dad-stare, and turned for the stairs.

Sam took the chair farthest away from Louis, crossed her arms, and remained silent until she heard the door latch behind her father. Her gaze remained locked with Louis's. "You too, Iris."

Iris stepped from her concealed location in the

dining room. "But—"

"No buts." She nodded towards the hall. "Take a hike."

"Man!" Iris huffed, but she moved down the hall. She turned and looked daggers at Louis. "Sam shared your pathetic story with us. Just so you know, I don't believe a single word."

Louis responded to Iris with a shrug, shifting uncomfortably under Samantha's continued scrutiny. His tongue slipped out to explore his split lip, and his fingers clenched in suppressed fury. If he ever caught up with loverboy, he'd more than return this favor. He struggled to rein in his anger. His initial threats had put such a look of disapproval on Sam's face that he'd faked a second blackout to divert her attention. More verbal threats wouldn't get the reaction he needed.

A door slammed down the hall. Sam leaned forward in her chair. "OK, Louis, let's have it. Be advised, I'm not in the mood for any of your garbage. You've got five minutes to explain yourself, and I'm watching the clock."

Where was his docile, innocent Sam? "Sweetheart, I didn't come back here to cause you any trouble—"

Sam snorted. "Your middle name is trouble." She glanced at the clock over the mantle. "Four minutes and fifty seconds."

Louis swallowed. *Slow and steady now.* He tried again. "Sam, you were the best thing that ever happened to me. I've thought about you and our child every day since I was forced to leave. All I want is a chance to show you that I've changed. The gambling is a thing of the past, the threat to you and our child is gone." Sam's doubt was tangible enough to feel. He forced a little more pleading into his voice. "I know my timing looks suspicious, but it's just coincidence. At the very least, I deserve a chance to be a part of my daughter's life." He studied her stony expression. *Maybe just a little hint of a threat.* "I don't want to resort to legal measures to get what's mine, but I will."

Sam's eyes widened. *Bull's eye.*

He rushed forward to soothe her ruffled feathers with the smooth tongue that had always served him so well. "I've never stopped loving you. I want to build a family with you. I know that can't happen overnight. I have too much to prove, but I *will* prove it if you give me the chance."

"Are you proposing to me, Louis?"

"As much as I love you, I know you're not ready for that." He plucked the small box from its place on the cushion beside him. "It's not a ring, Sam." Louis ducked his head. "I didn't have a lot of money, and"— he gestured to the slightly bedraggled larger package— "I wanted to buy a gift for my daughter, too." He stood, crossed the room, and held out the brightly wrapped gift. "It's more of a peace offering than anything else. Consider it the final piece of my heart. You've had the rest for almost five years."

Sam brushed his hand aside and shoved up from her seat. She paced the length of the room. *Jesus, help me. I need You to tell me what I'm supposed to do.* When she reached the mantle, she studied the clock, watching the second hand tick away Louis's five minutes. Several beats of silence stretched into the room. Her eyes closed in resignation when no answer materialized. She prepared to turn, ready to offer her nemesis any excuse to get him out of the house in order to give herself, and God, some more time.

Danger!

The hair on the back of her neck stood up and she froze in place. She felt the word more than heard it. She tilted her head and turned all her senses inward.

Danger!

Her eyes fluttered closed, and she breathed a quick prayer of thanksgiving. *Thank You, Father.* Samantha turned to face Louis. "I don't think so." Louis opened his mouth, obviously ready to plead his case. She shook her head.

"The Bible says that I have to forgive you. I've tried really hard, in the last few days, to think of reasons why I shouldn't, but really, I forgave you a long time ago. Your actions gave me Bobbie, and for the life of me, I can't be angry about that. Even your dishonesty and the situation you left us in worked out for the best. If not for your deceit, Iris and I would have continued on our own. You forced us into a position that ultimately reunited our family." She shrugged. "So consider yourself forgiven."

"Sam..." Louis took a single step in her direction. Samantha's raised hand stopped him cold.

"Forgiven but not forgotten. I forgive you, Louis, but regardless of all the positive things your actions caused, I will never forget what you did to me and my sister. Our memory is what keeps us out of trouble. And just like a child avoiding a hot stove once he's been burned, I'll be cutting a wide path around you."

Louis's expression slid into anger. "Wrong answer."

"I beg your pardon?"

"Wrong answer." It was Louis's turn to pace. "I spent a lot of time and money tracking you down and moving out here. I worked and saved for months so that I could start paying you back for what I took. I don't intend to be brushed aside like yesterday's garbage. I deserve a chance."

Sam crossed her arms. "Oh, you're doing a fine job of showing me what you deserve."

Her sarcastic response pulled him up short. She watched him struggle to regain control.

"What about my daughter?"

"What about her?"

"She's my flesh and blood, and I have rights." He motioned to the gift on the sofa. "I want to see her."

Sam shook her head. "An hour ago I wasn't sure how I'd answer this question when the time came. I've been praying about this, a lot. I thought about the years I went without my own father, and I worried about putting Bobbie in the same situation. But, the more I think about it, the more I realize her safety, now, is more important than what she might think twenty years down the road."

She looked him in the eye, her voice even and calm when she continued. "Where were you when I couldn't afford diapers? Where were you when Bobbie was drinking milk instead of the baby formula she needed? Where were you when I was forced to leave *our* daughter in the care of a child so I could work?"

She paused, shrugging when he didn't answer. "You gave up any claim you might have had to her before she was ever born. You can't breeze in here with gifts and sweet words and make up for that."

"I'll get a lawyer—"

"Threats won't win you any battles either." She crossed to the door and pulled it open. "But you go right ahead and hire a lawyer. I already have one. If you can convince a judge that you deserve to be a part of her life, we'll talk, but until then, you need to leave."

Louis stepped out into the cold night air. "You haven't heard the last of this."

"No, I don't expect that I have, but I've heard all I intend to listen to tonight."

Sam closed the door in Louis's face, forcing him to take a quick step back. When she turned, she spied the larger of the two gifts still on the couch. She crossed the room, yanked the box up by the mangled bow, and hurried back to the door. Louis took a step forward when the door swung open. Sam shoved the gift into his chest. "Take this with you."

Sam leaned against the closed door. Two men expressing their undying love in one day. Her dream and her nightmare. Her gaze drifted down to the hand where the beautiful emerald ring had resided so briefly. She closed her eyes and a single tear escaped to run down her cheek.

Patrick.

CHAPTER FOURTEEN

Patrick took the turn toward Garfield's lake at forty miles an hour. The truck fishtailed in the loose gravel.

Get back on the road, you worthless piece of junk! He punched the gas, sliding some more before the Chevy's tires found purchase on the broken pavement.

He skidded to a stop in the parking lot, slammed out of his truck, and hit the deserted walking path that wound around Garfield's little lake. His breath fogged around him as he ran, but the emotions churning in his gut and the physical exertion required to keep his pace kept him plenty warm. He ran until the cold threatened to choke the very air from his lungs. Stumbling to a stop, he bent over and braced his hands on his thighs. The labored wheeze of his gulping breaths was the only sound in the cold night air. His heart rate slowly returned to a normal rhythm, settling down to throb in time with the pain in the knuckles of his right hand.

He stepped into a circle of yellow light cast by one of the well-spaced pole lamps and examined his hand.

No broken skin. He flinched when he touched it with the tentative fingers of his left hand. That's was gonna hurt tomorrow. An unbidden smile played around his lips. Not as much as that loser's face.

"I can't believe I did that." Patrick's murmured words were for his ears only. He shook his hand at his side and stared across the dark surface of the water. "My momma didn't raise no sissy," he whispered to the lapping waves.

She didn't raise a hothead either.

Patrick pushed the small voice of reason aside. "Jerk had it coming, and then some."

Maybe, but did Bobbie need to see you do it?

He brought his hands to his face and tried to scrub the memory of her little face away. He'd been so angry...hurt...over Sam's refusal of his proposal, he hadn't really even seen Bobbie until it was too late. But he saw her now, tagging after him, trying to get his attention. Now, he heard her frantic cries in his memory and tried to justify his actions. It was just a punch in the face. But Bobbie sounded scared to death. She had no experience with violence...until now.

Patrick kicked at a stone in the path and sent it skipping into the water. He pictured his butt painted on the rock as it disappeared beneath the surface.

"Yep, that's me, sinking a little deeper every day."

Well, no one forced you to hit him.

He cocked his head as he tuned into his conscience once more. "Oh, you're a lot of help. Where were you before I slugged him?" The next rock he kicked ricocheted off a tree ten feet away. "I'll be lucky if Mr. Evans ever lets me in his house again after tonight."

He looked up at the star-sprinkled sky, clear as glass

in the December cold. Anger renewed itself, finding a target in the One supposed to be in control. "And where are You in this whole mess?" His heart constricted in guilt at his irreverent tone. Patrick brushed a lifetime of teaching aside, determined to have an answer once and for all. "Oh, don't play Your guilt card on me. What do You care, anyway? When have You ever done a single thing for me except ignore me? You talk a good story, but with every day that passes, that's what I'm convinced it is...just a story."

Patrick stopped. Surely if God was up there, He'd defend Himself. The wait stretched out. No answering voice rumbled from the heavens. No lightning bolt zipped down from the sky. The ground didn't open up to swallow him and his disrespectful words.

"That's just what I expected." Patrick waved a dismissive hand at the sky and began the cold, solitary trudge back to his truck on feet that grew more leaden with each step.

The silence around him remained unbroken. More silence greeted him as he climbed into the seat. No father. No Samantha. Once Mom had the facts, she wouldn't take his side in this. Sisko had been his confidant for the last year, but he had enough on his plate right now. Patrick refused to add to it with his problems. Talking to God was a galactic joke.

A wave of stifling heat ignited in his chest and bloomed outward. He struggled to draw in a breath. He was alone for the first time in his life. When the sensation passed, he leaned his forehead against the steering wheel and cried like a girl.

Louis pressed a cold washcloth to his bruised chin.

The threadbare terry cloth scraped like sandpaper. He jerked it away. The fleabag laundry for this rattrap hotel had obviously never heard of fabric softener. A snort of disgust followed the rag into the sink.

"If I ever get my hands on that...that...punk kid, I'll..." Do absolutely nothing. He couldn't afford any trouble with the law for the same reasons he couldn't call Sam's bluff and take her to court. There were outstanding arrest warrants with his name on them. A con or two gone wrong. Nothing life threatening, but enough to earn him a long vacation behind some very steep walls.

He worked his jaw, flinching when it popped. His hands fisted in an automatic response, and he forced them to relax. No, nothing violent for loverboy. The best revenge he could deliver on that tab would be taking Samantha away from him. Sorta like killing two birds with one stone.

Samantha...he shook his head. He'd been so sure of himself, especially after loverboy laid him out. He raised his hand, holding his thumb and index finger centimeters apart. "This close...I was this close." The way she'd held him...ushered him into the house...her words of forgiveness...

He threw the blown opportunity aside. "I need to get serious, and sometimes the best way to move forward is to take a step back." Carson had given him ninety days, and he had eighty-five of those left. He paced the small room and thought aloud. "I pushed her too hard, put all my cards on the table too quickly. I expected to find my pliable little Samantha." *Stupid.* "She grew up on me." Louis stopped at the mini-fridge, pulled out a lukewarm beer, and popped the top. He frowned at the temperature but took a swig anyway, swiping foam from his mouth with his sleeve as he mapped out a plan.

I'll take a few days off, and I'll get serious about finding a job. This is obviously going to drag out longer than I expected, so I'll need the cash. He snagged a can of chicken noodle soup out of the tiny cabinet and opened it with a crank can opener. He dumped it into a paper bowl while he outlined his plans to the four walls of the room. "A step back will give her some time to cool off. The job will impress her."

Telling her I'm a changed man hasn't worked, so maybe I need to show her. Louis nodded as he waited for the microwave to heat his dinner. His thoughts clouded. It was a good plan, except for Carson's muscle man. As if conjured by some sixth sense, Louis's cell phone began to ring. A shudder slithered up his back as he picked it up.

"Hello."

"Hey, Nancy, how's your face?"

The sound of sniffling and small feet shuffling on the carpet brought Samantha out of a light sleep. She rose up on one elbow. "Baby?"

The answer she received was a low, frightened whine. She sat up, her eyes adjusting slowly to the dark room, and held out her arms. "Come here, sweetheart."

Bobbie came running, bounced onto the bed, and landed in her mother's arms, bringing her stuffed penguin with her. Bobbie burrowed deep with a shuddering breath.

"What's wrong?" Samantha asked.

"I sleep with you?"

Samantha rearranged herself, her midnight visitors, and the blankets, tucking her baby to her side. She smoothed the sleep-tangled curls away from Bobbie's forehead and used a kiss to check for any leftover fever from last week's cold. The skin under her lips was smooth, dry, and no warmer than it should have been. "Of course you can. Tell me what's wrong."

"I'm scared."

Sam held her tight, knowing the answer to the question before she asked. "Did you have a bad dream?"

"Patty hit the bad man." Bobbie twisted and sat up in the bed. "Is Patty a bad man too?"

Samantha pulled her daughter back down, silently condemning both men to a life in a cold, dark place. Was there any way to explain this situation to a four-year-old? "No, Patrick isn't a bad man. I'm sure he's very sorry that he scared you."

"It's mean to hit. Seth hits me sometimes. G-ma puts him in time-out."

"Well, Seth is a baby. A time out helps him learn when he does something wrong."

Bobbie nodded against her shoulder. "I get time-out sometimes. Will Nana Kate put Patty in the corner?"

The child's simple logic brought a much needed smile to Sam's face. Oh, to be four and have everything so black and white. *Wait 'til I tell Patrick...* She didn't finish the thought, but answered her daughter's question instead. "No, grown-ups don't get time outs."

"I want to be growed up, then."

Oh, baby, be careful what you wish for. Sam rested her cheek on Bobbie's head, almost wishing to have the worries of a four-year-old again.

"But growed ups have to do hard work and go to school and stuff." Bobbie yawned. "So I'll stay me."

The bedroom grew quiet as Bobbie's breathing evened out, and she drifted back to sleep.

Sam closed her eyes as well. *You'll stay you, huh?* She pulled her sleeping daughter just a centimeter closer. "That's good. I'd like for you to stay my baby for just a while longer."

The cramp yanked Chick out of a sound sleep, squeezing his newly healed thigh muscle like a vice. He tossed the covers aside and scrambled to his feet, anxious to get his foot on the floor and relieve the vengeful muscle. A hiss of pain escaped his lips when his leg took his weight. "It'll get better...it'll get better." The first few steps were a misery, but the pain gradually faded, leaving just the ghost of an ache behind.

Chick made his way to the bathroom, the limp he'd learned to live with was always more pronounced after one of these episodes. He filled a glass with tap water and searched his travel bag for a bottle of painkillers. He shook the contents into his hand. *Just three left.* One more reason to put this job behind him. He'd need a refill soon. Chick swallowed the pill, sat down on the closed toilet, and rested his head in his hands. A harsh groan escaped as memories played havoc with his sanity. Would he ever be allowed to forget? The condescending tone of Mr. Carson's unexpectedly mild reproof for a job not-so-well-done. The look of calm on his face as he talked, turning the .38 over and over in his hands. The disbelief when the gun was turned on him, the pain of two bullets piercing his leg in quick succession. The damage was up close and personal. A nick to his thigh bone and some muscle damage, but nothing broken. Nothing lost but Chick's dignity. Nothing gained but the limp and a deeper respect...fear...for the man Chick called Boss.

"*But PopPop...*" He shook the memory from his head. The beating PopPop delivered years ago couldn't hold a candle to being shot. He'd run away back then. Why did he stick around now? Chick smirked. Easy answer. PopPop didn't have the mob at his beck and call to track him down.

Chick levered himself up. "And now?" Nancy boy was messing up his second—and last—chance. Chick made his way back to the bed.

Seeing Louis laid out on the porch had been entertaining and laughable. Seeing him hauled into the house by the skirt had given Chick hope. Seeing the door slammed in his face fifteen minutes later turned those hopes to dust. The kid was a royal screw up, and it was just a matter of time before he messed this up too. Problem was, when that happened, Louis wouldn't face the consequences of Mr. Carson's wrath alone. *If the boss don't get his money back, a bum leg'll be the least of my problems.* The boss's next bullet would be aimed at Chick's head.

I'm not gonna let that happen.

CHAPTER FIFTEEN

"Mommy, come on!" Bobbie stood at the foot of the stairs, a bundle of pent up energy after being cooped up in doors for several straight days. Outside, the frigid weather continued, while inside, tempers had threatened to boil over more than once. The promise of some time in the indoor play area at the local fast food restaurant had the little girl bouncing from one foot to the other.

Samantha was in wholehearted agreement with her daughter's impatience. The basement apartment provided a generous living area, and Bobbie also had free run of the whole upstairs, but there was no space big enough for an energetic child going on a week of housebound play. Home or day care, the walls came with rules. Bobbie needed a chance to run and scream and stretch.

With Party Palace relief still two days away, Sam considered an hour out of her Thursday evening schedule a small price to pay in exchange for her sanity.

The slides and tunnels of the play area would go a long way in wearing Bobbie down and maybe—Sam slid her arms into a heavy coat and pulled up the zipper—maybe tonight, Bobbie would go to sleep at a decent hour and stay that way. Between her own sleepless nights, lack of appetite, and Bobbie's rambunctiousness, Sam's reserves of patience and energy approached an all-time low.

She stopped next to her daughter and the ever-present penguin. "Frosty needs to stay here." Bobbie's lip jutted out and Sam hurried to avert the meltdown. "You know those little bouncy balls you like so much?"

Bobbie hugged the penguin closer and nodded her head.

"Leave Frosty here, and I'll give you two quarters to get two balls."

"Two?"

"Um-hmm, but Frosty stays here. You only have enough hands for the balls."

"But..."

"One or the other. Frosty or bouncy balls. If you take Frosty, no balls."

Bobbie looked from her mother to the penguin. After an exaggerated sigh, she propped the toy on the sofa and patted it on the head. "Stay here, Frosty. I'll bring you a ball." She sidled back to the stairwell and gave her mother an innocent smile. "Race you!"

Sam never got off the starting block. She followed her daughter at a normal pace. Bobbie reached the top and tumbled through the door and into the kitchen.

"I win!"

"Yep, beat me fair and square."

Iris spun at their entry and leaned against the

counter, a bag of chips smashed to her chest. "You guys scared me to death." Her eyes brightened at the sight of their outdoor gear. "Where ya goin'?"

"McDonald's for fries and an hour of playtime." Samantha motioned to her daughter. "If she doesn't work off some of this energy, one of us will not survive the night."

Iris discarded her snack. "Can I go?"

Sam shrugged. "Grab your coat." She looked at Bobbie. "Go with Iris while she gets ready. I'm going out to start the car."

The sound of a racing engine broke the silence of the winter evening as she started down the porch steps. She looked up and found the source. A white van careened around the corner and sped from view.

Chick wrestled the wheel of the van as the tires spun on a patch of ice. *Way to keep a low profile.* One quick drive-by on his way to dinner, and the skirt comes out the front door. The tires found traction on the asphalt, and he loosened his grip a bit. "This thing sure don't handle like my Charger." His statement was a mutter as he looked in the rearview mirror. *Did she see me?* It didn't really matter. The van might handle like a brick on wheels, but the nondescript color and design made it hard to track. With that stingy bit of praise barely out of his mind, the van died. He pounded his hands on the wheel in frustration. That was three times in the last week. He coasted to the curb, slammed the gearshift into park, and turned the key. *Nothing.*

He did a slow count to ten and tried the key again. The van purred to life. *I have got to get this thing looked at.* He couldn't do his job with an unpredictable vehicle.

A hungry grumble from his stomach pushed thoughts of the van from his mind and prompted him to look at the clock in the battered dashboard. *Way past dinner time.* He snorted. "And the choices are so plentiful in this dumpy little town." He was sick of eating out, sicker of alternating three meals a day between the limited choices available. He might not be a gourmet chef, but he knew his way around a kitchen, and he couldn't wait to get back to the one in his Vegas apartment.

A drive down Garfield's main street produced no interesting options. *I'll be glad when this gig is over.* A defeated sigh accompanied his decision. He turned the corner and headed for the golden arches just visible over the tops of the naked trees.

The parking lot was full this time of the evening, forcing him to circle the building twice before a slot opened up big enough to accommodate his oversized vehicle. The door of the van hit the car parked next to him. He shrugged at the white mark it left on the red paint of the SUV. *They shouldn't park so close to the line.* He leaned back into the van to retrieve his phone and the newspaper, scraping the red SUV a second time.

Chick stood in line with whining kids and frazzled adults. He kept his head down, shuffling forward when he could. His faded blue jeans and tan shirt made him as unremarkable as the van. One key to success in this business was the ability to blend into the background. He took his tray from the perky teenager behind the counter, paid in cash, and scoped out a booth. He unwrapped the first of two cheeseburgers and dumped the large order of fries onto a napkin. His shoulders slumped on a long exhale. The food held no appeal.

Tonight, his meal was more about fuel than enjoyment.

While he chewed, Chick punched Nancy boy's number on the cell phone. It rang six times before going to voice mail. Chick jammed his finger on the screen to disconnect the call. Punk had figured out how to program his voice mail and hadn't answered his phone since Monday. Probably thought he was being cute by ignoring the repeated calls.

Chick slurped his soda, head bent over his crossword puzzle. *Kid doesn't know who he's messing with.* Mr. Carson had given Chick one line of instruction before he left the country on vacation. "Protect my investment." There'd been no mention of the ninety-day agreement Nancy boy kept harping about. Mr. Carson was of out touch for ten more days. Chick would deliver good news to the boss when he returned, even if it killed...well, not him, but Nancy boy, maybe.

Headlights swept across the plate glass windows as a car slid into the newly vacated parking space next to his van. The black Mustang turned his idle glance into an unexpected fit of coughing.

Samantha cut her engine and stared out the side window. "Is it my imagination"—she turned to Iris—"or are there a lot of white vans around town all of a sudden?"

Iris released her seatbelt and leaned forward to study the object of her sister's question. "What do you mean?"

She turned back to the van. "It's just weird. I saw one behind me most of the way to church on Sunday. I've seen one a couple of times this week going back and forth to school. There was one in front of the house earlier tonight, and now..." She motioned out the window. "Here's another."

"Hmm...The same one each time?"

"Who can tell? A white, unmarked van. It's pretty generic."

"And probably just a coincidence," Iris said. "

Yeah, probably. This whole thing with"—she paused to glance at Bobbie in the rearview mirror—"L-O-U-I-S has me spooked."

It was Iris's turn to frown. "You don't think it's his van, do you?"

"It's not really his style, but..."

"I suppose he could be following you, and even if he isn't, he has to eat somewhere. Do you want me to sit here with Bobbie while you go in and take a quick look?"

Sam reached for her door handle. "That's a great idea." She opened her door and squeezed through the narrow space. "Get Bobbie out on your side, will you? Whoever parked this behemoth needs a refresher course in driver's ed."

Bobbie came to life when her mother's car door opened. "Yay! Time to play."

"Just a second, baby. They're pretty crowded tonight." *That's no lie.* "I'm going to run in and see if there's an empty table."

She stepped inside the building and looked around. The place was every bit as crowded as she'd told Bobbie. There were a few friends from school in the mix, but nobody suspicious. She saw one free booth on the near side of the building. Sam shrugged out of her jacket and tossed it on the empty table, grateful that the only door in and out of the play area was just four tables away.

She returned to the door and motioned for Iris and Bobbie to join her, watching while Iris wrestled Bobbie out of the booster seat. Released from her confinement, Bobbie came running through the door her mother held open, grabbed Sam's free hand, and swung her arm as she bounced up and down.

"Quarters...quarters."

Sam stooped down and removed her daughter's bright red coat. "After your playtime. If you get them now, you'll lose them. What do you want for a snack?"

"Purple bouncy balls." Bobbie's squealed reply bounced around the noisy room like the balls she was so fond of.

"You *are* a bouncy ball. Now tell me what you want to eat and you can take your outdoor voice to the play area."

"Fries?"

"Got it. Scoot. I'll come get you in a bit."

She watched her daughter race for the play area. The noise level doubled as the door opened. Seemed Bobbie wasn't the only housebound child using the area to run off some extra energy. The weather might prove to be the death of parents in the area, but it was an obvious boon to McDonald's. The door closed slowly, blocking out all but the worst of the childish screaming.

Sam took a seat on the side of the booth that allowed her to keep an eye on the door. "Thank God for McDonald's!"

Iris slid into the opposite side of the table. She grinned. "I say the same prayer every time I order up some super-sized fries."

Sam fished her wallet out of her bag and flipped her debit card across the table. "Make that two large orders, one regular, diet soda for me, apple juice for Bobbie, and whatever you want to drink. Food's my treat, but you get to go stand in line."

Iris caught the card and scooted from the booth. "No prob."

Alone in the booth, Sam sat back and tried to force some of the tension from her body. *Yeah, that always works for me.* She kept her eyes on the door to the playroom. It was the only way in and out, and Bobbie knew the don't-talk-to-strangers drill. But the world was a mess, and now that Samantha had a choice, she didn't take chances where her daughter was concerned. *I took enough chances when she was a baby to last both our lifetimes.*

The stray thought pulled her mind back to Louis and the grim realities Iris and she faced after he'd worked his con. Mom dead, Dad as good as, more than half their money gone, a baby on the way, unable to go to the authorities for fear of being separated, afraid to apply for any sort of help for the same reasons. *Jesus, thank You so much for being with us before we even knew You existed.*

Sam watched Bobbie through the windows, following her daughter's progress as she climbed, slid, and ran around to start the process again. *Knock yourself out, girlfriend. We're both sleeping tonight.*

Bobbie climbed to the top of the highest slide and stood at a precarious angle.

Sam started to rise. *She knows better than that.* She stopped when Bobbie turned, blew her a kiss, sat, and slid out of view on the corkscrew. *Imp.* But Sam smiled.

Father, you really did give me beauty for ashes.

She lost track of the circuits Bobbie made while she waited for Iris to come back with their food. As hard as their life had been back then, as frustrating as the last few days, there was nothing she would take in return for the smile she saw on Bobbie's face.

Her little sister came around the corner with their snack.

What would I have done without Iris? "I love you, sis."

Iris scooted into the booth. "OK. What brought that on? I mean, I love you back, but..."

Sam reached across the table for her soda and fries. "Just feeling a little reflective, I guess, dwelling on the past. I was watching Bobbie and thinking about how far we've come and how I'd have never made it without you." She shrugged. "Chalk it up to Louis."

Iris grinned as she munched on her fries. "Yeah, well, you sent him packing, smashed face and all. I think we've seen the last of him."

Sam glanced back to the playroom as she shook salt on her own mound of crispy potatoes. "I wish it were that easy, but something just keeps nagging at me." She shivered. "It's creepy, like I'm being watched or something." She waved at the white van sitting outside the door. "You saw how suspicious I was over that van. The whole situation is just weird beyond words."

She caught Bobbie's eye through the glass and held up the apple juice. "Here comes the munchkin. Time to change the subject."

Since he couldn't run the risk of leaving and being connected to the van, Chick slumped in his seat and kept his back to the girls in the other booth. He tried to focus on his food and his puzzle, but the voices of the skirt and her companions kept pulling his attention. Some of what he heard caused him to cringe. He needed to be more careful if he wanted to remain anonymous. His ears perked up as the kid joined the group.

"I heard Dad say it was supposed to warm up this weekend."

"Yeah, I heard that too." Laughter from the skirt. "If you consider forty warm. I think we're in the deep freeze for the duration. Thank goodness for places like this and Party Palace. These indoor play areas are a parent's best friend."

"I wanna go play at the party place."

"Not tonight, but if you're good, we'll go on Saturday."

Chick felt his eyebrows climb and thanked his lucky stars as possible disaster turned into a chance to gather valuable information. He wrote Party Palace on the edge of the newsprint and circled it. He had no idea what or where it was, but he intended to find out. He angled further into the corner of the booth, trying to hear more of the conversation without being obvious about it.

"Want some company?" the younger girl asked.

"Sorry, Iris. Lisa and the kids are meeting us. I think she needs to talk, and so do I."

"No sweat. I'm sure I can find something to do. Maybe I can talk Dad into dropping April and me off at the mall for a couple of hours."

"Mama, quarters now?"

"Only if you're ready to go home."

There was rustling in the booth as the kid scrambled

to her feet.

"Ready, Freddy."

"You're a clown." The skirt stood next to the table. "Iris, can you clean up? I promised her bouncy balls."

Chick bent his head over the paper but watched them cross the room to the gum and candy dispensers. The kid snatched the coins from her mother's palm and danced in place as she twisted the crank to dispense the small rubber balls. She turned in his direction and raced to the table.

"Iris, Iris, I got two purple ones!"

The kid stumbled in her haste and one of the balls flew from her hand and bounced from the floor onto Chick's table. He caught it out of reflex and found himself face to face with small, vivid blue eyes.

The little girl held out her hand. "They are slippery bouncy balls."

He leaned over and dropped the ball into her outstretched hand. "Not a problem. Better hold tight."

The skirt came to stand behind her daughter. She placed her hands on the kid's shoulders and nodded in his direction. "Sorry. They're her favorite and she gets so excited." She bent over the little girl. "What do you say?"

"Thank you."

Chick nodded and feigned interest in the remains of his dinner. Mom bundled the kid back into her coat. The three girls left, cold air from their exit mingling with the warmth of the burger joint. His gaze tracked the Mustang out of the lot before he turned to study the dispenser filled with brightly colored balls.

CHAPTER SIXTEEN

"All right!"

The two words worked magic on the tearful symphony issuing from the back seat Saturday morning. Samantha turned off the engine, climbed out of the car, clicked the car's locks into place, and headed back into the house, leaving her daughter safely locked in the back seat, her expression calm beneath the tears on her cheeks now that she had her way.

Pick your battles...pick your battles...pick your battles. The mantra rang in Samantha's head these days. She wouldn't trade motherhood for anything in the world, but there were days, especially as Bobbie grew into some independence, when she missed the baby who didn't ask questions, only threw a fit when she was hungry, and never challenged her mother's wisdom.

Sam hurried down the stairs and grabbed the stuffed penguin from the sofa. *She probably misses Patrick as much as I do.* Five days seemed like an eternity to Sam; it must feel like forever to a four-year-old. She supposed it was normal for Bobbie to cling to this final gift. Sam climbed the stairs, hugging the toy to her chest. *Is it final, Father?* What if Callie was right and God was taking him out of their lives? The thought tangled her feet on the steps and brought her to an abrupt halt on the top riser. The prayer for Patrick and their future came without thought. *Father, please find a way to reach him. Please make a way for us to be together.*

She returned to the car and handed the toy across the seat.

"Thank you, Mommy."

"You're welcome. Now, can we please have a peaceful afternoon?"

"Uh huh. Pizza?"

Sam put the car in gear and met Bobbie's eyes in the rearview mirror as she backed out of the drive. "Seriously? You just ate french toast and bacon an hour ago."

"I'm really hungry."

One more thing no one ever told her about a growing child. Bobbie was *always* hungry these days. "We'll have pizza at lunch time. Trust me, once you start playing, you'll forget about eating."

"OK. Can we listen to my music? Jem wants to sing."

Jem again. Sam nodded and punched the power button on the Mustang's CD player. The car filled with tales of animal crackers, magic dragons, and weasels that popped. Bobbie sang along to the songs she loved. Sam boosted the volume on the CD player, adding her voice to the serenade. The car filled with off-key singing and laughter for the short drive to Party Palace. And even though Sam listened closely, she never heard the mysterious Jem utter a single note.

Chick spent five dollars' worth of quarters before the contrary machine dispensed a purple ball into his eager hands. How in blue blazes had the kid gotten two in a row the other night? He walked out of the burger joint and tossed the other nineteen balls into the trash barrel beside the door.

Nancy boy still wasn't answering his phone and, as far as Chick could tell, he hadn't made any effort to approach the skirt in the last five days. Chick was tired of the wait, tired of being ignored, and tired of this little town. Plan B would become plan A before the end of the day.

He arrived at Party Palace and scanned the lot for the black Mustang, pleased when he didn't see it. *Good, I beat her.* Chick parked the van behind the motel two businesses away. Mindful of possible security cameras he pulled on a baseball cap and slipped on a pair of sunglasses. Not much of a disguise, but he needed the kid to recognize him when the time came, and since he'd never been arrested, his face wasn't on file anywhere. *Let's check this place out.* He pulled open the heavy glass doors and ran headlong into a solid wall of ear shattering noise. On one side of the cavernous room, a massive indoor playground swarmed with screaming kids, sliding, crawling, jumping, and running. On the other side, video games in the arcade exploded, whistled, or revved their virtual engines. It was enough to make him long for the solitude of his van, but despite the racket, the smell of popcorn and chili made his mouth water. He crossed to the concession stand and purchased a chili dog and a soda. Not much of a breakfast, but a good cover as he strolled the inside perimeter of the building. He took in the lack of any sort of safety device on the outside doors, the widely spaced security cameras, and the silent cop watching over it all with constantly roaming eyes.

Chick chased the final bite of the dog with his drink, turning casually from the officer. The cop would be a problem. He threw his trash away, like the responsible citizen he was, and exited through the back door of the facility. Empty batting cages, a silent go-cart track, and a mini-golf course stretched out before him, frozen and barren. A quick trip through the gate leading to the attached driving range took him into a vacant delivery area. *Perfect.*

He belched chili, hunkered deeper into his jacket, and took a seat in the empty picnic pavilion. *I can make this work if I can distract that stupid cop for five minutes.*

A trio of older boys tumbled through the back door talking trash and jabbing at each other good- naturedly. Chick studied them, a plan taking shape in his mind. He settled the cap lower on his head, pulled his wallet from his back pocket, and removed three twenty-dollar bills. He held the bills up like a fan and waved them in the air until he got the attention of one of the boys.

"Can we help you with something, mister?"

Chick put on a long face. "I hope so. I'd pay you for your time."

"What'cha' need?"

"I need to see my little girl. Her mama is mad at me and won't let me take her for an ice cream cone."

The tallest of the boys, red hair moussed into spikes, stepped forward. "That stinks."

"Yeah. It's my baby's birthday today, and all I can

do is watch from out here. If I go in, my wife'll pitch a real fit." He nodded at the cop, barely visible through the finger-smudged door. "That cop will take her side, and my baby's day will get ruined."

The three boys exchanged looks and seemed to come to a silent agreement. Spike took the lead again. "What do you need us to do?"

Samantha held tight to Bobbie's hand as they entered the cavernous play area of Party Palace. The decibel level on this side of the door hovered somewhere between make-your-ears-bleed and an unshielded jet engine. She steered Bobbie towards the open seating area located between the arcade and the teeming play area. Several of the large tables held cakes and brightly wrapped gifts, evidence of multiple birthday parties in progress. The festive balloons reminded Sam that she needed to make party arrangements for Bobbie soon. *I don't want her birthday getting lost in the Christmas rush or the Louis uproar.*

Her grip on her daughter's hand tightened as Bobbie struggled to make a break. "Wait just a minute." She continued to scope out the tables, smiling when she saw Lisa sitting in a back corner, close enough to keep an eye on the kids, but as far removed from the noise as they were likely to get. Sam kept a firm hold on Bobbie as Lisa motioned them over.

"This place is packed."

"Yep, it's a madhouse," Lisa said. Her eyes cut to the crowded play area. Sam followed her gaze and located the Sisko's three-year-old twin boys.

"Jared and Jordon look like they're having a good time. Where's Alex?"

Lisa shook her head. "Alex needed some daddy-time today. She's been real clingy since the fire, hardly lets Dave out of her sight. I think it's because he wasn't there when the fire started. We could tell she didn't really want to come today, so Dave offered her the chance to hang with him. We're hoping that some one-on-one attention will help put some of her fears to rest."

Sam shook her head. "Bless her little heart."

Lisa nodded at Bobbie. "I hope she isn't too disappointed that Alex stayed home."

"She'll be fine. She has a penguin and a new imaginary friend to keep her company if the twins aren't enough."

Bobby tugged on her hand. "Mama, I'm hungry."

Sam looked towards the pizza counter and the patrons standing six deep waiting to place their orders. "Oh, boy..."

Lisa held out her hand. "Give me the munchkin. I'll help her with her coat while you wait in line."

"Works for me." Sam slid out of her own coat and tossed it across a chair. She bent down eye-to-eye with her daughter. "I'm going to order our lunch. Tell—"

"Frosty and I wants to play."

"Frosty and you can go play. But first, what are the Party Palace rules?"

Bobbie's nose wrinkled in concentration while she rocked from foot to foot. "Stay where you can see me."

"And?"

"Don't talk to 'trangers."

"Good. Last one?"

"Don't leave the playground unless I ask."

Sam smiled at her daughter. "Good girl. Let Sister

Lisa help you with your coat. I'll be right back."

Bobbie beamed a smile. "OK."

Fifteen minutes later, Sam wound her way back to the table loaded with a pitcher of soda and a stack of thick plastic cups. She sat across from Lisa. "It's going to be a while on the pizza."

"Not a problem for me, and I'm pretty sure the kids are too busy playing to think about food."

Sam took a second to locate her daughter in the mass of kids. "I don't know. Bobbie's been eating everything in sight for a month now. She's probably getting ready to grow another four inches."

"Don't you hate that? When we shopped for new clothes the other day, I had to buy a bigger size for all three of them. My mom used to threaten to put a brick on my head. Now I know why."

Satisfied that the kids were busy and safe, and determined to focus on something other than her own problems, Sam turned her attention to her friend. "So, how's things? Any word yet from the fire department or the insurance company?"

Lisa's brown eyes sparkled and a smile lit her face. "You are not going to believe what I'm about to tell you."

Sam tilted her head, trying to decipher the look on Lisa's face. She'd just lost her house in a fire, her kids were having issues, and they were living in a travel trailer. *How can she smile through all of that?* "Try me."

Her friend took a deep breath. "New house, new furniture, plenty of immediate cash to replace necessities, and the money we're saving by staying in the RV for the next few months will be banked for some cool upgrades. We're going to have the house of our dreams when this is over."

"Wow."

"Major wow! We were a little worried about having enough coverage, but we got a nice surprise there."

Sam raised her eyebrows and waited.

Lisa picked up the pitcher and nodded to the stack of cups. When Sam nodded back, Lisa poured them both a drink. "Valley View pays half of our house payment and all of our insurance as part of Dave's salary package. We didn't know it, but they increased our coverage six months ago. With the current housing market..." She shook her head. "God's grace and provision continues to astound me. The fire was the most horrible thing we've ever been through, but what Satan meant for evil, God just turned it right around for our good. When this is done, we're going to be better off than we ever dreamed."

"That's so amazing!" Sam lifted her glass and Lisa clinked hers against it. "I smell shopping."

Lisa laughed. "More than one trip. I'm already combing catalogs and online sites. I'm a little like Santa. Making a list and checking it twice."

"Well, don't get too carried away, I'm gonna throw you guys a huge house-warming party. It'll be the social event of the year, we'll—"

A scuffle broke out across the room. Three older boys began pushing and yelling. The cop on duty started across the room.

Chick took a position between the front door and the play area. He located the skirt's kid and nodded at the boys stationed at the other end of the building. The three boys moved into action, shoving and name-calling. Once the cop headed in their direction and most of the attention in the room was on the disturbance, Chick went into action.

He ditched the sunglasses, pulled the purple ball from his pocket, and approached the kid. "Hey, sweetheart. Remember me?" He held out the ball. "I think you dropped this again."

The little girl smiled and patted her pockets. "Those slippery balls." She held out her hand. "Thank you."

Chick reached to drop the ball into her hand.

Instead, he grabbed her arm, yanked her forward, and hustled her out the door. Her screams were simply one more noise buried by the clamor of the room.

CHAPTER SEVENTEEN

Sam shook her head as the cop waded into the middle of the scuffle and separated the boys. *Where are their moms and dads?* What sort of parents just dropped their kids off at a place like this for others to deal with? Her eyes roamed back to the play area. She didn't see Bobbie, but Jared and Jordon were headed towards the table at a dead run. They slid to a stop in their stocking feet, identical faces flushed with exertion, their words coming in unison.

"Is it time to eat?"

"I'm hungry."

Sam looked from one boy to the other. They were three-years-old, and she still couldn't tell them apart. "Our pizza should be ready any minute. Where's Bobbie?" She received two shrugs in response.

"Samantha Evans, your pizza is ready at window three. Samantha Evans, your pizza is ready at window three."

Lisa held out her hand. "Give me the receipt. I'll settle these two and grab the pizza while you round up

Bobbie."

Sam scooted the cash register slip across the table and went to retrieve her daughter. She poked her head through the mesh of the ball pit. "Bobbie?" Four kids whooped down the slide and into the colorful sea of plastic spheres while she waited. Her shoulders lifted in a shrug. Lots more equipment to check out. No telling where she was hiding. Regardless of the rules, it was impossible to keep any child in sight a hundred percent of the time during these play sessions, and calling her would be a waste of breath in this noise. She stooped and retrieved a pair of pink and blue Nikes from the jumbled pile of discarded footwear at the base of the slide. The purple laces made Bobbie's shoes easy to identify, but just to be safe, she checked for the initials inscribed on the underside of the tongue. Terri's rule for everything that went to Tiny Tikes. Clothes, toys, bags, coats, everything had to be initialed in permanent ink.

Sam checked out the obstacle course with its swinging bags, padded pylons, and slippery slopes. Not there. Moving next to the entrance of the overhead maze of tunnels and turrets that ran the width of the building, she walked from window to window, looking through the scuffed Plexiglass, hoping to see Bobbie's curly black hair. By the time she reached the exit at the other end, frustration threatened to bleed into her patience. *I'm not going to be happy if I have to climb up there and crawl through this thing.* Back to the ball pit, she made the rounds a second time. Worry began to niggle at the edge of her frustration. Sam returned to the table where Lisa had just deposited the bubbling pizza.

"Where's the munchkin?"

"I hoped she'd come back to the table."

"Nope." Lisa glanced over at the running, screaming kids. "Easy to lose her in that. Let me get the boys started on lunch, and I'll help you track her down."

Sam waited impatiently as pizza was distributed along with a command to the twins to stay put. She and Lisa crossed the room, pausing at the low wall surrounding the play area. Sam made a circle in the air.

"I'll go this way, you go that way, we'll meet by the door."

They separated, and Sam looked into every corner, through every window, and under every slide. She pulled her boots off twice to climb inflated slopes. Nothing. Every empty spot nudged her maternal temper up a notch. Bobbie knew better than to stray away from the play area.

She rounded the last corner and saw Lisa coming in her direction, empty handed. Their eyes met and Lisa shrugged. Sam put her hands on her hips and turned in a complete circle. The door to the new laser tag annex opened, spilling more kids into the main area.

Sam stared into the darkened room. The fog, mechanical music, and blinking lights would probably be very enticing to a curious little girl. Would she go in there without asking? *It's possible.* She took a step forward, half turning to motion for Lisa to join her.

A snatch of red and blue caught Sam's eyes. She crossed to the vending machine just inside the front door, stooped down, and pulled a stuffed penguin from behind it. In the space of a breath, her irritation shifted to panic. Sam clutched the toy to her chest, eyes roaming the facility anew as Lisa joined her. She turned to the wide glass front doors and her gaze went to the busy interstate that ran in front of the building. Sam pushed out the doors, her hands slick with sweat on the metal bar.

Lisa followed close behind. "Any sign of her?"

Sam shook her head, eyes darting, looking for any sign of her daughter. She held up the toy. "Just this."

"Bobbie's?"

For a second Sam entertained doubt. She bit her lip and turned the animal over to examine the tag. Black initials, B.L.E. jumped out at her. Sam's breath froze in her lungs. Her head lifted back to the busy highway, the step she would have taken halted by Lisa's grip on her arm.

"She wouldn't have come out here, not without her shoes and her jacket. We need to go back inside and get some help."

A horn sounded out on the highway and jammed Sam's heart into her throat. Sweat soaked her clothes from every pore in her body; her pulse pounded in her ears. She nodded and tried to force her shaking legs to move. *Jesus, show me what to do.* Finally she managed a step, and then one more, shouldering through the door and straight to the officer.

Sam found him perched on his stool, phone held to his ear. She grabbed his forearm, her knuckles white against the dark blue fabric of his shirt.

He stood. "What?"

"My daughter..." Her voice was a squeak. She stopped and cleared her throat. "I can't find my little girl."

The officer's expression went from annoyed to professional. He put his phone away and guided Sam to a seat at a nearby table. He snagged the attention of a passing Party Palace employee. "I need the manager."

The teenager nodded to the tray of discarded dirty glasses balanced in his hands. "Just let me put these in the back and I'll—"

The cop took the tray and slid it onto the other end of the table. "Now!"

The youngster shuffled back a step or two, his voice a little higher when he responded. "Yes, sir!"

The officer perched on the corner of the table and pulled a notebook from his pocket. "How old is she, what is she wearing, and where have you looked?"

Sam took a breath and struggled to keep her voice steady. "She's four, almost. She has on blue jeans and a purple sweatshirt." She motioned to Lisa. "We've looked everywhere, three times. We haven't looked in the laser tag area yet."

The manager arrived, a bit out of breath. "Is there a problem?"

"We have a missing child, age four, blue jeans, purple sweatshirt." He glanced back to Sam. "What's her name?"

"Bobbie Evans."

He nodded. "How long since you saw her?"

Sam looked to Lisa for verification. "Fifteen minutes. We've been looking for most of that time." She offered the stuffed penguin to the officer. "I found her toy by the front door."

The manager stepped away. "I'll announce the code Adam and get some help to look for her."

The police officer shook his head. "Let's move to lockdown."

"But—"

"Don't argue. Lock the place down, now. We've

already exceeded your five minute code Adam threshold."

The manager nodded and sprinted to the counter area. He spoke to a couple of young people behind the desk. Sam watched from a detached distance as Party Palace employees scrambled to guard exits and clear players out of the laser tag arena and arcade.

A male voice came over the PA system: "We have a code Adam, I repeat, code Adam. Missing child is female, aged four, wearing blue jeans and a purple shirt. If you've seen this child, please report to our security officer immediately. No one is allowed out of the building at this time. We apologize for the inconvenience and appreciate your patience. If everyone will please have a seat in the food court, complimentary sodas will be provided shortly."

Panic hovered on the edges of Sam's consciousness. *This can't be happening. Dear God, please let this be a bad dream.* She lowered her head to the table and fought for composure. Hysterics wouldn't help her or Bobbie.

Her head came up when a hand touched her arm. The officer crouched before her. "I need a physical description of your daughter."

A shiver ran up Sam's spine as she straightened. She clutched her arms around her middle and rocked back and forth. Sitting still seemed wrong. She needed movement, needed to help look for Bobbie. Her eyes rose to the officer's face and snapped down to his shirt pocket and the name badge pinned above it. *BLACK.* Karla's comment about her son's part time job echoed in her mind. Her gaze went back to his face, locking on intense blue eyes beneath a shock of curly, sandy hair.

She tilted her head. "Black...Nicolas Black?"

The cop leaned back with a puzzled frown. "Do I know you?"

Sam grabbed on to his hand like a lifeline. "No," her voice broke, "But I know your parents." She slumped. The elephant on her chest lost ten pounds. Karla said he was a good cop, one who didn't quit. Not just a cop but the new detective on Garfield's police force. Sam breathed a small prayer of gratitude. "Oh, thank God."

The cop looked at his notes. "Bobbie Evans...you're one of Mom's friends...Terri's stepdaughter?"

She nodded. "Samantha."

He squeezed her hand. "OK, we're going to find her, but I need you to answer some questions for me. Do you have a recent picture of your daughter?"

Sam dug her phone case out of her pocket and flipped through photos and credit cards. She withdrew a snapshot. "They took this at the day care Halloween party last month. She's wearing her costume, but it's a good clear picture underneath the bunny ears."

Nicolas accepted the picture and motioned to the manager. He passed over the picture. "Show this around to your employees." He turned back to Sam, pen poised against paper. "Height and weight?"

Sam provided figures, watching as he made careful notes. She looked at the clock on her phone. Ten minutes had passed since she'd grabbed Detective Black. How long did it take to search a building?

As if to answer her question, the manager approached, a frown on his face, hands wringing at his waist. "We've cleared the arcade, the laser tag arena, and the play area. My employees have combed all three. The outside attractions were checked as well, even though they're closed for the winter." He turned sympathetic eyes on Sam. "There's no sign of her."

His words left Samantha breathless and shaken. *That's impossible. She has to be here.* Not finding her wasn't an option. Sam squeezed her eyes closed, unable to hold back panicked tears. Hands massaged her shoulders. She looked back at Lisa. The worry in her friend's eyes did nothing to calm the pounding of her heart. "What do we do now?"

"I'm going to get a couple of patrol cars out here and—"

"Man, he said you'd throw a fit. You need to calm down, lady. They'll be right back."

The officer's attention went to a trio of boys standing on the other side of the table. Sam recognized the boys who'd been scuffling a few minutes ago.

The redhead of the trio shook his head. "All he wants to do is buy his kid an ice cream cone for her birthday."

Sam stood on trembling legs. "Who? What are you talking about?"

"Your husband."

Sam shook her head at Nicolas's questioning glance. "I'm not married, and Bobbie's father..." Her voice trailed off. *Louis.* She grabbed her phone and started punching numbers. "I'll kill him." The phone rang, unanswered, as she paced beside the table.

Nicolas pulled out a chair and motioned the boy into it.

The phone went to voice mail a second time. Sam stabbed the redial button, one ear to the phone, one ear tuned to the conversation at the table.

"Tell me what happened," the officer demanded.

"We," the kid pointed to his two friends, "were

outside a while ago and this guy was sitting at the table lookin' all sad and stuff. He said he wanted to take his kid for ice cream, but his wife was mad and wouldn't let him. We felt kinda sorry for him, I mean, not gettin' to see your kid on their birthday sorta stinks." He stopped and fished in the pockets of his jeans, drawing out a piece of crumpled currency. "He gave us twenty dollars each to act like we was fightin' so he could sneak in and take his kid for a treat. He promised he wouldn't be gone long." He stood with a shrug. "So now that you know it's not such a big deal, will you tell them to open the laser tag back up? We've got a tournament to finish."

Detective Black pulled out two more chairs and crooked a finger at the other two boys. "You three sit here. Your tournament is finished." He ripped a sheet of paper from his notebook. "I need your names, addresses, and phone numbers."

The redheaded boy sat back and crossed his arms. "Why? We didn't do anything wrong."

The cop pinned them with a no nonsense stare and dropped a pen next to the paper.

"Whatever." The kid huddled with his friends and started writing.

He turned to Sam. "Do you know what they're talking about?"

"Oh, I think so, and if I'm right..." She hit redial again. The knot of tension between her shoulder blades had loosened. Louis was a jerk, but he wouldn't hurt their daughter. This was just his way of getting what he wanted. "Answer the phone you slimeball."

"Who—"

She held up a finger as a click sounded on the line.

Her hand shook as a new recording took the place of Louis's standard voice mail greeting. *We're sorry, the person you are calling cannot accept messages at this time. Their mailbox is full.* Anger solidified in Sam's stomach. Good! Better to be motivated by anger than paralyzed with fear.

"You know who has your daughter?"

"I'm pretty sure." Sam continued to pace, giving him an abbreviated version of the history between her and Louis. "He's been after me to see Bobbie, and I told him to take a hike." She tried the phone again. "He isn't picking up, and I have no idea where to find..." She stopped and remembered the napkin hanging on her fridge at home. "But I know how to find him." She snatched up the penguin, yanked her keys from her pocket, and sprinted for the door, pushing past the employee who tried to stop her, ignoring the cop's shouted demand that she wait, and forgetting Lisa and the boys in her haste.

Samantha dialed a different number on her phone as she slid into the seat of the Mustang. *Pick up, pick up, pick up.* She jammed the key into the ignition as the phone call connected.

"Samantha?"

"Patrick, I need you to meet me at the house. Louis has Bobbie."

CHAPTER EIGHTEEN

Louis rolled over with a groan. He opened one eyelid the barest slit, whimpering when light from the window speared into his head. The hangover monster with the steel hammer and the iron anvil increased the rhythm of the up close and personal pounding behind his eyes. Louis pulled a pillow over his face and tried to drown out the metallic clanging ringing from the inside of his skull. *Major fail.*

His mouth was cotton, his tongue snaked out over dry lips. He needed water and aspirin. *Do I have aspirin?* The effort it took to come up with an answer sent the monster in his head on a frenzied spree.

Louis pulled himself to a sitting position on the side of the bed. He dug his fingers into the edge of the mattress until the room ceased to spin. The room stopped spinning, but his stomach began. He had to get to the bathroom.

He stood and the world fell out from under him. He waited for balance before he shuffled across the room.

His feet sent empty beer cans crashing into each other like marbles hitting obstacles in a pinball machine. *Did I drink the whole case?* He couldn't remember, didn't really care. He shielded his eyes with one hand and kept the other outstretched as he walked. If he ran into the wall, he'd die where he fell.

His stomach lurched and his bladder threatened to explode. It was a crapshoot to see which would give up first. He quickened his pace. Once in the bathroom, he sat on the john, because his legs wouldn't hold him upright, dragged the dingy trash can into his lap, hung his head over the edge, and let nature take its course.

When he stumbled from the bathroom minutes—hours—later, his stomach and bladder empty of the poison he'd ingested the night before, he was weak as a newborn rat. He filled a glass with water from the small sink. His shaky hands clattered it against his teeth as he took the first cautious sip. He hesitated, waiting to see if his stomach would reject the water. When the water stayed down, he tempted fate with four aspirins before returning to the side of the bed.

Louis sat, elbows on his knees, head in his hands. *I should have closed the curtains while I was up.* He cracked his eyelids and risked a glance at the clock. One in the afternoon. The last thing he remembered was his eighth beer and turning on the ten o'clock news the night before. The TV was off and, even though he didn't count them, he was pretty sure an entire case of empty beer cans littered the floor. *When was the last time I binged out?* The effort to recall the answer made his head hurt worse. As if that were possible.

His phone came to life, dancing across the top of the old wooden nightstand. Louis snatched it up out of self-defense. Thankfully the ringer was still off. Carson's thug was going to drive him crazy with the constant calls. He swiped an unsteady finger across the screen. The sight of Sam's number jerked him upright. *Samantha?* The unintended motion brought on a fresh wave of nausea. He drew in a few slow, deep breaths and waited for it to pass.

He scrolled through the list of missed calls. Plenty from the goon and a half dozen from Sam in the last half hour. *I knew it was just a matter of time before my girl came to her senses.* He put the phone aside. He couldn't talk to anyone feeling like this. Forcing himself up again, he swayed on wobbly legs. He'd grab a cold shower while the aspirin had a chance to work. Sunlight stabbed his eyeballs as he turned to the bathroom. He'd be lucky to make the drive across town in one piece.

Chick drove. He had the kid. He needed a plan. He'd have a plan just as soon as the wailing from the back seat stopped. The kid had been screaming bloody murder for almost thirty minutes. She had to get tired soon, didn't she?

"Kid, kid. Please stop crying."

"You're a bad man and I want my mommyyyyyyyyy..."

Chick squinted as the last word dissolved into an ear splitting howl. A sign beside the road caught his attention. *Food.* If she was eating, she couldn't cry.

"Little girl." He yelled to get her attention. "Hey! Are you hungry?"

There was a moment of peace from the back of the van. "Yes."

"Do you like hamburgers?"

"Do I have to?"

The child's words confused him. "No, you don't have to like burgers. I can get you a taco."

"He's a bad man." The child's wailing started anew.

Aw, not again! "I'm sorry, I'm sorry. No tacos." His eyes searched the billboards growing out of the roadside. *Where's a Sonic when you need it?* "We can get a corn dog instead."

An abrupt silence met his suggestion. Then a whispered, "I really don't want to."

The kid's words weren't making any sense. Who was she talking to? Chick frowned into the rearview mirror. The kid sat sideways in the seat, looking for the world like she was carrying on a conversation with someone. The small hairs on the back of his neck came to attention. There wasn't anyone else back there. He refocused on the road, confused but grateful for the reprieve.

Shuffling drew his attention back to the mirror. The kid was on the move. She climbed between the seats, over the console, and settled into the front passenger seat. She reached for the seat belt.

"Jem says I can stop crying and buckle up. He won't let you hurt me."

Jem? Chick's eyes roamed the back of the van a second time. "Good. That's good. Jem is right, I'm not going to hurt you." He wasn't sure what he was going to do, but for now, as long as she wasn't crying, Jem, whoever that was, was right. "We're just going to have an adventure. What's your name?"

The kid's mouth puckered. "Bobbie Lee Anne Evans."

Chick held his breath, waiting for the crying to

resume.

Instead, the child crossed her arms and stared out the side window. Her giggle startled him. "Really?"

Chick frowned. The kid must be looney tunes. Who was she talking to?

"OK. *Jesus loves me this I know, for the Bible tells me so...*"

Oh great. The singing was worse than the crying, Especially Jesus songs.

The childish voice echoed through the van. Chick marked the time with the mile markers he passed. Ten miles down the road her shoulders finally slumped against the seatbelt, her eyes closed, and she slept.

He used the silence of the next several miles to work out the plan he probably should have had before he snatched the kid. *Would have had if Nancy boy hadn't forced my hand.* The boss had a small house he used as a hidey hole in Tulsa. It was empty right now and would make a good home base. He pondered ways to make his demands and considered just what those demands would be.

Nancy boy owed Mr. Carson a hundred k, but why think so small? If he made the ransom an even two hundred thousand, Mr. Carson would be happy and Chick could vanish to a nice tropical island somewhere. Chick rubbed his damaged leg. Every time he limped across the room, retirement sounded better and better.

He ticked off the things he'd need. A burn phone topped his list.

Samantha jerked her car to a stop in the drive. Some level of her consciousness registered the police car following close behind her and Patrick's blue truck approaching from the opposite direction, but all her concentration narrowed at the site of Louis, standing next to a beat up Ford parked at the curb in front of the house. *Bobbie had better be in that car!*

She bailed out of the Mustang and rushed Louis like a she-lion deprived of her cub, claws and teeth bared. "You twisted freak. Where's my baby?" She swung at Louis's bruised chin and missed, but her booted foot connected with his shin before strong arms wrapped her from behind and pulled her away.

Detective Black's calm voice rumbled in her ear. "Ma'am, you need to stop. Now."

"He has my child." Sam struggled in the cop's grasp, straining to see inside the car, losing some of her fight under a load of fear when she didn't see Bobbie. She stared at Louis through a veil of windblown hair. Her breath clogged in her lungs. "If anything happens to Bobbie, I swear by all I hold holy, I'll kill you with my own hands."

Patrick stepped to her side, gently easing her from the cop's grasp and into his arms. "You won't have to."

The cop took a step back, thumbs hooked in his belt. "Everyone needs to calm down so we can get to the bottom of this." His gaze traveled from one to the other and settled on Louis. He took out his notebook. "Name?"

"What?"

"What is your name?"

Louis smirked, ignored the cop, and turned to Samantha. "I came because you called me."

"I called you because you have my daughter."

A young voice came from the window of the patrol car. "That's not the guy."

Chick pulled the van into the department store parking lot. They were just a few miles from the house, and they needed supplies. He turned off the engine and looked at the kid. He was tempted to lock her in the van, but if she woke up and caused a scene, this gig would be over.

He shook her shoulder. "Wake up, kid."

Bobbie sat up and rubbed sleep from her eyes. She looked around, her mouth puckered in pre-scream. "Mom—"

"Wait." Chick held up his hands. "We're gonna go get a phone to call your mommy, but only if you don't cry."

She stared at him with liquid blue eyes. "Promise?"

Chick nodded. "If you don't cry."

Bobbie sat back. "I'm still hungry."

"And we'll fix that too, but you have to make me a promise. Can you do that?"

Bobbie stared at him, then looked out the window. She sat for a few seconds before nodding. "Jem says I can promise."

Chick rubbed his hands together. Whoever Jem was, he liked him. "Great. We're gonna go into the store, but I need you to promise to be good and not cry. We're gonna play a little game. Do you like pretend games?"

She nodded.

"Good. We're gonna play house. I'm the daddy and you're the good little girl. We'll get a phone and some food, and if you play the game real good, I'll get you a toy."

Bobbie nodded again. "Jem says I need some shoes."

"Yeah, well, we'll see."

The kid sat back and crossed her arms. "Jem says I need shoes and a coat."

"Listen, kid, *Jem* ain't the boss here."

Bobbie unbuckled the seat belt, her smile almost as creepy as her docile obedience. "That's what you think."

Louis perched on the edge of a chair, head in his hands once more. Sam sat on the sofa, her father on one side, her mother on the other. Loverboy paced the area behind the sofa. Louis tried to think, but everything was drowned out by one sick certainty. Carson's thug snatched the kid. There was nothing left to salvage of this con. If they ran his record... *I've got to get out of here.*

The cop stepped closer, towering over him with crossed arms. Louis squirmed as the stern-faced officer invaded his personal space.

"Mr. Cantrell, I need you to tell me where you were this morning between eleven and one."

"Home." Louis's hands muffled his response. He looked up. "Home."

"Any witnesses who might confirm that?"

"Why?" Louis pushed out of the chair and was forced to take a hasty step to the side when the cop refused to move. He motioned to the silent redheaded kid sitting across the room. "He's already told you that I'm not the guy you're looking for."

The cop nodded while his fingers tapped on the wide leather of his belt. The sound of the tapping cut straight into Louis's brain.

"Let me share something with you, Mr. Cantrell.

Every inch of Party Palace property, inside and out, is monitored by security cameras."

Louis met the officer's stony stare with one of his own. "Yeah?"

"We're in the process of downloading those videos now. If I find your face, for even a millisecond, on any of those camera feeds, it's going to be all the evidence I need to charge you with conspiracy to kidnap."

Louis shrugged. "Go for it. I wasn't there, I don't know anything about what happened, or why."

Sam lunged forward. "You...you...creep. You come back here, honey oozing from your pores, trying to convince me that you're a changed man. You were a liar five years ago, and you're a liar now." Her voice broke as her father pulled her back to his side. She turned her head into her father's shoulder. "Make him tell me where she is."

The cop cleared his throat. "Mr. Cantrell. I have a child that's been missing for ninety minutes. Your child. Every minute that passes is vital, so I'm going to give you one more opportunity. If you have any light you can shed on the matter—"

"No!" Louis spun to face the cop. "How many times do I need to say it? I don't know where she is. I don't know who took her. I don't have any information for you." A niggle of guilt pricked at his conscience. The kid was his too. Shouldn't he feel something? He did an internal inventory and found nothing except an overwhelming need for self-preservation. Louis ran his hand through his hair. "Look, officer, you know what I know. You have no reason to keep me here."

"Detective."

Louis frowned at him. "What?"

"It's detective, not officer...something you'd do well to remember."

"Whatever. I'm still out of here."

Detective Black met his stare. He never broke eye contact as he motioned the young boy to his side. He put an arm around the youngster's shoulder. "Kurt, I want you to take a good look. I know you said that Mr. Cantrell isn't the guy who paid you boys to fight. Did you see this man anywhere around Party Palace today?"

"No, sir, but my friends and I were playing laser tag most of the morning."

The cop nodded. "I understand. Go back and sit down. Your mom should be here to pick you up in a few minutes."

Louis took a deep breath. "Satisfied?"

"Not really."

"Well, I can't help you." He looked at Sam. She met his eyes in an ice blue stare.

"Louis, please, she's all I have."

"The brat's gone and I didn't take her!"

Sam leaned her head back on the cushion. "God was right when He warned me not to trust you."

Louis took a step toward the door. "Well, He is supposed to know everything, right?"

Loverboy stopped pacing, placed his hands on Samantha's shoulders, and glared at him over her head. "How can you be so unconcerned about your own child?"

Louis smirked. "I have some doubts about that too. You know girls. Once they give it up for one..."

Fire lit the younger man's eyes, and he started around the couch.

The cop stopped him with a pointed finger and a

shake of his head.

Louis rubbed his jaw and nodded. "I'd listen to him if I were you. You already took the only shot at me you're gonna get." When no one spoke or tried to stop him, Louis shrugged. "I'm out of here."

"You stay where I can find you."

"Oh, yes sir, *Detective*, sir." Louis slammed the door behind him and sprinted for his car. As far as he knew, he still had ten thousand dollars in the bank. He hoped that was enough to put a safe distance between him and everything connected to this plan gone wrong.

CHAPTER NINETEEN

Chick pushed the loaded cart through the department store aisles. The kid walked beside him, calm as a pup on a leash, munching on a box of animal crackers. *So far, so good.*

She took a new cookie from the box and held it in front of her. "You want one?"

He rolled his eyes and ignored the question. He'd already figured out she wasn't talking to him. *Spooky* didn't begin to cover what this kid was.

"OK." She stopped in the aisle and popped the cookie into her mouth. "They're really good, though." Oh, this kid was nutso. He nudged her shoulder to get her moving again. "Come on, kid."

She shuffled forward in her socks. "Jem isn't hungry."

Oh good grief. "Kid, there's nobody there."

Bobbie stopped once again. "Don't say that!"

Several people looked their way, and he winced.

Great, let's make a scene. He pasted a fake smile on his

face and patted her on the head. "Well, if your little friend isn't hungry, that leaves more for you, right?"

"Jem's not little. He's an angel and he's bigger than you."

"Whatever. Let's..." Chick stopped as the kid raced away. He rushed after her with a string of whispered expletives. "Kid, get back here," he hissed.

She stopped in front of a rack of tennis shoes and began to point. "I want the blue ones and the green ones and the pink ones."

"Pick one."

The little girl crossed her arms, rebellion plain on her face. "Jem says I can have what I want."

"*Jem* ain't payin'."

The kid plopped down on the floor and turned her back to him. Her shoulders began to heave and Chick knew wailing was coming. A quick look around confirmed that it was just the two of them in the aisle. *Time to show this brat who's boss.* His intent to snatch her to her feet and retake control of the situation ended with her whispered words of warning. "You shouldn't touch me."

Chick stared down at the militant kid. Did she have eyes in the back of her head?

"Jem says that if you hurt me, you'll be sorry."

As if to accent her words, a box of shoes slipped from the top shelf and grazed his shoulder, before landing in the floor at his feet. Goose bumps crawled up the back of his neck. He looked to his left, his right, and then behind him. Nobody in sight except the little girl, who couldn't possibly have nudged that box. "What...?"

His sputtering drew the girl's attention. She scooted

around to face him. Giggles erupted as she clapped her hands in obvious glee. "That was Jem!"

Chick stepped back, looking from the shoes to the empty spot on the shelf and back to the kid. "What...?"

A young woman peeked around the corner of the aisle. "That box didn't fall on you, did it? I was trying to reach a pair of shoes on one of the upper shelves. I must have knocked that one loose. I'm so sorry!"

Chick's heart slowly regained its normal rhythm. He flashed the woman a smile of gratitude. "Nope, missed us by a mile."

The woman returned his smile before she disappeared back around the corner. Chick looked at Bobbie. "Jem, huh?"

Bobbie stood and resumed her study of the shoes. She pointed to the rack. "He says I can have what I want."

Chick stooped to pick up the box of shoes, then reached high to return them to their place. *Just a fluke.* He took a few deep breaths and swallowed hard, reining in the harsh words and actions he'd intended to deliver. A happy kid, after all, was much less likely to draw unwelcome attention. There would be plenty of chances to show her who was boss once they reached the safe house.

"Sure, kid, sure. Pick out whatever you like. I'll help you try them on so we get the right size."

Shoe issues settled, they continued through the store. The girl walked beside him, obedient once more, obviously content with a new pair of shoes on her feet and two more pair in the cart. She still worked on her cookies, all the while carrying on a one-sided conversation. They made the promised stop in the toy department, and because he was leery of denying her anything, he waited patiently while she selected a jacket. *I'm not giving in...just protecting my investment. And it is pretty cold outside.* His attempts at self-justification didn't do much to calm his nerves.

Chick steered them to the electronics department and tossed three cheap prepaid phones in the basket. He stood in line at the counter, chafing to be back on the road. His nervous glance took in the rows of television screens lining the wall next to the checkout. It was just a matter of time before the news stations lit up with pictures of this kid and he wanted to be tucked into the safe house before that happened.

The kid behind the register greeted them with an eager metallic smile. The overhead lights glinted off his braces. "Will that be all for you, sir?"

Chick nodded. "Yeah."

The clerk smiled down at Bobbie. "Did you help your daddy pick out these phones?"

Bobbie smiled in response. "He's not my daddy. He's a bad man, but we're gonna call my mommy."

Chick's heart stopped. *I'm a dead man.* The girl's words, delivered with a matter-of-fact calm, seemed to hang in the air. He offered the boy behind the counter a forced grin. "I think I need to have a talk with my wife about her TV time."

The clerk's smile made a repeat performance as he rang up the rest of Chick's purchases and handed him the receipt. "Instructions on how to activate the phones are in the packages. Y'all have a nice evening."

Chick's mumbled response was lost under the rush to the front entrance. He had to get this kid out of this store.

The slamming door accented Louis's departure.

Seated between her dad and Terri, with Patrick's hands kneading her shoulders from his place behind the sofa, Sam raised her eyes to meet Detective Black's. "So that's it? He just walks out? What happens now?"

Nicolas Black crouched in front of Samantha. "What happens now is probably the hardest thing you'll ever do in your life." His gaze shifted from Sam and moved in turn to take in the other three. "You wait and let us do our jobs. Asking for your trust is a lot, but we know what we're doing." He paused with a slight shrug. "I'm sorry if that sounds harsh, I don't mean it to."

He stood and dug his notebook out of his pocket, making notes as he spoke. "It's obvious, from witness testimony, that we're dealing with a legitimate abduction..."

Sam doubled over, her groan lost under the detective's list of procedures. *I won't be sick...I won't be sick.*

"...so an AMBER Alert has been issued. Bobbie's description will be flashed on road signs statewide, and there'll be news alerts on all local TV and radio stations. We have a decent verbal description of the guy who paid the boys to stage their fight. Kurt's mother will be taking him to the station to work with an artist. Between that and what the security videos give us, we should be able to broadcast a picture of our perp before the night is over. Party Palace is shut down while investigators look for evidence. All individuals present during the incident have been questioned and released with instructions to call us if they think of anything pertinent to the case. We have a second team canvassing the neighboring businesses to see if any of their employees noticed any suspicious activity this morning."

The detective paused, and Sam looked up in time to see him glance at the closed front door. "And, despite Mr. Cantrell's denials, he'll be under constant surveillance until this is resolved." Black stooped in front of Samantha for a second time.

Sam straightened, scooping her hair away from her face with an unsteady hand. She met his eyes.

"You don't know me, but you know my parents. You need to trust me, just like you'd trust them. I'm going to make you two promises. One, I won't lie to you, ever. Two, I'm going to do everything I can to bring your daughter home, but I need you to help me."

Sam sniffed and nodded.

"Good. Now, I want you to think. Have you noticed anything suspicious over the last few days? Vehicles that don't belong. A stranger that showed up more than once. Odd phone calls."

"I've been thinking, but nothing—"

"Yes!" Iris jumped up from her seat in the corner of the room. She wiped her face on the sleeve of her sweater and crossed to join the rest of the family. "Yes, Sam. Remember the white van?"

The officer looked from one girl to another. "What white van?"

Sam surged from the sofa and grabbed Iris by the hand. "The white van..."

"What white van?" Detective Black repeated.

Sam let go of Iris, pacing as she spoke. "Just a plain white van...like a delivery van but no business markings. So plain, I'd forgotten about it. I've seen it a couple of times while I was out in the car. Even in front of the house, and the other evening when I took Bobbie to McDonald's."

"You thought it was following you," Iris reminded her.

"Not seriously, sis. It was just a passing thought." She turned to Nicolas. "I did worry, for a few seconds that it was Louis, but he wasn't around. I double-checked before I allowed Bobbie out of the car. Do you think...?"

"Why didn't you mention it, Sam?" her father asked.

Sam rubbed her brow. "Once I knew it wasn't Louis, I wrote it off as paranoia and forgot about it."

Detective Black pulled her back on course. "Any description other than 'a white van'?"

She looked at Iris.

Iris shrugged. "Not really."

"License plate?"

"It was always behind me," Sam said

"Any impression of the driver?"

Sam shook her head. "None...wait...it has really dark tinted windows!"

The detective scribbled in his notebook. "We can go with that for now, but you need to let me know ASAP if you remember anything else, or if you see the van again. If you do see it again, try for that license plate number, but don't approach the van to get it."

Sam put her face in her hands. "I can't believe I might have had part of the answer to this, and I ignored it." The emotions of the day slammed into her like a tidal wave and almost drove her to her knees. Her tears flowed in uncontrollable torrents. "Why is this happening? She's just a baby."

Patrick hurried around the sofa and pulled the woman he loved into his arms. He rubbed her back as she melted into his embrace. "Shh, baby, shh. We're"—his own voice broke on the uncertainty of the promise he needed to make—"gonna get her back." He faced Black. "So that's it? We sit on our butts and wait for the phone to ring with news?"

The cop crossed his arms in front of his chest. "If you have a better option or an avenue we aren't exploring, I'm open to suggestions."

Patrick rested his forehead on the crown of Sam's head. It broke his heart to admit it, but he had nothing to add. He tightened his embrace and heard Sam whispering. He leaned in to hear what she was saying.

"Jesus take care of my baby. Please take care of my baby. You're all I have. Jesus..."

It took everything inside of him to hold back a snort of unbelief. He faced the cop. "No, I don't have anything to add to what you're already doing."

Detective Black nodded and turned his attention to Samantha's father. "Ransom is another reality we need to prepare for. You're a successful public figure. It's likely that the man who has your granddaughter knows this. You might want to have a conversation with your financial contacts. Get a plan in place. We probably won't have a lot of time to work once a demand is made."

Steve's expression was grim as he accepted the cop's advice.

Patrick raised his head. "I want to help with that when the time comes."

The officer acknowledged Patrick's offer with a nod before he stepped away to admit Kurt's mother and hold a whispered conversation with her.

At least I can help with that part of it. The thought of Alan's money mingled with Sam's prayer and formed an ugly taste in his mouth. Yeah, he could help because his father was dead. His father was dead, twice. Dave Sisko, one of the most dedicated Christians he knew, just lost his house, Sam's life was in shambles, and now Bobbie was in danger. If God was trying to convince Patrick of His ultimate benevolence, He sure needed to try harder.

Samantha continued to sob into his shirt. Patrick murmured more assurances to her as he led her to an overstuffed chair, sat, and pulled her down into his lap. He rocked her like a child, not caring that his own tears mingled with hers. *OK, God. Pretty much everyone I know right now is in pain, and the way I see it, if You really are in control, then You've got a plan. And if You aren't...*His thoughts stumbled over the "and ifs," no longer sure what he believed...or didn't.

His breath shuddered in his chest as he reached for a hope he'd always denied the need for. *Sam can't do this. I can't do this. We need something bigger than the cops. God, if You're up there. If You're listening. If You care. Please bring Bobbie home.*

CHAPTER TWENTY

The house overflowed with people. Benton and Callie had come first, followed by Karla and Mitchell. The four of them stood in a corner, talking quietly with Nicolas. Now that they stood next to each other, Sam could see the family resemblance between Mitch and Karla and their oldest son. His face was round and just a bit boyish like Mitch's. The curly hair had to have come from Karla. Maybe it would help if she thought of him as Nicolas, the son of her friends, instead of the detective trying to find her daughter. Their whispered conversation failed to reach Sam's ears. She didn't care. Pam and Harrison arrived later, bearing a casserole and a cake. The offering scared Sam to death. Cooking might ease Pam's mind, but people brought food to funerals. She closed her eyes. *I won't go there!*

Kate was here, her face streaked with tears, her quiet words of reassurance lost in the haze cocooning Sam.

Sam saw and heard things from a distance, almost in slow motion. Bobbie had been missing for five hours now. Sam needed to pee, but she couldn't summon the energy to get up. She declined offers of food. *How can I eat when my baby might be hungry?* Terri left a plate of her favorite snacks on the table next to her, anyway. The very thought of food sent Sam's stomach rolling and threatened to clog her throat with bile. She remembered the Scriptures from Pastor Gordon's sermon on Sunday. Well, not the ones he'd preached on, but the ones that had caught her attention. *Is this how David felt while he waited for word about his child? While he waited for his baby boy to die?*

"Am I being punished?" Sam had no idea she'd spoken aloud until Callie and Karla came to sit beside her.

Callie picked up Sam's limp hand and pulled it into her lap. "What did you say?"

Sam drew her brows together and released a shuddering exhale. "Do you think I'm being punished?"

Karla put an arm around Sam's shoulders. "Punished for what, sweetheart?"

Samantha looked up, her words slow and measured, the effort to speak almost requiring more energy than she had. "You know...punished. Like David and Bathsheba."

After hours of silence, her words acted like a magnet, drawing Mom, Kate, and Pam into the conversation. Sam raised her head and tried to make the others understand the fear that was squeezing the life from her heart. "David and Bathsheba slept together, and God took their son from them as punishment." She swallowed, almost afraid to put her fears into words. "What if he's doing the same thing to me? I slept with Louis, and we weren't married. What if...what if neither of us deserves the child we made."

The question elicited a groan of despair from Terri, and Pam pulled Terri into a hug. The rest of the women were silent as Sam continued. "I mean, I know God loves me, but we reap what we sow, right? If He took David's baby, why should I expect any different?"

Callie's grip on her hand tightened. "Samantha, no..."

Kate knelt at Sam's knees. "Look at me."

Sam focused her eyes on the woman she'd hoped to call mother-in-law someday.

"Yes, God disciplines his children"—Kate shook her head—"but this isn't one of those times."

"How—?"

"You were a baby when you slept with Louis. An innocent baby taken advantage of by an experienced con man. David and Bathsheba were adults. David was king over God's people and he broke the law in a very public way. Then instead of repenting, he had Bathsheba's husband murdered. The two situations don't even begin to come close, so you put that thought out of your mind."

"But—"

"No buts." Kate stood and held out a hand to the women on either side of her. Callie and Karla each took one of Sam's hands and closed the circle. Kate offered up a prayer. "Father, I know that You have not ignored our prayers this afternoon. We need Your comfort and Your peace. We're human, and we're afraid. Don't let us be hopeless. God, calm Sam's heart. Please let her feel Your love for her in this moment of despair. Proverbs 24:10 tells us, 'The fear of the wicked, it shall come upon him: but the desire of the righteous shall be granted.'

"Fill this man's heart with fear, Father, and grant our desires. Peace in this place, calm in Sam's heart, wisdom for the authorities, and an angel of protection for Bobbie. We claim these things by Your word and in Your name."

With whispered amens, the women dispersed back into the room, leaving Sam to her peace and quiet. An angel? Sam kept her eyes closed as tears continued to flow down her cheeks. Bobbie called her new imaginary friend an angel. *What did she say his name was? Jeb...Jim...no...* She remembered the printed letters on Bobbie's drawing...*Jem.* Sam retrieved her phone, connected it to the Internet and did a quick search on a baby naming site for male Hebrew names. *There it is. Jem...Sent by God.* Bobbie's simple memory verse floated into her mind. *He will order His angels to protect you.* She wrapped her arms around herself, and surrendered to a fresh wave of tears. *O Father, make it so.*

Run.

Louis threw his belongings into a battered suitcase with that single word echoing through his mind. Run far and run fast. Well, as far as his remaining cash would take him. Sweat prickled his brow as a new string of swear words peppered the air. Banks...bureaucracy and red tape.

His first stop, after leaving Sam's, had been the bank. He needed quick cash, and since Mr. Carson would be out for his head after this, one more offense didn't seem to matter. If Sam hadn't cashed that check, an additional ten thousand dollars would, at least, get him out of the country.

He'd begged, pleaded, threatened, caused a scene...*nothing.* The bank teller, the vice president, the president all sang different verses of the same song. Too bad, so sad, Mr. Cantrell. That money was tied up tighter than his granny's stockings. The cashier's check had not been cashed, but the bank couldn't release the funds to him without an official stop payment request from him, followed by a ninety day waiting period. *Ninety days?* He planned to be out of Garfield, Oklahoma, in ninety minutes.

Louis, anxious to be gone, looked around the shabby, impersonal room. Never had a con blown up in his face so completely. He knew exactly where to lay the blame. Carson's stupid goon.

That goon has your daughter.

The thought stopped him in his tracks. Louis made no internal bones about the fact that he was a con man. He lifted his shoulders in a shrug. It is what it is. But he had rules to his own game, and those rules stopped well short of physical harm. He'd taken money from Sam, would have taken more. But even though he had no use for kids and no particular feelings for Bobbie, seeing her harmed had never been a part of the plan.

He plucked his phone from his pocket and bounced it in his hand. Calls had been ignored on both ends over the last few days. There wasn't any guarantee the thug would pick up the phone now, but he'd make the effort, ease his meager conscience, and hit the road. Louis scrolled through the numbers and pushed redial. The phone rang once before it connected.

"What's shakin', Nancy?"

Anger threatened to boil over, and Louis struggled

to focus. His grandmother's ancient saying about flies and honey became a silent mantra. "Do you have my daughter?"

"Maybe. Have you developed some sort of attachment to the kid, cause I gotta tell you, she's nutso."

"That sounds like more than a maybe. What are you planning to do with her?"

"What difference does it make?"

Louis flinched at the sneer in the thug's voice. "You had your chance. You blew it. Best thing for you to do is tuck your sissy tail between your legs and make room for the pros."

"If you hurt her—"

"You'll do squat, and we both know it. You're a sniveling coward with no attachment to any skin 'cept your own. So, leave me alone. I'll take this from here."

The phone went dead in Louis's hand. Several redials later, he gave up with a shrug. *I tried.* He stuffed his phone in his pocket and continued to pack, overcome with a serious need to see Garfield in his rearview mirror.

Chick leaned in the doorway and studied the sleeping child. Nancy boy's question occupied his mind. What was he planning?

Chick would be the first to admit that he'd jumped the gun just a bit. He should have prepared the house beforehand and taken better measures in regards to his identification *before* he acted. As it stood, the kids at Party Palace could probably identify him, as well as a number of people at the department store. And the kid? Well, she was little more than a baby, but he had no doubt that she could point him out in a group. Snuffin' her hadn't been a part of the plan, but no way could he just take her back home once he got his hands on Grandpa's money.

He remembered the incident in the shoe aisle and his flesh crawled. He rolled his neck on his shoulders. All the kid's angel talk had him spooked. Chick shook himself. "You need to get a grip. The kid was yapping about angels and that woman knocked a shoebox onto the floor. Human accident...no angel involved." At least he was ninety-eight percent certain that angels had nothing to do with it.

He approached the bed. Time to wake her up. She had a phone call to make, and he had to get his demands on the table. Chick nudged the bed. "Kid."

Bobbie rolled over, taking her new doll with her, eyes still closed in sleep.

Chick shook his head. This kid was a stinkin' puzzle. Granted, she was the first kid he'd ever snatched, and there wasn't exactly a how-to manual with step-by-step directions, but he'd had some logical expectations. Tears, terror, and obedience had topped his list. There'd been plenty of tears, but otherwise the kid was spooky calm, and obedience? Only when it suited her own agenda.

Chick reached out to shake her awake, jerking his hand back at the last minute. "I'm only going to wake her up," he whispered to whoever or whatever might be listening. "See, nice and easy." He reached out a second time, holding his breath until his hand made contact with the tiny shoulder. "Hey, kid, wake up. You want to talk to your mommy?"

Her blue eyes popped open. She looked around,

looked at him, and her lower lip trembled. A sign of the tears he expected. Instead she took a breath and looked past him.

"You promise?"

Once again the hair on his arms stood to attention. Who was this kid talking to? She nodded in response to something he couldn't hear. He took a step away from the bed as she bounced to her feet, all signs of an impending meltdown gone.

"OK, let's call my mommy."

CHAPTER TWENTY-ONE

Please, can't they all just go home and let me fall apart without an audience? Sam pulled her feet up into the chair, wrapped her arms around her legs, tucked the phone between ear and shoulder, and rested her forehead on her knees. *Would this day ever end?* The brief escape to her apartment had proved disastrous. Bobbie's clothes, Bobbie's toys, *Bobbie's smell... Father, I can't do this.*

Police came and went. She forgot their names. They mostly held quiet conversations with Detective Black and headed out to follow new leads or instructions. Her phone rang off the hook. She'd have ignored the calls, but Detective Black needed each one answered, by her. "We can't take the chance," he said, "that the kidnapper will call and be put off by someone else's voice."

So she sat in a dark corner of the living room, trying to ignore the bustle and the occasional tearful, well meant, but useless words of encouragement and compassion. At least no one had said that they knew how she felt. That really would have been the final nudge over the edge of her sanity. No one could know what this felt like. Her child was missing. Her life for the past four years, gone. Was Bobbie hungry? Was she cold? Was she scared? Was she—Sam struggled to breathe—was she still alive? Sam chewed her nails, fielded phone calls, and answered the same questions a hundred times.

Samantha heard a throat clear on the other end of the phone. She'd zoned out of the current conversation. "Dave, I don't know anything yet." She closed her eyes and nodded. "Yes, I know you'd be here with Lisa if you weren't watching the kids." *I'm so glad you aren't here.* The call waiting beeped with another incoming call. She pulled the phone away to look at the number and sighed. Another number she didn't recognize. *Where are these people coming from?* "Dave, I've got to take this call." She waited through his words, added, "Yes, I know you're praying. I appreciate that," and clicked the button to accept the new call.

She tried to sound less tired than she felt. "Hello."

"Mommy?"

Sam's heart skipped a beat, then revved beyond its normal rhythm. Heat flushed her face and gratitude galvanized her actions as she jumped to her feet. "Bobbie!" Her excited shout drew everyone in the house to her corner. Detective Black sat on the arm of her chair, notebook in hand, scribbling furiously. He held it up for her to see. *Deep breath. Get all the info you can.*

She nodded and turned away. "Bobbie, are you all right?" Sam wiped tears from her face with her free hand and read the new note Detective Black held in front of her.

Put it on speaker.

She complied with the cop's instructions, amazed that all the noise in the room had disappeared so fast. Suddenly, all she could hear was the sound of her daughter's beautiful breaths.

"Baby, can you tell me where you are? Mommy will come get you." The sound of Bobbie's muffled sniffle weakened Sam's knees, driving her back to the chair.

"The bad man taked me away."

"Oh, baby, I know. But can you tell me where?"

"A long way." Bobbie's voice cracked. "Jem says to be brave, but I'm scared." The sound of her tears flooded the room, accented by muffled grunts and scraping noises. The sound of a door slamming echoed from the phone.

"Bobbie?"

Sam shrank in her seat as a strange voice replaced her daughter's.

"Do I have your attention?"

She nodded and swallowed the lump in her throat. It lodged in the pit of her stomach and pressed against her heart. "Yes."

"Good. I wanted you to know that your kid's OK. I plan to keep her that way if you do what you're told."

She looked up at a tap on her shoulder. Detective Black drew his hands apart in a stretching motion. Sam acknowledged with a single jerk of her head. She wanted to scream into the phone, wanted to make demands. Instead, she forced a deep breath into her lungs, striving for a calm she didn't feel. "I understand. I'll do whatever I have to do to get my daughter back. Just tell me what you want."

A harsh cackle filled the room. "Well, let's not get ahead of ourselves. I think we all need to sleep on things. I need some time to think about what I want. You need some time to think about what'll happen if I don't get it. We'll talk again tomorrow."

"But..." A tone. Then silence filled the room. Samantha bowed her head over the dead phone. "He's gone." Tears made rivers down her cheeks as she stared at her lap. "He hung up."

Patrick knelt in front of her, took the phone away, and pressed tissues into her hand. Nicolas Black rubbed her back from his perch on the arm of the chair.

"You did real good, Sam."

Samantha wiped her eyes and looked up at him through a curtain of hair. "Good? *Good?* How—"

"Yes, good. You did exactly what I needed you to do, and we learned a lot."

She smoothed her hair back and frowned up at him.

"We know Bobbie's OK. He hasn't hurt her, and he knows he won't get what he wants if he does. As hard as it seems, we know we can stand down for the night and you can get some rest while the team gets to work. He said he'll call back tomorrow, and he will." He laid the notepad in Sam's lap and tapped a portion of his notes. "Who's Jim?"

Sam shook her head in confusion. "What?"

His tapping drew her eyes to the scribbled transcript of the conversation and a single circled word. "Bobbie said that 'Jim' was telling her to be brave. Who's Jim?"

She picked up the paper and ran a trembling finger over the circled name. Her lips ticked up in spite of everything she was feeling. Her words were shaky and full of exhaustion. "Jem, not Jim." She spelled it for him. "Jem is Bobbie's imaginary friend."

Patrick took her hands in his and gave a reassuring squeeze.

Sam looked up and focused on Patrick. "Bobbie told me that Jem was her guardian angel."

Chick leaned against the closed door of the bedroom. He ignored the sobbing from the other side as he took the phone apart. The cheap device should be untraceable, not equipped with the sophisticated tracking so standard on more expensive models.

"Kid, stop that noise!" He banged on the door to emphasize his command before he crossed to the bathroom, broke the phone's circuit board into pieces, and flushed them one at a time. The water swirled around the last piece. *Trace me if you can.*

His nerve endings began to vibrate as the wailing from the other room intensified. Chick pressed his fingers to his temples. The kid was giving him a headache. He hustled back across the hall. "Come on, kid. Give me a break already." He yanked the door open, prepared to be intimidating from a safe distance.

Bobbie barreled out of the room. Her hands slammed into the still tender wound on this thigh, sending Chick to his knees in pain. Bobbie's tennis shoe-clad foot landed a solid kick to the other leg.

"You were mean to my mommy!"

Chick scrambled to his feet and reached out to grab the little spitfire. The barest brush of something against his bare arms raised sudden goose bumps. He backed away instead. "Kid...Bobbie...are you hungry? I can make you a sandwich." Maybe if he fed her some dinner she'd calm down and go to sleep.

"No!"

"OK...OK. It's late. If you don't want to eat, you need to go to sleep."

Bobbie's small blue eyes narrowed. She crossed her arms. "I want cookies and milk and a bedtime story. Mommy and I always have a story before I go to sleep."

"I can do that." *I can do anything if you'll just be quiet.* "Umm...why don't you make a trip to the john...?"

Her confused stare had him backtracking. He pointed to the bathroom. "Go to the bathroom while I get the storybook and your snack."

Chick rustled through sacks on the kitchen table until he found the cookies and the book. When did kidnapping become babysitting? He shook his head. This was not going as he'd envisioned it. He was pretty sure he was supposed to be the one in charge.

He shuffled back to the bedroom. Bobbie was already there, sitting against the pillows at the head of the bed. She held out her hands for the promised snack without meeting his eyes. With the glass held steady between her thighs, she twisted the cookie apart and licked out the cream before dunking the chocolate wafers in her milk. She completed the exercise with surprising neatness. Her stormy expression seemed to calm a bit with each bite. When the last of the four cookies was gone, she drank down her milk, set the glass aside, and reached for the book.

Chick fidgeted while the kid flipped through the pages. "Just pick a story already."

Bobbie looked up at him with a cheery smile and handed him the open book. "This one." She scooted beneath the blankets and turned her back to him.

"Jesus Blesses the Little Children." Chick sat back, folded the book closed, and looked at the cover. *Aw, man...Bible stories.* Why hadn't he noticed that when she'd picked it out at the store earlier?

"I'm waiting."

He took a deep breath. "One day after Jesus finished talking to the mommies and daddies in a crowd of people, he sat down on a big rock and motioned to the children in the crowd. When they began to move forward, his disciples tried to stop them. 'Let Jesus rest. Can't you see how tired he is?' When Jesus heard what his disciples said, he was angry with them. 'Don't tell them to stay away from me. My kingdom is made up of many little children.'" Chick rolled his eyes. *Who writes this stuff?*

Bobbie rolled over to face him. "Is that all?"

Chick shook his head and turned the page. "Jesus spent the next few minutes talking and laughing with the children. Before they went home for dinner, he put his hands on their heads and prayed with each of them."

Bobbie yawned. "You can be done now." Her eyes cut to a dark corner of the room as if she saw something he couldn't. She flopped to her back, arms crossed in a pose of stubbornness. "I don't want to. He's a bad man!"

The hair on the back of Chick's neck lifted, and he suppressed a shiver. He studied the corner. There was nothing there. He tilted his head and listened to the silence. Not a whisper. His skin crawled as the kid's expression calmed.

"OK." She looked back at him with a very adult

sigh. "Jem told me to tell you..." She cocked her head. "Jesus loves you, even if you are a bad man." Bobbie frowned. "He wants you to know that Jesus is very sorry because your grandpa hurt you." With the blanket pulled up to her chin, she turned her back to him in dismissal. "Good night."

Kicked out. Patrick shrugged as he drove. He understood that Sam needed some rest, but leaving her had been the hardest thing he'd ever done.

After the kidnapper's call, Sam's dad had thanked everyone for coming, for their prayers, and moral support, and asked that everyone go on home so Sam and the rest of the family could have some peace and quiet.

Patrick didn't like it, but he got it. His fingers drummed on the steering wheel. The motion caught his attention. Despite the circumstances, a half-hearted smile lifted one side of his mouth. The hand was bare. Sometime in the last few hours, by his actions or Sam's—he wasn't even sure which—the class ring had slipped from his finger back onto Sam's. *Where it belonged.* Had that happened before or after he'd prayed?

Patrick tilted his head in the on-again, off-again light as he drove under the street lamps of Garfield's deserted streets. Could that brief admission of helplessness, that desperate cry for help, be considered prayer? *Did I mean it as a prayer?* And if it had been a prayer, would God listen, much less answer, after his years of denial? *Am I ready to change everything I've believed and said?*

Maybe not for himself...maybe not even to have a

future with Sam...but for Bobbie? Was Bobbie's welfare more important than all of the things he'd refused to pray about over the years?

I held those needs in My hands in spite of your denial, just like now. I've always cared.

Warmth spread across Patrick's heart. The heaviness that followed in its wake left him struggling to breathe. A groan filled the cab of the pickup. He pulled the truck to the side of the road, shifted into park, and rubbed at the spot on his chest where his heart threatened to pound through his skin. Sisko probably...*probably?*...didn't need Patrick's problems stacked on top of what they were going through in their own lives right now, but Patrick needed to talk, and Sisko wouldn't turn him away. He thumbed his cell phone to life and waited for the call to be picked up on the other end.

"Patrick. Is there news?"

"No, I..." He stopped when his voice cracked, forced to swallow around a melon-sized lump in his throat. Even then, the words stuck in his throat, forcing another swallow. "Man, I know you've got your own stuff going on right now, but I seriously need to talk."

The young pastor answered without hesitation. "Sure, come on over. We'll go sit in my office—"

"No!" Patrick let go of the wheel for a second and ran his hand down his face. What's wrong with me? "I mean, yes, I'm on my way, but could we just go sit in the sanctuary?"

"The sanc..." He heard Sisko clear his throat. "Sure, I'll meet you there. Just come around to the front doors. I'll have them unlocked."

Patrick swiped the call closed, tossed the phone into the passenger seat, and headed toward the church. He couldn't explain the need for Valley View's sanctuary, didn't understand the urge to hurry. But as surely as a man knew finding water in the desert would save his life, Patrick needed answers he could only find within those four walls.

He jerked his truck to a stop in the winter-dark parking lot and stumbled out, driven by a growing hunger that filled his whole being. His hand trembled as he reached for the door. *What's wrong with me?*

Sisko came around the corner as Patrick stepped into the entryway. He rushed forward and grabbed Patrick's shoulders. "Patrick, what's wrong?"

Patrick fell into the arms of his friend, his body wracked by sobs. "I don't know. I can't breathe. I think I might be dying." He drew in a shuddering breath. "I need to talk to God."

CHAPTER TWENTY-TWO

Patrick sat in the front pew, staring at the softly lit cross that hung on the back wall of the platform in Valley View's sanctuary. "Wow."

Sisko leaned forward. "Wow?"

Patrick nodded. "Just wow. Samantha told me once that I wouldn't get it until I got it. I get it now."

The other man nodded. "Are you feeling better? You were pretty shaky when you came through the door."

Patrick took a deep breath and exhaled slowly, probing his feelings like a child sticking their tongue into the socket of a recently pulled tooth. "I'm still terrified over this thing with Bobbie."

"I'd be checking your pulse if you weren't. But dig under that."

Patrick shoved to his feet, pacing the open area between the pew and the altar. "Light," he finally said. "Like I could climb Everest without a rope. Like I should be standing on Valley View's roof telling the world about what I just found." He stopped in front of his friend with his head bowed. "But..."

"There's always a 'but' with you analytical types. Get it off your chest."

"There's a lot of guilt down there too." Patrick raised his head, a fist clutched over his heart. When Sisko didn't respond, he continued, "How can God love me when I threw His love back into His face for so many years?" He sank down to sit on the altar. "I said some ugly things to Him a few nights ago, pretty much challenged Him to show me His stuff. What if this thing with Bobbie is—?"

"Hold it right there. Are you arguing for the defense or the prosecution?" It was Sisko's turn to pace. He retraced Patrick's footsteps in silence before coming to a halt in front him. "There are some things you need to understand. God forgave you for every single sin. Gone, vanished, zip. What He can't do is make you forgive yourself. That's all on us and sometimes..." He spread his hands in a helpless gesture. "Well, let's just say Satan is an expert at tormenting us with things God doesn't even remember. Now, about Bobbie."

Sisko sat on the altar next to Patrick. A heavy sigh escaped before he continued. "Patrick, you have to understand something. We're all praying they find her, but there are no guarantees. You have to accept, here and now, that even if this thing with Bobbie goes south, it won't be because God is punishing you. We live in a fallen world where bad things happen to good people every day." He leaned forward and thumped Patrick's chest. "This is new and light and filled with hope right now. Regardless of what happens over the next few days, you need to hang onto that."

Louis cracked the blinds and peered out into the parking lot. Flurries danced in the spotty light, but beyond the snow, nothing moved. His ninety minute exit plan had given way to caution. Just like gambling, life was a game of chance. You didn't run a successful con or survive in this life by being stupid.

If he stayed put, he ran the risk of the local cops finding the Las Vegas warrant. He balanced that possibility against the certainty that he was being watched, and if he took off, he handed the cops all the excuse they needed to take a closer look. Better they thought him an obedient citizen than a hasty fool. The third possibility was that they would watch from a distance, assuming that he knew more than he was telling, hoping that if he had enough rope he'd hang himself. *Crapshoot.*

So, he'd hunkered down in his room while afternoon turned to dusk. He ate his dinner with his suitcase resting by the door. He watched TV with one eye on the clock. Each hour that passed without a knock on the door bolstered his courage. At ten o'clock, he turned out the lights. *That's right. Just an ordinary Joe with nothing to hide, nothing to be ashamed of or worried about.* Instead of going to bed, he sat in a chair and drank coffee, the only light in the room the illuminated digital clock on the abused old nightstand.

At midnight he risked another look through the blinds. The snow had stopped and everything remained still and dark. His eyes roamed. "That's right, nothing to see here. I'm all tucked in for the night. If you're out there, you might as well go on home."

He gave it another hour before opening the door

and creeping outside. For months, he'd cursed the burned-out dome light in his car. Now as the driver's side door opened without disturbing the dark, that liability became a blessing. Louis tossed his suitcase into the passenger seat, double checked the external light settings to make sure nothing was on automatic, and turned the dial for the dash lights down to their dimmest level. As long as he didn't step on the brake pedal or use the turn signals, the car would operate in complete darkness.

Louis started the car and shifted it into reverse. "Don't touch the brakes...don't touch the brakes." He gave the gas the slightest tap to start the car rolling and nudged it into drive just as soon as he cleared the parking spot. With a warrant hanging over his head, he'd schooled himself to be a careful driver. He didn't plan to sacrifice his freedom on a preventable traffic stop. Tonight was different.

"No blinkers, no brakes." The whispered words became his refrain as he crept along. "Take it slow and dark for a couple of blocks, and then, get out of Dodge."

He paused at the intersection where the city road met the state highway. Five miles would see him out of Garfield's city limits. Louis peered through the foggy windshield. No other traffic was visible in any direction.

"Saturday night in the big town." He delivered the statement with a sarcastic sneer. With a twist he switched on the lights and prepared to leave Garfield in the dust.

"Stupid Podunk cops." He pulled onto the state highway. "If I was tailing me, I wouldn't let me outta my sight." The chuckle at his own joke died in his throat as the night began to strobe with red and blue lights. Louis pounded a fist on the steering wheel as he tromped the gas. His tires lost traction on a patch of black ice and fishtailed all over the road, driving his stomach to his knees. A layer of cold sweat covered his brow by the time he regained control of the car. He jerked the car to a stop. A black police cruiser sailed past him and blocked his path.

Louis squinted through the glare of the headlights at the bulkily clad figure approaching his door. The cop tapped the window with his flashlight, prompting him to roll it down. Louis muttered under his breath. It was the same jerk cop who'd questioned him earlier in the day.

"Going somewhere, Mr. Cantrell?"

Louis swallowed and grasped at any straw he could use to redeem the situation. "Just going for a pack of smokes, Detective. Sorry about that ugly skid. Your lights startled me."

Detective Black swept his light through the interior of the car, hesitating briefly on the suitcase. "Mm-hmm. I need you to step out of the car."

"But—"

"No buts, Mr. Cantrell." He took a couple of steps back and rested his free hand on the gun holstered at his waist. "Step out, now. You are under arrest for an outstanding grand larceny warrant in the state of Nevada. There are some very angry people waiting to see you again. We're arranging a reunion." Black offered Louis a condescending smile as he leaned forward to open the car door. "You have the right to remain silent..."

Chick tossed in the unfamiliar bed. *Jesus is sorry your grandpa hurt you.* What was that supposed to mean? How could she know anything about that? She couldn't. Who knew what was going on in that whacked-out kiddie brain of hers?

It had all started with that stupid Bible story, bringing up those ugly memories from his childhood.

Chick, you can't run from Me forever.

Ahhh...now he was hearing voices. Suddenly hot and sweaty, he threw off the blankets. He lay there for a few seconds, hoping that the cool air would wick the uncomfortable moisture from his skin. What cool air? Chick rolled out of the bed. The room was muggy with heat and musky with the sour odor of his own nervous sweat.

Nervous? He didn't get nervous. He made people nervous. He turned on the ceiling fan as he shuffled from the room. "This day just keeps getting better."

He trudged to the front room, muttering under his breath the whole way. "I just need to get control of that kid. She thinks she's running the show. Well, she's not."

Mind made up, he turned on the TV out of habit but muted the sound. He needed to think. His hand brushed against the storybook, still lying on the sofa where he'd tossed it earlier. He picked it up and began turning the pages absently in the flickering light. He stopped in the middle of the book and studied one of the pages. *I remember this.* His lips twitched up. *I guess some of these pictures just get moved ahead from printing to printing.* Chick searched his mind for the story that went with the illustration. The prodigal son—that was it. A story about a boy who ran away from home, lived a hard life, and decided he needed to go back.

The book slipped from his hands and fell to the floor. "What am I doing?"

He rested his head against the back of the sofa. If he couldn't sleep and he couldn't read, he'd plan. *I'm supposed to call the kid's mother in a few hours and tell her what I want. "What do I want?"* His chuckle was a harsh bark in the darkened room. *Money.* The kid's granddaddy had some, and he wanted it for himself. And the price had gone up. The kid was making him crazy, and sanity was expensive.

"Two hundred and fifty thousand dollars." He whispered the number to the four walls and nodded at the sound of it. It was a nice number, one that would satisfy Mr. Carson and enable Chick to retire to a tropical location. Far away from vengeful bosses, lazy con men, and spooky kids.

You can't hide from your heart, Chick.

He rubbed his face and pushed the thought aside. "I'll buy a boat and take tourists out to fish." He closed his eyes, imagining the sun on his face, an ocean breeze in his hair, and a gently rocking vessel under his feet. Cozumel, Belize, Jamaica. An American with cash could live well in places like that. There was just one fatal flaw in that plan.

He had no idea how to make it happen. Oh, he understood the basics. Ransom money transferred from a US account, to one off-shore, via so many computer links that it became nearly impossible to track. He had the kid and all the leverage he needed to get the ball rolling. But, Chick was hired muscle, not hired brains. This was his first...

Jesus still loves you.

His eyes darted to the dark corners of the room. Chick turned up the sound on the TV in an effort to drown the annoying voice in his head.

This was his first and last kidnapping, and he certainly wasn't computer savvy enough to set the plan in motion. He straightened. "But I know people who can do those things." He narrowed his eyes at the light shifting on the TV screen. "People who owe me...big" He nodded. He'd take tomorrow...*today*...to call in some favors and make some threats.

He thought about the child sleeping in the next room. Strange didn't begin to cover what she was, but at least she was cooperative. He'd get everything in place before he contacted Samantha Evans again.

Chick laced his fingers behind his head and propped his feet on the worn coffee table. The skirt was expecting to hear from him tomorrow. He could see where putting that call off for twenty-four hours could play to his advantage. By the time he put his plan in motion and got around to contacting her again, she'd be only too willing to follow his instructions.

"What am I supposed to do now?" Samantha roamed her small apartment, Bobbie's stuffed penguin clutched against her chest. She had the peace and quiet she'd craved earlier, but now she longed for the company of her friends. The apartment was too quiet, Bobbie's absence too glaring. She clutched the penguin tighter. "O God, I can't do this. I really can't do this."

Sam swiped at the pointless tears. They hadn't helped earlier in the day and they weren't helping now. She continued to prowl and pray. "Father, please. If you aren't punishing me, then help me understand why this is happening. Bobbie's a baby. I know she's scared. Is she cold or hungry? How am I supposed sleep or rest or breathe without those answers? She's my heart, Father. My very heart." Sam leaned against the wall and sank to the floor. The room danced with the flickering lights from the small Christmas tree in the corner. "I don't know what to do." She lowered her head to her knees and cried tears she didn't know she had left. "What do I do without her?"

With this round of tears spent, she crawled to her feet. Too restless to sleep, too empty to cry, too alone. Her Bible beckoned to her from the side table. She picked it up, switched on a lamp, and allowed it to fall open in her lap. The verse she'd chosen last year as her favorite encouragement stared up at her, highlighted and underlined. Psalms 37:4 "Delight thyself also in the lord: and he shall give thee the desires of thine heart."

Reading it now washed a fresh wave of anguish over her heart. "Really? My desires? They're so simple, Father, and I've done everything I know to do to trust You for them. A good life for my baby, a future with Patrick." She shoved the Bible aside and lowered her face into her hands. "Did I get that all wrong?"

Her cell phone trilled to life from the other room. *Bobbie!* Sam rushed to pick it up, despair mingled with gratitude when she saw Patrick's number on the screen.

"Hey."

"I know it's late, but I didn't figure you'd be asleep."

Sam lowered herself to the edge of her mattress and sniffed. "I may never sleep again."

"Tell me what I can do to help."

"Noth..." Sam's tears transitioned to hiccups.

"Nothing. There's nothing anyone can do."

"Go wait by the front door. I'm coming over. I'll be there in ten minutes."

"Patrick, you can't—"

"Yes, I can. Not being there when you need me is breaking my heart. Be up there to let me in. I don't want to ring the bell and wake the whole house."

The phone went dead in her hands. Sam forced her leaden limbs up the stairs. The house was quiet, her youngest siblings asleep, and the rest? Probably being quiet in the hopes that she'd sleep. *As if.*

She spent the time making hot cocoa for the both of them. *Maybe the warm milk will help me sleep later.* She heard Patrick's truck in front of the house and hurried to let him in.

Patrick didn't say anything. He held her at arm's length. With one hand, he reached up to brush the hair out of her face before he placed a kiss on her forehead. "You're so worn out. You need to rest."

She let her head fall to his chest. "I told you, I can't sleep."

Patrick took her hand and pulled her towards the kitchen. "You don't have to sleep, but maybe you'll rest better if you aren't by yourself."

I doubt that. She shook free of his hands, followed him into the kitchen, and retrieved the cups. "I made us some cocoa."

He took the steaming mugs and nodded to the door. "Lead the way."

Sam shrugged, descended the steps, and crossed to the sofa. She moved the discarded Bible and collapsed into the cushions. "I need my baby. Nothing else matters."

Patrick deposited the cocoa on the coffee table. He sat and gathered Sam into his arms. "Babe."

"Patrick?" Sam shuddered as she voiced her deepest fear. "What am I going to do if she doesn't come home?"

"We aren't going to let that happen."

"Can you promise?" She sat up, motioned at her Bible, and answered her own question. "You can't promise that. God won't even promise me that." She bowed her head, her next words a bare whisper. "It's a reality I have to think about...be prepared for. How do I do that?"

Patrick shifted and framed her face with both of his hands. His thumbs brushed the tears from her cheeks. "I love you so much. Maybe I can't make promises about Bobbie, but..." He brushed his lips across hers. "But I can promise you this. Whatever happens, we'll face it together. You, me...and God."

Sam sat back and studied his face.

"You heard me. I had a long overdue conversation with God tonight. I finally get what you and Sisko and everyone else have been trying to pound into my heart for the last year."

"Oh, Patrick." Fresh tears overwhelmed her. "That's...that's the best news..."

Patrick pulled her back into his arms. "Sam, we have so much to talk about. I wasn't sure I should even tell you about this right now. I don't want you to think that my decision to give my life to Christ is just something to pacify you or—"

Sam raised her head. "I don't. I can see it in your eyes. I'm glad you told me. It helps...a little."

Patrick lowered his lips to hers, their kiss tender and

comforting. He raised his head, tucked her under his chin, and settled in the cushions. "Shh. Just lean on me, OK?"

Sam nodded, snuggled into his embrace, and gave in to the sleep she'd considered impossible.

CHAPTER TWENTY-THREE

Patrick's eyes snapped open as Samantha stirred beneath the covers and shifted out of his arms. She muttered unintelligible words, obviously trapped in the fog between asleep and awake. Two words came through loud and clear. They almost broke his heart.

"Weird dream."

The absence of windows kept the basement rooms dark, but the nightlight in the corner provided enough illumination to allow him to see Samantha's face. He watched as she frowned, and shook her head. His hand trembled a bit when he reached out to brush her dark hair from her face. He longed to smooth the crease between her eyes, but he didn't want to wake her. The automatic prayer that filled his heart caught him off guard. *Jesus, just let her sleep a little longer.*

Patrick scooted into a more comfortable position on the sofa. He didn't want to disturb Sam, but his neck had a crick in it from sitting up all night and he'd lost all feeling in the arm where Sam's head rested. He hadn't meant to spend the night. He'd only come back to keep her company, tuck her in once she slept, and leave.

After she'd fallen asleep on the couch, he'd stood to leave. But her eyes snapped open the second he'd left her side, and the tears had started again. He'd retrieved a blanket and some pillows and returned to the sofa. He'd tucked the blanket around her and pulled her back to his side, just to hold her, just to comfort. They'd fallen asleep in each other's arms. *Not how I envisioned our first night together.*

Her head snapped back and forth on his arm once again. "A bad dream," she mumbled. "It was all a bad dream." Suddenly she stiffened and tossed the blanket aside, her attempt to rise from the sofa arrested by his arms.

Samantha slapped at him. "What are you...? Let me go!"

"Shh, Sam. It's OK."

"Let me go," she repeated. "I need to go check on Bobbie."

Patrick held her tighter. "Sweetheart, be still and take a deep breath."

Her struggles stopped. With a defeated sob, she rolled into Patrick's arms. A keening wail filled the room. "I wanted it to be a dream."

Patrick rubbed her back, whispering assurances in her ear. "Sam...babe...it's going to be OK. We'll get her back."

Sam raised her head. "I—"

Light flooded the windowless room, framing Sam's father in the doorway at the top of the stairs. Steve Evans descended the stairs and looked from one to the other. "Patrick, what are you...?"

Patrick released Sam and scrambled to his feet. "Nothing. Absolutely nothing." He motioned to the tousled blanket. "I mean...I called her and she was crying and I couldn't stay away..." He shoved his hair out of his face. "Nothing happened. We fell asleep."

Steve crossed to the sofa, sat, and gathered Sam into his arms. "Calm down, Patrick. I've watched you both struggle for a year to keep your relationship on this side of pure. I trust you. I was just surprised to see you." He turned his attention to his daughter. "I was making coffee in the kitchen and heard you crying. Did you get any sleep at all?"

When Sam didn't answer, Patrick did. "She tossed most of the night, but I think she got a couple of hours."

Sam's tears were fading, and Steve nodded. He held her away and pushed the damp hair out of her face. "Sweetheart, Nicolas called my phone first thing this morning. They picked Louis up late last night."

Her face regained a bit of animation. "Has he told them where Bobbie is?"

"They're questioning him right now, but Nicolas doesn't think he knows anything." Sam slumped in his arms. "He's coming over here as soon as they're done. You need to change and eat something before he arrives."

"I'm not hungry."

"Babe..." Patrick started.

Steve silenced Patrick with a look and turned stern eyes on his daughter. "You aren't helping Bobbie by tearing yourself apart." His voice took on a no-nonsense, fatherly tone. "Pancakes with the family in thirty minutes. Patrick, you've been drafted to fry the bacon. Samantha, we'll see you upstairs."

Louis prowled the interrogation room, angry after spending an uncomfortable night on a lumpy cot in a cell smaller than the hotel room he'd recently abandoned. His stomach growled, empty, after his refusal to eat the runny eggs and stale toast that passed for breakfast in this place. The idea that this was just the first of many uncomfortable nights and bad breakfasts lurking in his future did nothing for his mood. He stared at the mirrored wall to his left. He'd seen enough TV to know that someone watched from the other side. He leaned against the glass, braced on both hands. "Can I at least get a hot cup of coffee?"

He whirled when he heard the sound of the locks engaging on the door. Detective Black stepped inside, accompanied by a second man in a cheap black suit. The two men took a seat on one side of the table and motioned to the single chair on the other side.

"Have a seat, Mr. Cantrell," Detective Black said.

Louis threw himself into the chair. "I. Need. Coffee."

The cop shrugged. "And I need information. You play nice with me, I'll play nice with you." He took a recorder out of his pocket, placed it in the middle of the table, and turned it on. "Detective Nicolas Black, Garfield PD, and Detective Oran Charles, Las Vegas PD, in interview with Louis Cantrell." He looked up. "Mr. Cantrell, please acknowledge that you have been read your rights and that you understand them."

Louis sat back in the hard metal chair and crossed his arms. "Coffee, two sugars, no cream."

Both officers mirrored his pose, silent and staring. No one spoke for several moments. The officers looked at each other and shrugged. They pushed back from the table, their chairs scrapping shrilly on the worn tile floor. Both men turned for the door without further word.

"Wait! Where are you going?"

Detective Black turned and reached for the recorder. "Mr. Cantrell, I have a missing child to locate. I don't have time to play your power games. If you have nothing to say, I have no recourse but to release you to Detective Charles for immediate transport to Nevada."

"You can't—"

"Can, will, have. If you're no good to my investigation, they can have you for theirs."

"There's nothing I can tell you."

"Fine, but I want you to remember this conversation, because it's the only time we'll have it. You're a gambler, Mr. Cantrell. You should know what it means to be out of cards." He nodded to Detective Charles. "You're looking at ten years in a Nevada prison on a grand larceny complaint. If we find out later that you could have helped us recover your daughter, and you didn't, that's another five years for obstructing justice. Fifteen years is a long time for a young man. On the other hand if you tell us what we need to know, the extra five years is off the table. The original ten could be reduced to five if you behave yourself. You've got sixty seconds to decide."

Louis put his head on the table. "You don't understand. I never saw him. I don't know his name. I don't know where he took her."

The two cops sat back down. Detective Black

tapped the recorder. "Please verify that you've been read your rights and that you understand them."

Louis sat up. "Yeah...OK, whatever."

Detective Charles sat back, silent as a stone. Detective Black leaned forward with hard narrow eyes. "Now, tell me what you know about the person who took your daughter."

Patrick stood in front of the stove next to Sam's father. He shuffled sizzling strips of bacon in one skillet while Steve flipped pancakes in another. The moment seemed surreal. How could life carry on, so normal, while Bobbie remained missing?

Sam's father hadn't said a word since coming up the stairs. Patrick watched him from the corner of his eye. He noticed a small shake in Steve's hands, and the usually smiling mouth was tight at the corners. The lines around his eyes seemed more pronounced than usual. Maybe normal was just an illusion.

Patrick turned a few slices of bacon and cleared his throat. "Did Detective Black have anything to say other than they'd picked up Louis?"

Steve used a spatula to loosen the edges of a pancake before he flipped it. He added two others to the growing stack on the platter before he answered. "No."

The single word drew a sigh from Patrick. "I feel so helpless."

"I understand. Bobbie is Sam's baby, but Sam is mine. As hard as it is to function without answers, I have to do what I can to keep Samantha propped up." He scooped up the last pancakes. "That includes some tough love and breakfast."

Patrick ducked his head. "Prayer, too? I've been praying, off and on, all night."

Steve took a step back and cocked his head. "Have you, now?"

Patrick looked up, unashamed of the tears clouding his eyes and the tremor he heard in his voice. He swallowed. "Yes, sir. I made a commitment to Christ last night. I know it was this whole situation that forced my hand...heart." A shrug accented his words. "Even though I've just accepted the faith I've been taught all my life, I'm trying really hard to stand on it with both feet."

Sam's father stood in silence as Patrick forked up the remaining bacon from the skillet, laid the slices on a stack of paper towels, and turned the burner off. When he turned, Steve slipped an arm around his shoulders and steered him to the table. "That's awesome news, son." His voice was raspy, and he stopped to clear his throat. "If nothing else positive comes out of this mess, that, alone, is a cause for celebration."

Patrick rubbed his chest through his shirt, still amazed at how different he felt, even in the face of disaster. "I think my insides are celebrating without me."

"I know the feeling. Did you share this news with Sam?"

"Yeah. I wanted her to know that I was praying, too. That I finally got it." He tilted his head to listen for movement on the basement stairs. When he didn't hear anything, he continued, "This isn't the right time, but I want you to know...once this is mess is settled and Bobbie is back..." He stopped, forced to clear the emotion from his throat before he could finish. "Once

Bobbie's back where she belongs. I want the two of us to have a talk. I want to marry your daughter."

Steve nodded. "When the time is right, that's a discussion I've been looking forward to for a long time now."

Patrick opened his mouth to continue the conversation, but snapped it closed when he heard Sam shuffling up the stairs.

Surrounded by her family, Sam picked at her breakfast, rearranging more food than she ate. The rest of the family kept abnormally quiet, except for the chatter of Lilly and Seth. At least they were enjoying Dad's breakfast.

Iris bent over her plate, eating without the normal enthusiasm for the pancakes that were her favorite. Mom fussed with the babies and Patrick and her father continued to watch Sam as if she were one step from falling over an unseen cliff. *Maybe I am.*

Sam wanted to give up the pretense, but every time she started to lay her fork aside, Dad cleared his throat and stared at her plate. Then she'd force herself to take another bite, even if just to placate him. She knew how worried he was about Bobbie and her.

When the stack of two pancakes was half gone and she'd finished a whole piece of bacon, she pushed the plate aside and looked at her father. "Can I please be finished now?"

Dad sipped his coffee and studied her over the rim of his cup. "You sound about six years old."

"I feel about ninety."

Terri stroked her arm before wiping Lilly's mouth and scooting Seth's cup of milk closer to the two-year-old. Seth, unaffected by the tension around the table, delivered the next knife to Sam's heart.

He swiped milk from his mouth with the sleeve of his pajamas. "Sammy, where's Bobbie?"

Her brother's simple question cut straight to her soul. *He doesn't know...he doesn't understand.* Sam opened her mouth but found she couldn't force any words past her constricted throat. The doorbell rang, saving her from the pain of answering. She pushed back from the table with a quick, "I'll get it," and bolted out of the room.

Sam opened the door to find Kate standing on the porch. She came across the threshold and held out her arms. Sam simply fell into them.

"Still no word?"

Sam shook her head. "No, I'm just...Kate, I'm going to go crazy if I don't hear something soon."

Gravel crunched on the road, drawing the attention of both women. Sam disentangled herself from Kate's embrace as Detective Black climbed from his police cruiser and came up the walk. She raced down the porch steps to meet him halfway.

"Please tell me you have news about my daughter."

CHAPTER TWENTY-FOUR

A place for food, a place for discussion. Sam took a seat at the hastily cleared table. She bowed her head over her clenched hands. *Please God, let it be a place for answers.*

The family took seats around her. Terri placed a mug of hot, black coffee in front of the cop, and its steamy fragrance rose to mingle in the air with the lingering scents of bacon and syrup.

Nicolas sipped and studied each person in order until his gaze rested on Sam. "I have some news. Not as much as you're probably hoping for, but progress."

Sam leaned in. "Dad told me you picked up Louis. Was he able to tell you anything?"

The detective pushed the cuff of his shirt sleeve aside and looked at his watch. "Mr. Cantrell will be boarding a plane soon to begin a nice long vacation in a Nevada cell. Our background check led us to an outstanding warrant for grand larceny. There were some other complaints on record with no charges filed.

That's likely to change once word of his arrest gets out. I don't think he'll be in a position to bother you again for a long time."

"That's great, but what about Bobbie?"

The cop shrugged. "He pretty much spilled his guts in interview, but there wasn't a lot that will be of immediate help. Louis is tangled up with a pretty rough group in Vegas. Owes some major money to some very ugly people." He lifted his cup in a silent salute to Steve. "He pegged you and your daughter for a lifeline."

Sam's snort filled the room. "Not likely. I'm not sixteen anymore."

"And you probably could have sent him packing if you'd stuck to your guns. He wasn't in a great position to bargain or even threaten. The outstanding warrant made him a target if he'd pursued any sort of legal action to insinuate himself into your family." Nicolas removed a small notebook from his breast pocket.

"But this thing is like an iceberg. The little bit you can see is nothing compared to what's hidden just under the water." He flipped pages. "Those very ugly people I mentioned? Mob money-men. Louis owes them a hundred K. He was able to convince them that if he had some financial backing, he could come back here"—Nicolas nodded at Sam—"marry you and, through that union, gain access to your father's money to repay his debt."

Sam's hands clenched into a white knuckled ball on top of the table.

Patrick eased them apart and held one. "And when that failed, he stooped to kidnapping?"

Detective Black shook his head. "No. We don't

think he had anything to do with the kidnapping, other than being incredibly stupid. When he came here, he didn't come alone. Louis didn't know it, but the money man he was working with sent some hired muscle along to make sure Louis got the job done. Louis claims he never saw him, only spoke to him over the phone a couple of times. Their last conversation pretty much confirms that this unknown person is the one who has your daughter."

Sam bolted to her feet. "The mob has my baby?"

Patrick stood and pulled her into his arms. "Easy now." He rubbed her back, his next words addressed to the cop. "This helps us get Bobbie back *how*?"

"Because we know what they want, and, by his actions, we know the guy who snatched your daughter isn't the sharpest knife in the drawer. He gave Louis two weeks to pull off a delicate con. He's impatient and greedy. We'll hear from him again." Nicolas unfolded a sheet of paper. "And we have this." He handed it to Steve.

Steve frowned over it for a few seconds. "Who is this?"

Nicolas sat back and pulled his coffee closer. "That's our perp. Compliments of a very observant teenager. Kurt was able to give us a good description. A good thing, since the feeds from the Party Palace cameras were either too grainy to be useful or only caught him from the back. That flier is being circulated all over the state in conjunction with the AMBER alert."

Iris angled in for a look. She took the paper and studied it for a second before it fell from her hands. She snatched it from the air. "Sam, you need to look at this."

Sam stepped out of Patrick's embrace. "What?"

Iris pushed the paper across the table.

Sam examined the sketch. She looked at Iris.

"What are you seeing that I'm not?"

"Look harder. Try to picture him without the hat and glasses."

Sam covered her mouth as recognition set in. "Oh no..."

Detective Black straightened in his chair. "Do you know him?"

"Yes...I mean no...I don't know him, but I've seen him." She shoved the drawing into Patrick's hands. "He spoke to us. He spoke to Bobbie."

"Where?"

Sam sank into her chair. "Last Thursday night. Do you remember that I told you we went to McDonald's?"

Nicolas nodded.

"Before we left, Bobbie wanted one of those balls out of the vending machine." Sam looked up when Patrick rested his hands on her shoulders. "You know how much she loves those things. I promised her two if she'd leave the penguin at home." Sam put her face in her hands. "She had her balls and one of them got away from her and bounced on top of this guy's table. He caught it and handed it to her. I made Bobbie thank him."

"That's not all, sis."

Sam looked up at Iris.

"He was in the booth behind us the whole time we were there. He knew where you and Bobbie would be yesterday, because there's no way he didn't hear you talking about taking Bobbie to Party Palace for a play date with Lisa and the kids."

Nicolas looked at both of the girls. "I need one of you to come down to the station. We'll get to work with the artist and get an updated picture out ASAP."

Sam started to rise, stopping when Iris scrambled to her feet.

"I'll go. Just let me grab my jacket." Iris hurried from the room.

Nicolas tapped the table and drew Sam's attention back to the sketch. "What more can you tell me?"

Sam picked up the paper, closed her eyes, and tried to get a mental picture of the man. "The sketch is pretty good. The hat keeps you from seeing his hair though. It was a dirty blond, not curly, but wavy. Average build...about...forty, maybe?" She shook the paper in her hands. "I just wasn't paying attention."

"Yes, I have a complete set of new identity documents." *That was the first thing I did when I got out of the hospital.* Chick's insides clenched at the painful reminder. He had no illusions about where Mr. Carson's next disciplinary bullet would go. Getting out of the country had been nothing but a desperate hope until now. "So, the first thing I need is a new bank account?" He nodded at what he was hearing while he scribbled notes. He'd been at this for several hours. Calling, writing, planning.

A noise in the doorway drew his attention. The kid stood there, rubbing her eyes.

"I gotta go. How long 'til we can make a move?" Another nod. "Roger that. I'll call you tonight." He shivered under the kid's intense blue stare. "What?"

"Is it time for breakfast?" She rubbed her stomach.

"My tummy's empty."

Chick levered himself out of the sofa. *I'm gonna write a book on the top ten reasons not to kidnap a little kid. One: They throw tantrums.* He paused to think about what might come next. His memory landed on three pair of shoes and a coat. *Two: They're expensive.*

"I'm hungry!"

"And three: they're impatient." He was almost afraid to think about the seven remaining reasons. He led her to the kitchen, took down a bowl from the cabinet, and placed it, the box of Fruity Berries cereal she'd demanded, and a gallon of milk on the table. He waved at her breakfast. "Knock yourself out. I got calls to make."

"But..."

"What?"

"Mommy doesn't let me pour it by myself."

"Kid, I ain't your mommy."

Bobbie shrugged and picked up the box. Chick left her to it as she turned it over in her hands. He settled back on the couch with his notes and his phone. He ignored a muffled "Uh-oh" from the other room, but sprang back to his feet at the sound of cereal bouncing on the tile floor. He rounded the door to the kitchen just as she lifted the gallon of milk. The first drops missed the bowl by six inches. *Four: They can't do anything for themselves.* "Wait, kid..." He grabbed for it, catching it just as it slipped from her hands. The plastic container was slippery with condensation, and he fumbled it. Milk sloshed down the front of his jeans.

Bobbie's giggles mixed in the air with Chick's muffled curses.

"Jem says you shouldn't swear."

"Is Jem going to come clean up your mess?"

Bobbie sat back in her chair with crossed arms. "I told you to help."

Chick rubbed both hands down the length of his face. "Yeah, yeah..." Cereal crunched under his feet as he searched for a broom. Finally locating it and a dust pan in a small corner closet, he swept up the mess. She had so much cereal in the bowl, there was no room for milk. He tipped half of the cereal back into the box and poured milk on the rest. "Now, is there anything else you need?"

Bobbie shook her head then looked at the empty space across the table. "Where's yours?"

"I don't like cereal. Just eat, OK?"

The spoon clattered into the bowl. Bobbie puckered. "Mommy always eats breakfast with me." Her chin quivered and the last word rose in a howl. "I want my mommy!"

Not the crying again. "Look, kid..." Chick grabbed a second bowl and sat in the empty chair. "I'm eating, OK? I'm right here, and we're gonna eat breakfast together." He poured a bowl full of the multi-colored berries, doused them with milk, and shoveled up a bite. "See?"

Bobbie's tears dried instantly and a cheerful smile transformed her face. "Jem says you're gonna need your strength."

Chick bent his head over his bowl. *Five: They're spooky.*

The door closed behind Iris and the cop. Sam jumped to her feet, hurried to the closet, and snatched out her own coat.

"Where are you going?" Patrick asked.

She waved the copy of the flyer in his face. "Nicolas said he'd be back in about an hour. I'm taking this guy's face, and I'm going to check out some places around town. Restaurants, fast food places, convenience stores. He was here to watch Louis. He had to eat, had to buy gas, didn't he? Maybe someone remembers him. Maybe someone heard something helpful. Maybe he had a meeting with Louis and Louis is a lying pig." Sam shoved her arms into the sleeves of her coat. "I'm gonna find out."

Patrick put a hand on her arm. "I'm sure the cops—"

"Yes, I'm sure the cops have already covered all of these bases." She jerked her arm from his grasp. "But they aren't me."

"Sam..."

"Why are you trying to stop me?"

Patrick ran both hands through his hair. *Why was he?* "I'm not trying to stop you. I just think we need to wait..."

Sam reached for the door.

"Just a minute."

She turned to face him, arms crossed.

Patrick searched her face. Determination had replaced tears. Purpose lit her eyes instead of fear. *Two positives replacing two negatives.* It might be a useless mission, but what could it hurt?

"Do you have your phone?"

Samantha gave him the look women seemed to be born knowing how to use.

"Of course you do." He opened the door and pulled out his own jacket.

"What...?"

"I'm going with you. I can tell this is something you feel you need to do, and I'm not letting you go by yourself."

Sam rose up on her toes and brushed a kiss across his lips before turning to race up the stairs.

"Where are you going now?"

She stopped halfway up and leaned over the banister. "To scan a second copy of this picture. We'll cover more ground if we each take a side of the street."

They started at one end of Garfield's Main Street. He took the east side, Sam the west. It took less than the allotted hour to visit the two restaurants and four convenience stores open on Sunday morning.

With time to spare, they drove the five miles to the truck stop just on the edge of the city limits. A city cop car pulled out of the lot as they pulled in. Patrick watched Sam's gaze follow the car out of the lot. He frowned as some of the fight drained from her features. He grabbed her hand and kissed her fingers through her gloves. "None of that now. What do we have so far?"

Sam drew her hand back with a sad smile and turned her copy of the picture over. It was covered with scribbled notes Patrick couldn't read. "He was a regular at Harding's Café, mostly for breakfast, but occasionally for dinner."

Patrick nodded. "And Thursday wasn't his first visit to McDonald's. He's been there several times over the last few days."

Sam chewed her lip. "Yeah, and Sonic a time or two. I think he must have hit every gas station in town, at least once, always in a big white van. He was always alone, never flashy, but not hiding."

"And..."

Sam drew a deep breath. "Every place we've been, the cops were there first." She met his eyes. "You were right, but I had to try. Doing nothing was killing me."

"I know. I think we'll both rest easier knowing we did what we could do." He nodded to the glass doors of the store. "Do you want to go in?"

"We're here and I'll feel like I gave up if we don't, at least, ask. You go ask in the store, I'll take the diner and I'll get us something hot to drink."

Patrick nodded and parked. He helped her down from his side of the truck, squeezing her fingers before heading into the store.

Sam pushed through the doors of the diner. She approached the woman behind the counter, waiting for her to finish with the customer she was helping. She smiled when the woman looked in her direction.

"What can I get you?"

"Two coffees to go."

The woman in the crisp white uniform moved to the coffee machine. "Anything else?"

Sam laid the sketch on the counter and slid it across. "I wondered if you'd seen this guy around."

The customer at the counter turned a puzzled look in Sam's direction. "Them cops was just here asking the same question. I gave them all the information I had."

Samantha's heart kicked up a notch. "You've seen him?"

"Sure did. I work the night shift in the garage. He brought a big white van in a few nights ago. Said it was sputtering and dying on him. Wanted me to check it out."

"Did he say anything else? Anything that might tell us where to find him?"

"Naw, he was just a little frustrated that I didn't find a thing wrong with the van. Paid the bill in cash. I didn't charge him very much. There wasn't anything to fix."

Sam slid a pan of chocolate chip cookies into the oven and transferred the previous batch to the cookie jar. Her detective work had proved futile. Now, she could cook, or she could pace while she waited for the phone to ring. Since she'd already worn furrows into every available patch of carpet in the house, it was time to focus on something else. A stack of cookbooks waited for her on the kitchen table. If the kidnapper didn't call soon, the family would be enjoying a gourmet meal tonight all in an effort to save her sanity.

She sat, crossed her arms on the stack of books, and bowed her head. *Jesus, I'm trying to have faith...trying to trust Your will. Do You have any idea how hard that is? How scary it is for me to say 'have Your way' when I don't know what that means?* She swallowed, searching her heart for words to express what she was feeling. The search came up empty. *Jesus, I don't have words. If this is a lesson, then make me a quick learner. Bring my baby home...*

A noise in the doorway drew her attention. She looked up to find the ever-present Nicolas Black. They'd beaten him back to the house this morning, barely. He'd been here ever since, waiting, as she was, for the kidnapper's call.

"Sorry, I didn't mean to intrude. I just never could resist a warm chocolate chip cookie, and yours smell amazing."

Sam jumped up from the table as the timer for the current batch started beeping. She grabbed a paper towel, wiped her streaming eyes, and motioned to the cookie jar. "Help yourself."

The cop tore off a towel for himself and stacked a handful of cookies on it. He took a seat at the table. "The waiting is always tough."

Sam shrugged, afraid to speak because of the tears that hovered just behind her eyes. She scooped spoonfuls of fresh dough onto the pan, trying to keep her attention on the repetitive actions.

"Samantha, I know this is hard—"

Sam whirled to face him. "Really? How many children do you have? How many times have you had your heart ripped out of your chest?"

The officer kept his eyes steady on hers, refusing to back down in the face of her angry outburst.

"Sorry." She crossed to the set of cabinets next to the fridge, removed two glasses from one and a package of chocolate sandwich cookies from another, and poured them both a tall glass of milk.

She set a glass in front of the cop, reclaimed her seat, and tore open the chocolate cookies. "Sorry," she repeated. "You're right. The waiting is hard—it's driving me crazy." She dunked a cookie in her milk.

Nicolas followed suit with a homemade cookie. He bit, chewed, and swallowed, motioning to the open bag of store-bought cookies. "Why would you eat those when you have these?"

Sam dunked another cookie. "It's...a very long story." She leaned forward. "Nicolas, I know you've known Terri for a long time. You guys are friends. Can we be friends?"

He studied her with a frown. A hesitant nod followed.

"Great, You promised never to lie to me and I need you to be straight with me right now. Forget all the procedural things you're supposed to say to someone in my situation." She glanced at the clock over the stove. "It's almost two. He said he'd call back today, and the day is half over. What happens if he doesn't call back today?"

"Samantha—"

"No! No platitudes, no empty assurances, no sympathetic..." She waved her hand for lack of words. "Whatever. I want to know...need to know. From your experience, if he fails to keep his word, and doesn't call today, what are the odds of getting my baby back? What more can be done that isn't being done?"

The cop scrubbed his hands down the length of his face before answering. "I can answer the last part of your question easier than the first. Everything that can be done is being done. Every law enforcement agency in the state is aware of the situation and prepared to offer aid if we request it."

Sam nodded. "What about the FBI?"

He shook his head. "That the FBI is involved in every child abduction is a common misconception. But, if we get one shred of evidence that he's taken your child out of the state, they will deploy a CARD team immediately."

"Card?"

"C-A-R-D. Child Abduction Rapid Deployment team."

"OK." She held his gaze with hers. "What about the first part of my question?"

"That's harder." He looked down at the table and rubbed the back of his neck. When he continued, he seemed to be weighing each individual word. "There are no absolutes in cases like this. The fact that his initial call came quickly was a good thing, and pretty typical when ransom is being sought." He reached across the table and laid a big hand on Sam's arm. "But if we don't hear from him again today, as promised..." His words dwindled to nothing as he shook his head. "That's not usually a good thing."

CHAPTER TWENTY-FIVE

Patrick kept vigil with his mother in the living room of the Evans's home. Every minute that ticked away without the promised phone call eroded another layer from his sanity. Mom's red eyes and white knuckled hands, clasped into a tight ball in her lap, told him better than words ever could that the hours tore at her heart as well.

He put an arm around her shoulders and squeezed. "Is this wild internal swing from peace to panic normal?"

"What do you mean?"

Patrick lifted a shoulder. "Just...I know God's got this, and when I let myself focus on that,"—he drew in a deep breath—"my heart rate slows down a bit, and I can breathe. But I look at Sam...or you, and I see the hurt and terror in your eyes, and it speeds right up again." He stopped. "That didn't come out the way I wanted it to. I don't mean you guys aren't acting the way you should, just that I don't want to act the way I

253

shouldn't." He shook his head. "Never mind."

Kate unclenched her hands and patted his knee. "I know what you meant. You want to be strong for Sam. We all do, but saved or not, we're still human. God sees our lives from an eagle's viewpoint, a path from start to finish and every obstacle in between. So, He's never surprised at what comes our way. We're not granted that luxury. We only see the moment we're living in, and peace isn't always easy to find." She looked up at him and a smile momentarily transformed her expression. "Have I told you how proud I am of you? There's been so much going on with Sam and the baby. I don't want the fact of your salvation to get lost in the shuffle." Her eyes filled with tears. "Somewhere underneath all of my concern for Bobbie is a very happy mom."

"I—" Nicolas Black came into the room. Patrick looked at his mom and received a slight nod in return.

He motioned to an empty chair. "Detective, could we have a word with you?"

Nicolas took the indicated seat and waited for Patrick to continue.

Patrick wagged a finger between himself and Kate.

"We've talked it over. We want you to know that we're prepared to meet any ransom demand this guy might make."

The detective leaned forward and braced his elbows on his knees. "You're the boyfriend, right?" His eyes moved to Kate. "I'm sorry, there have been so many family friends in and out of the house, I've lost track. You are...?"

Kate held out her hand. "I'm Kate Archer, Patrick's mom." The cop straightened and took her hand in his as she continued, "I'm friends with your mother." She laid her left hand on top of their clasped right hands. "That probably puts me at a slight advantage. Karla brags on you, a lot."

Nicolas Black laughed. "No one ever accused my mom of being an indifferent parent."

Patrick frowned at the sight of their still joined hands. Umm...His brows arched as the cop's gaze lingered on his mom's left hand where a wedding ring would be, and wasn't. He shook his head. *This waiting is driving me more than a little crazy.* He cleared his throat, and the two older adults pulled apart.

The cop returned his elbows to his knees and focused his attention on Patrick. "You mentioned helping with the ransom yesterday. I'm sure the family is grateful for your offer." He lowered his face into his left hand and massaged his temples. "We have everything in place to move on his demands. He just needs to call back and tell us what he wants."

Sam slid the clean cookie sheet back into the cabinet. *If I spend one more second in this house...*She glanced at the clock and weighed her options. More of the fruitless pacing, crying, baking, and hand wringing, or a strategic retreat to a place where, even if she didn't find answers, she'd find distraction from the thoughts that had become her worst enemy. Mind made up in favor of distraction, Sam wiped the counter down, tossed the damp towel over the rack, and searched for the cop.

She found him in the living room, carrying on a conversation with Patrick and Kate. Patrick patted the cushion next to him.

Sam gave him a smile but shook her head. "No

thanks." She addressed Detective Black. "Do I have to stay here?"

Detective Black sat back. Sam read confusion on his face. "Where do you want to go?"

"I'm going crazy in this house with nothing to do but wait. It's Sunday night. I want to go to church." She motioned to Patrick and his mom. "I think we should all go."

The cop frowned. "If he calls..."

Sam fished her cell phone out of her pocket. "If he calls tonight, he'll call this number, and it won't matter where I am when I answer." She sank to the couch. "I really need to do this, unless you can give me a good reason why I should sit here and go silently crazy."

Nicolas pondered her request. "It's not my first choice, but I can't keep you here."

"Great!" Sam stood and tugged Patrick to his feet. "You and your mom go home and get cleaned up. I'll go tell Mom and Dad to do the same. A little time in God's house will do wonders for us all."

A short time later Sam took a deep breath, squeezed Patrick's hand, and walked into the sanctuary of Valley View Church. The praise and worship team were already on the stage when Sam and Patrick slipped into the back pew. Peace washed over her soul like thick, warm honey.

Sam surrendered again to tears, tears of worship, submission, and brokenness. With her hands raised, her face lifted, and her eyes closed, she simply opened her heart to her Heavenly Father. Calm took the place of despair. She had no words, but the Holy Spirit in her heart conveyed her pain, agony, and fears to her Father on His throne. With her eyes still closed, she heard

Pastor Gordon's voice over the PA.

"I just saw Samantha and her family slip into the sanctuary. I know we've all been praying for Bobbie's safe return, but let's take a few moments from our routine, gather around this family, and lift them up in personal prayer."

Hands came to rest on her shoulders and back. Sam drew strength and encouragement from their presence and the knowledge that this fight was not hers alone.

She wept as one friend after another took her into their arms and whispered words of love and support in her ears. This place, those words, the love she received—that was what she needed. Not to be the center of attention, but to be the center of prayer.

In response to the pastor's words, spiritual warriors moved to close ranks around Samantha, ready to fight this battle with her.

Sam heard Patrick's whispered prayers beside her and glanced over. The men in her life, Benton, Sisko, Harrison, and Mitchell surrounded him, offering praise for his salvation and strength for this fight. Her heart flooded with gratitude. *Father, thank you. In the middle of these horrible two days, you've already worked a miracle. Will you please work one more?*

Those words barely left her heart before she found herself enveloped in Lisa's arms. Her friend leaned down.

"Can you hear me?"

Sam nodded.

"Good. I have something I need to share with you. The Lord just laid a verse on my heart. Isaiah 41:10. 'So do not fear, for I am with you; do not be dismayed, for I am your God. I will strengthen you and help you; I

257

will uphold you with my righteous right hand.'" Lisa pulled back and pressed a clean tissue into Samantha's hands. She sniffed as she wiped her own eyes. "I know that telling you not to worry is a total waste of breath, but you aren't fighting this battle alone. Do you remember when you gave Bobbie to the Lord in dedication?"

Sam nodded and used the tissue to blot away the mascara she was sure was running down her cheeks in twin rivers.

Lisa pointed to the front of the sanctuary. "Look."

Sam followed Lisa's pointed finger and swallowed a gasp. Someone in the projection and sound booth had loaded the disc of pictures used during Bobbie's dedication service almost three years earlier. Photos of her baby scrolled on the screen accompanied by a banner that read, *Pray for Bobbie's safe return.* Sam lowered her head to Lisa's shoulder.

"That morning you placed your baby in God's protection. I can't say what I'd do if I were in your shoes, but I do know that God knows your heart is broken. Worry if you need to, but temper that worry with the knowledge that God has a plan."

"I need a drink."

The kid's voice was starting to grate on him like nails on a chalkboard. Chick buried his head in his hands. Five steps...he'd managed to get five whole steps down the hall before the kid's most current request. He retraced his steps. "Look, you've had a snack, I got your doll, you've been to the john, I checked the closet for monsters, and I left a light on. Go. To. Sleep."

"I'm really thirsty."

His hands clenched into fists, and Chick forced them to relax. He spun, marched to the kitchen, filled a glass with water, and returned to the bedroom. Water sloshed from the glass when he plunked it down on the bedside table. "There. Are you happy now?"

Bobbie scooted up in the bed and took a tiny sip of the water. She sat back and looked up at Chick over folded arms. "No."

"No, what?"

"No, I'm not happy. You're a bad man, and you lied! You told my mommy I could talk to her today." Her chin began to quiver. "You lied," she howled. "I need to talk to my mommy!"

Chick's hands went to his ears, as much in defense of the noise as the words. "Kid...kid. Tomorrow...I promise, we'll talk to your mom tomorrow."

"Liar, liar. Pants on fire." Bobbie flipped onto her stomach and buried her face in the pillow as the howl became a shriek.

PopPop, I swear it wasn't me that left the gate open.

Don't you lie to me boy!

He shoved the memory away, anxious to calm the child. "Kid!" Chick forced himself to gentle his voice. "Bobbie. I'm sorry. I just got so busy today, and you didn't remind me..." *That's right, foist the blame off on the kid.*

She levered up onto her elbows, tears streaming from eyes clenched shut, covers churning as she kicked. "I want my mommy... I want my mommy!"

Chick backed away from the sheer fury of the tantrum. He ran his hands through his hair. *What do I do now?* Let her call her mom? Yeah, right. An idea bloomed. *Right!* He rushed from the room, grabbed a second disposable phone, and hurried back to the hysterical kid.

"Kid, look." He waved the phone. "We can call her right now if you want, but you have to stop."

Bobbie sat up and wiped her face on the sleeve of the two-day-old shirt. She nodded. "Yes."

Chick keyed in the numbers for the phone in his empty Vegas apartment, shoved the phone into the kid's hand, and waited for her to get tired of the endless ringing. He watched as the anticipation on her face changed to disappointment. "What's the matter now?"

Bobbie handed him the phone. "She's not home."

He nodded. *No joke?* "We'll try again tomorrow."

"But"—her lip trembled again—"It's my turn to tell the story."

"What story?"

"Mommy tells me a story one night, then I tell her a story next." Her little shoulders lifted in a shrug. "You told me a story, and now it's my turn." The last word threatened to dissolve into renewed tears.

"Aw, kid, please don't start crying again." He sat in the chair next to the bed. "I'll sit right here, and you can tell me a story. Will that work?"

She plopped back down in her pillows with a stuffy sigh. "I guess." She crossed her arms and closed her eyes. "One time, a long time ago, Jesus was very tired and hungry."

Chick's head fell back on his shoulders. Didn't this kid know any normal stories?

"He told his 'ciples to go to town and cook dinner for him." Bobbie's mouth stretched in a mighty yawn. "When Jesus got there, the 'ciples feet were so smelly,

Jesus couldn't eat. He filled up a tub and washed everyone's feet." She stopped and looked at Chick. "Do you think they forgot to wear their socks? Mommy tells me my feet will be stinky if I don't wear my socks."

Chick shook his head. "I have no idea."

Bobbie shrugged and continued her story. "Peter got mad when Jesus told him that he had dirty feet. He wouldn't let Jesus wash them, but he changed his mind and everyone sat at the table. Jesus said grace and shared his bread and juice with everyone and then went to say his prayers. While he was praying some bad men came to take him away."

She gulped what Chick was sure would've been a sob. "But Jesus wasn't afraid of the bad men 'cause the angels were with him. The end."

She stopped and narrowed her eyes at Chick. "You're a bad man, too. I miss my mommy, but I'm not afraid of you."

Chick stood up. Every time he thought this kid couldn't get any crazier, she proved him wrong. "Are we done?"

Bobbie nodded.

"Good. Go to sleep." Chick stepped to the door reached to turn out the light.

"Mister."

He stopped. "What now?"

"Jem wants you to know that Jesus still loves you."

CHAPTER TWENTY-SIX

Monday morning sunlight filtered through the windows as Chick opened the hidden compartment in his suitcase and removed the small zippered case concealed within. He fanned the items out on the bed. *The new me.* The idea almost made him giddy as he sorted through the documents. A passport, a birth certificate, a driver's license, a social security card, and two credit cards, all under the name of Jason Kirk, age forty-one. This was his safety net, more valuable right now than the considerable cash he'd paid for them.

Somewhere in all the phone calls and kid-induced frustration yesterday, his sketchy plan had solidified into a firm course of action.

Ralphie was in the process of setting up the money transfers that would route the ransom to its final destination in the Caribbean. Gone were the days when complicated ransom drops and pickups had to be orchestrated. Those operations could get you killed. In this computerized society, the money would be transferred straight from the kid's grandfather's account to his, and then routed on its complicated journey to his brand new account in a Grand Cayman bank. Once that process was underway, Chick would use part of his remaining cash to purchase a nice anonymous plane ticket to paradise.

The only glitch in his plan was the kid and what to do with her. Snuffin' her wasn't an option. Chick wasn't a murderer—he didn't even own a gun. He lived his life to the left of the law, but he'd never been arrested. His assignments were always completed with no fanfare and plenty of caution. His caution had only failed him once, earning him a permanent limp. He had no wish to repeat either. So, what to do with the kid?

"Jem wants you to know that Jesus still loves you." His snort of unbelief filled the room even as he shifted uncomfortably. "Loves me?" *Yeah, right.* "Still?" *Never.*

"Now Chick, don't act like that. Jesus will always love you." Not the voice of his sketchy conscience this time, and not some figment of his imagination, but a nearly forgotten piece of his past.

The bedroom faded away, replaced with an old Sunday school classroom and the teacher who ruled there, Mrs. Drumright. He shook his head. *I haven't thought of her and her homemade sugar cookies in years.* How old had he been? Nine? Ten? Didn't matter. It was years before he went to live with PopPop. Years before PopPop managed to beat the faith right out of him. Mrs. Drumright taught a very different religious experience than PopPop preached, accented with sugar cookies, love, and encouragement. Sort of like the kid...

Chick shook himself out of the memory. The sooner he got away from this lunatic kid, the better. He pondered his options and decided that the best action where she was concerned was no action. Once the ransom process started, he'd put one of his remaining pain pills in a glass of milk, lock her in the house while she slept, and get on a plane. He had no doubt the kid would raise a holy commotion when she woke up. Someone would find her and return her to her family.

Satisfied with his plan, Chick emptied his wallet of identification. He studied his picture on the old driver's license. *I always hated this picture. Makes me look like a convict.* He cut it into plastic confetti with an old pair of scissors he'd found in one of the kitchen drawers. Credit cards came next. He kissed the hefty charges on them goodbye and wondered how long the banks would pursue collection of Chick Malone's debt before they figured out that Chick Malone no longer existed. He scooped up the pieces of the man he used to be and scattered the bits and pieces of plastic over the trash. *So long Chick, hello Jason.*

He tucked the new items safely inside the worn wallet. It was after nine, so the banks would be open. The first step toward his tropical island getaway was a savings account, and that required a trip to the bank. He needed to get moving. He was sure that by now the cops were circulating pictures of the kid, and maybe of him. He'd get this done before someone had a chance to spot his face on the news and throw a wrench into his plans. Only problem was the kid. Nothin' to do about that, though.

"Kid, get in here."

Bobbie edged into the room. "Is it time to go?"

He glanced up, then down, then back up. The kid was standing there, already zipped into her coat. "What are you doing?"

"Jem said it was time to go."

Her answer raised the hairs on his arms. Chick closed his eyes. If he never heard the name *Jem* again, it would be too soon. "You about ready to talk to your mom again?"

The blue eyes sparkled. "Yes!"

"Well Jem was right, we have an errand to run, and if you're very good while we're gone I'll let you call your mom when we get back."

"Yay!" She turned to go back down the hall.

"Where are you going?"

She faced him with a cheerful smile. "I have to get my toys."

"We're not going to be gone that long."

Her expression turned stubborn.

"Come on, kid, give me a break. We'll be right back."

Bobbie shook her head. "I don't think so." She turned and skipped down the hall.

What does that mean? "Hey kid. What are you talking about?"

The only response he received was a muffled giggle.

He took a deep breath. If he didn't ditch this kid soon, he was going to be as crazy as she was.

Sleep, eat, worry, pray, watch the clock. Bobbie's kidnapping had reduced Samantha's life to the bare basics of existence. When the worry became too much, she prayed. She watched the second hand on the clock sweep away minutes of her child's life and tried to remember Lisa's words during service last night. *God has a plan.*

She stood and crossed to the window. A heavy lethargy accompanied every step she took, every movement of her hand and arm, every beat of her heart. Like a deadly ocean current, the constant waiting threatened to pull her under.

God has a plan.

Sam leaned her head against the cool glass. *Father I'm trying to hang on, trying to trust, but You're asking too much of me. If I need to learn faith or patience or some lesson I can't even name, give me an illness to battle or something else that's mine alone to fight. I might find strength or wisdom in that. All I'm learning here is despair.*

She drew a deep breath when an arm slipped around her shoulders. No need to open her eyes to identify the source. Sam leaned her head on her father's sturdy shoulder.

"Daddy..."

"I know."

He probably did.

"Was it this hard when you were looking for us? This waiting?"

Her father drew her into a full embrace. "I could say yes, but you guys were older and living with your mother. I only had a few weeks of searching, once I learned of your mother's accident, where I worried every day." He released her, took a step back, and tilted her face up to meet his eyes. "God is the only way I survived those weeks of uncertainty."

Sam's eyes filled as she nodded. "I know. I'm trying. I was just talking to God, asking Him to bring Bobbie home, telling Him to afflict me with something if there's a lesson I need to learn."

"Sam—"

It was Samantha's turn to step away. "Dad, I mean it. I'd give my life in place of hers if I had the chance. She's all I have. If I don't hear something soon, I'll—"

Steve held up a finger to interrupt her. "Get your jacket. Let's go for a walk."

"I don't want to."

"Humor me. Its warmer this morning than it's been in two weeks. A short walk will clear your mind."

She shrugged and went to do as her father asked.

A walk wasn't a bad idea, but something in her father's voice warned her that whatever he had on his mind this morning wasn't going to be something she wanted to hear.

They stepped onto the porch, and Sam unzipped her jacket and stuffed her gloves into her pockets. "You were right about the temperature."

Her dad nodded before taking her arm, leading her down the steps, and steering her onto the sidewalk. "Forty-five degrees, sunny, clear, and no wind. A brief reprieve from the icebox we've been in this month."

They headed down the block under a sky so blue it almost hurt her eyes. Trees, naked of their leaves, speared their gnarled branches heavenward, like greedy fingers reaching for the sunlight they'd been deprived of.

Her dad jumped in without preamble. "Sam, I love you and I love Bobbie almost as much as you do. Almost as much, because no one can ever love her as much as her mother. I'm telling you this first so that you don't misunderstand what I'm about to say."

"Dad, whatever it is, can it wait? I'm out of resources. I don't think I can handle anything else right now."

"I know, but it can't wait. I told Patrick yesterday that part of my job in this situation was dishing out some tough love." He faced her. His eyes, so similar to her own, turned serious. "You have to accept that Bobbie is in God's hands now." He stopped and took both of her hands in his. "Everything that we can do, everything that the authorities can do, is being done. But, it all boils down to God's plan, and we just don't know what that is."

"Oh, no. No. Do you think—?"

"I don't think anything, Sam. But I know that even if God doesn't answer our prayers in just the way we hope He will, we'll have to accept His decisions where Bobbie is concerned."

Sam yanked her hands free. "How can you say that?" She raked her hair from her face and tried to read his expression. "You've given up!"

"Sam, it's not about giving up."

"Well it sure isn't about keeping the faith."

"That's exactly what it's about. You're praying for Bobbie to come home—we all are—but while you're at it, you need to search your heart and prepare your soul for the chance that she might not."

Sam stared at him.

"Because if she doesn't come home, that doesn't mean that God doesn't love you. That doesn't mean that God didn't hear your prayers. It doesn't mean that there was something lacking in the way you've raised her, or in your relationship with God. It doesn't mean that you did anything wrong, or that you didn't do enough. All it will mean is that God had a different plan for Bobbie than we did. As much as I hope you don't ever have to face that possibility, you need to be prepared for it."

Sam absorbed his words, each one a body punch to her already wounded heart. She shook her head. "I can't. I'm not that strong. I never will be that strong. She just has to come home."

Chick helped the kid into the van and rounded the nose of the vehicle to take the driver's seat. He patted the paperwork in his shirt pocket. *Mission accomplished.* The account was open, and the kid had been remarkably well behaved during the forty-five minute visit. He'd be on a plane by dinnertime. *Look out, paradise, here I come.*

He climbed into his seat and inserted the key into the ignition. He glanced over at the kid who was strapped into the passenger seat. She turned the pages of the book she'd insisted on taking in with her.

"You did real good." He reached over and pulled the stocking cap off her head, releasing the too-recognizable dark curls. "Ready to go call your mom?"

She looked up and shrugged.

"You don't want to talk to your mom?"

"When I get home. I'm going home now."

Chick snorted. *Whatever.* He turned the key. Nothing happened. He cranked it again. No sound at all. No grinding of the starter, no engine struggling to fire, no clicking or beeping. After five or six attempts, he released the hood lever and slammed out of the van. The mechanic in that Podunk town had told him there was nothing wrong. He wiggled battery cables that were firmly attached and gave the tangle of wires, cables, and hoses a visual once over. *Looks fine to me.*

He retook his seat and tried the key again. Nothing.

His limited amount of patience ran out. The air in the van thickened with obscenities as he pounded his fists on the steering wheel. "You stupid hunk of junk—"

"Jem says you shouldn't say those words."

"Kid, this ain't the time."

Bobbie folded the book away and stared him down. "Promise you'll take me home."

Chick flinched under her steady blue eyes. "I told you. When we get back, you can call—"

"No!" Bobbie sat back and crossed her arms. "Jem says it's time to take me home."

His hands itched to shake some sense into this kid. He clenched his teeth. "Jem. Is. Not. Driving!"

Bobbie sat back and resumed paging through the book. She ignored him as she looked at the pictures and sang a song he vaguely remembered from childhood.

Chick stared at her. "Jesus may love the little children, but I'm not too fond of them right now." He climbed back out of van and did a second check under the hood. Nothing had changed in the last ten minutes. Back in his seat, he turned the key a single click. Gages and dials all sprang to life. He had plenty of gas, and the oil pressure looked good. Breath held, he cranked the key into the starting position. Nothing.

"You need to promise to take me home."

He glared at the kid. "Whatever. I promise, OK. I promise to take you home."

Bobbie looked up at him with a brilliant smile.

Chick kept his eyes fixed on hers as he reached for the key. This time when he turned it, the engine roared to life. Shock drove him back into his seat. "All right!" He dropped the gear shift into drive and headed out of the parking lot, serenaded now with the kid's version of another song from his childhood. This one about hiding your light. *Keep singing, brat. Just as soon as you talk to your mom, you're in for a nice long nap, and I'm out of here!*

At the corner, he signaled for a left turn. Not the direction that would take them back to Garfield, but the direction that would take them back to the safe house. The van died.

"What the...?"

Bobbie pointed in his intended direction. "Is that the way to my house?"

He rubbed his hands down his face. This was almost too much. "No," he admitted. "We need to go back to my house first."

"I don't think so." She sat back and stared out the windshield. "He's not listening."

A shiver crawled up Chick's spine.

Bobbie sighed. She faced him one more time. "You shouldn't tell fibs." She slowed her words. "Promise to take me home."

Chick held up his hands. "All right. I promise."

"You have to say the words."

He fumed. "I promise to take you home."

"Now?"

"Yes, now!" He muttered curses under his breath as he reached for the key. When he turned it, the engine hummed back to life. With exaggerated movements Chick switched the blinker to the opposite direction and turned the corner. Five intersections later, he relaxed, confident that things were back under his control. He sneaked a glance over at the kid. *I don't know how she's doing what she's doing, but I won't be told what to do by a kid...or some imaginary friend...angel or not.* He eased the van into the turn lane, intending to circle back to where he wanted to go. The van died in the middle of the busy intersection.

Bobbie leaned forward and put her little face in her hands. "You're not very smart, are you?"

CHAPTER TWENTY-SEVEN

"I don't believe this." Chick turned to Bobbie as car horns sounded behind him. He looked over at the kid, calm and cool in the seat beside him. *I kidnapped an alien.* "How are you doing this?"

"It's not me. It's Jem."

Chick closed his eyes and fought for control. *I just want to shake her 'til her teeth rattle...just one time.* "Kid, if you say that word to me one more time, I'm gonna make you sorry you were ever born. Your imaginary friends don't tell me what to do. You keep your trap shut and let me think." Something tapped on the driver's side window.

He turned to find a lanky teenage boy standing beside his van. Chick rolled down the window. "What?"

The boy held up his hands and took a step back. "Whoa, dude, take it easy. You're blocking traffic. Is there something I can do to help?"

Chick swallowed a growl. "Sorry, the thing keeps

dying." He cut a glance in Bobbie's direction. "I took a look earlier, but I don't know much about engines."

"This is your lucky day, pops." The boy tapped his chest with a thumb. "Gearhead at your service. Turn on your flashers and pop the hood. Let's look under her skirt and see what ails her."

Chick pulled the lever. "Thanks." While the boy moved to the front and bent to look inside the engine compartment, Chick turned to Bobbie. "Sit right there and keep that fresh little mouth of yours shut."

Bobbie shrugged and turned her attention back to her book.

The kid's failure to acknowledge him only amplified his temper. He crawled out of the van and slammed the door.

The boy's head peeked from under the hood. "Hey, are you trying to break my eardrums?"

"Sorry, I'm a little frustrated."

"Not a prob. But you have to remember. Vehicles are like women. They want kind words and soft hands."

Chick studied the boy more closely. He wore ripped jeans and a faded flannel shirt over a dingy white T-shirt. The hair stuffed up under the baseball cap might have been blond. As mechanics went, he didn't look like much, but his grease-stained gloves moved along the components of the van's engine with a confidence Chick would never feel. "What are you...sixteen?"

The boy lifted his shoulders as his fingers continued to probe. "Seventeen, but my dad races sprint cars at the local track on the weekends. I'm on his pit crew, and I've learned to never mistreat the thing I need to depend on." He took a step back, his examination obviously complete. "This all looks good. Get back in and try to turn her over, let me hear what she has to say for herself."

Chick climbed back into his seat and the boy leaned into the open window. Chick turned the key. Silence greeted his effort.

"That's not good. Trade places with me."

Chick narrowed his eyes at the boy's request.

"Dude, if I was stupid enough to jack a set of wheels, it'd be something with a lot more style than this. I need to check your fuse panel, and the compartment is under the dash."

Chick climbed out and the boy climbed in. Bobbie was a belated thought. Chick cast threatening glances her way from his place on the pavement while the boy did his thing.

The compartment popped open under the teenager's skillful hands, and he pulled the panel out for a closer examination. He unplugged a few of the brightly colored tabs and held them up to the light. "Hmm...it all looks OK."

Bobbie sighed and shook her head. "I tried to tell him it was the angel's fault, but he won't listen."

Chick closed his eyes, prepared to yank the boy out from behind the wheel before Bobbie could say anything else.

The boy flashed a grin at the the girl. "Angels, huh? Well, let's see if we can get some wings back under your daddy's van."

The boy snapped the panel back into place, replaced the compartment cover, and turned the key. The engine caught on the first try. "Well, look at that. Must have been a loose connection or something." He grinned at

Chick though the window. "Looks like you're good to go, but I'd take her and have her checked out before I went too much farther."

Chick grinned at the kid. The mechanic in Garfield never looked at anything on the inside of the van. He opened the door. "Thanks, I'll do that. Don't..."

The boy switched off the ignition a nanosecond before Chick could complete his request to leave it running. The youngster climbed out of the seat. "Don't worry, she's fixed."

Chick nodded. "Thanks for your help. Just stay right there while I make sure." He turned the key and was greeted by the sweet sound of a humming engine. The kid held out a fist, and Chick bumped it with his own. "Thanks for your help."

The boy lifted his hand in a wave. "Ya'll take care. Merry Christmas." He loped across the street to his own car. Chick rolled up the window and waited for the traffic light to cycle back to green. He stepped on the gas. The van died.

When the cloud of profanities cleared, Chick glanced in his rearview mirror hoping to signal the boy before he had time to leave. The boy's car was gone. In its place sat a police cruiser. Cold sweat prickled Chick's body as the cop climbed out and headed in their direction.

"Jem says you really ought to take me home."

With no time for argument, Chick surrendered. If he could get out of this intersection, and away from the cop, maybe he could come up with a better plan. "OK, kid, OK. No more games. I don't know how you're doing what you're doing, but I've had all I want."

"Do you really promise this time?"

"Cross my heart."

Bobbie studied him.

The cop tapped on the window.

Chick sweated.

The kid nodded.

He turned the key and the engine fired. "Thanks, kid." He looked around the otherwise empty van. "I'm taking her home now." He closed his eyes. *The kid's got me talking to the air.*

He rolled the window down. "Sorry, Officer, she's been giving me some trouble this morning, but it looks like we're good to go now." The light turned green and Chick didn't wait for a response. He moved through the intersection, looked for a good place to turn around, and pointed the van back towards Garfield. *I don't believe in angels...do I?* His internal question remained unanswered. Angels or not, Chick had seen enough of this little girl and her God to know that she was protected, somehow, by someone much greater than himself. Someone who Bobbie said still loved him, not that he understood how that could be. He looked over at the kid, serene in the passenger seat. "Sing me some more songs, kid."

The afternoon crept toward evening. Upstairs, dinner preparations were underway. The cops, here and gone throughout the day, were here again, this time they'd brought news. They were pretty sure her child and the kidnapper had been seen in Tulsa earlier in the day. Several witnesses had called in, recognizing both the man in the sketch and Bobbie. One Tulsa officer approached a white van just seconds before he received the updated reports. The van was long gone, but the news gave Samantha hope. In all accounts, the child involved appeared unharmed.

Why won't he just call?

Samantha paced across the small basement apartment, seeing signs of Bobbie everywhere. She paused next to the tree and removed the ornament that Bobbie had made a few days ago. The paper heart shook in her hand, sprinkling silver glitter across the carpet. *Jesus, please bring her home.* The words had become a mantra, spoken, whispered, thought, breathed, prayed, and repeated. Her dad's words from this morning haunted her. *All it will mean is that God had a different plan for Bobbie than we did.*

Father, I just need You to bring her home. How can I pray otherwise?

Sam slipped to her knees in the middle of the floor and clasped the heart to her chest. "Father, I can't. You know my heart and You know my soul. I kneel in Your presence, and I'm offering You everything I am, everything I'll ever be, my life for hers."

I want both.

The words knocked Sam back on her heels. "Father?"

I have a plan.

Samantha bowed forward, her face to the floor. "Father, show me. I'm so scared. I know it's human, but that's how You made me. Look into my heart, calm my fear, and help me understand how to accept Your plan and Your will."

For my thoughts are not your thoughts...

Sam scrambled to her feet, hung the ornament back on the tree, and grabbed her Bible. She skimmed through the concordance and found the reference. She whispered it over and over again while she sat and flipped through the pages. "Isaiah 55:8-9...Isaiah 55:8-9...Isaiah 55:8-9...here we are." She sat back and read the verses aloud. "For my thoughts are not your thoughts, neither are your ways my way, saith the Lord. For as the heavens are higher than the earth, so are my ways higher than your ways, and my thoughts than your thoughts."

She bowed her head over the closed Bible and wept. "Father, how can I release the most precious thing in my life to a plan I can't see? I want to, but...Do You have any idea how hard this is?"

Trust me.

Samantha sat still and focused on taking one breath at a time. Doubts and indecision wrestled in her heart, but they failed to drown out the resonance of those two words. *Trust me.* Did she trust? Where she was concerned, the immediate answer was yes. For Bobbie, she had to dig deeper.

Names flashed through her mind. Moses, Isaac, Samuel, each a child of promise, each parent forced to make a choice, each one safe in God's plan.

All it will mean is that God had a different plan for Bobbie than we did.

Sam swallowed and prepared to jump from the highest cliff she'd ever been on in her life. Hopefully, she'd find wings of grace before she did a face plant in the canyon below. "Your will, Father. Just Your will."

The peace that washed over her was immediate, incomprehensible, and undeniably from the Lord.

All the prayers for strength in the last two days paled in the light flooding her heart. The future was still uncertain, her arms were still empty, but even as she longed to hold her child, she was held. Worry crouched on the fringes of her mind, but for this second, for this moment, she could trust. Maybe that was the key. Focusing on the moment, praying for strength in the moment, trusting in *this* moment, and refusing to dwell on the *what ifs*, *could be's*, and *maybes* of the big picture.

She stood. Her knees no longer shook, and she was hungry for the first time since Saturday afternoon.

Taking the kid home was a one-way ticket to jail.

Chick tried not to dwell on that. He drove, and Bobbie sang every song she knew six times. Songs he remembered from long ago. Simple songs of love and faith. Somewhere along the way, he felt the ice cap over his soul crack.

He probed the fissure tentatively and allowed his heart to say the first prayer he'd prayed since he was fifteen. *God, this kid's religion is so not like what I grew up with. I'm not going to make excuses for anything I've done, I'm just going to plead guilty and throw myself on the mercy of the court, in more ways than one. Can You still love me like You obviously love her? I know that coming to You now isn't a get-out-of-jail-free card. I'm man enough to be accountable for my actions. I can't even blame this on following orders. But can I ask You to go with me?*

He released his white knuckled grip on the steering wheel, and each breath that left his lungs felt more cleansing than the one before. Chick felt like an old Christmas cartoon character as invisible bands around his chest broke free, allowing his heart to expand at least three sizes. A long, difficult path lay ahead, but he wouldn't walk it alone.

They entered the Garfield city limits. Dusk came

early this time of year. Houses on both sides of the street winked with multicolored Christmas lights. He looked over to the passenger seat and interrupted another chorus about hiding your light under a bushel. "Hey kid, do you know any Christmas songs?"

Bobbie nodded, her dark curls bouncing in the light of the dashboard. "Do you know the manger song?"

"I think I can remember it if you get us started."

The child's clear voice filled the van. On the third time through Chick pulled the van to the curb in front of her house. He glanced at the police cruiser parked in the drive. *I could just drop her and go. Good for her, better for me.* The van died as he contemplated.

The kid released her seat belt and reached for the door. She turned to face him. "Jem says not to be afraid. You have an angel, too." She climbed out of the van and raced for the front door.

Chick got out of the van and made his own way up the walk. He stopped when the kid threw the door open and screamed.

"Mommy! Mommy, I'm home."

A woman's shout of joy filtered out of the open door a second before a cop stepped onto the porch. Chick put his hands behind his head and sank to his knees. "It's OK, officer. I surrender."

The cop was on him in two seconds, yanking Chick's hands behind his back, snapping his wrists into cuffs. He flattened himself on the cold ground and allowed the cop to pat him down. Once the cop hauled him to his feet, Chick found himself facing a group of people. A multitude of emotions mixed on their faces, but there were tears everywhere he looked. He focused on the only person he recognized, even though he didn't know her name.

"I know 'sorry' don't cover it, but I want you to know what a great kid you've got."

The woman had a death grip on her child. Chick waited while she stared at him, knowing what he deserved, not sure what he expected. All he received was a nod as she turned away. The rest of the group followed her lead.

The cop nudged his shoulder. "Let's go."

Chick slid into the open back seat of the black and white car and looked up at the officer. "You've got a chaplain at the jail, right?"

CHAPTER TWENTY-EIGHT

Samantha sat in a chair next to Bobbie's bed and watched her sleep. With the blanket tucked under her chin, the stuffed penguin clutched to her side, and her freshly washed curls a dark stain against the pale pillowcase, she looked like an angel. *An angel...*

Sam leaned forward just enough to finger her daughter's damp curls. In the hours since she'd come bursting through the front door, Bobbie had been a whirlwind of nonstop chatter. Bad men, spilled cereal, and angels. Tomorrow they faced a round of appointments and interviews. Doctors, lawyers, police, counselors. Maybe those professionals could make some sense out of Bobbie's stories. But for tonight...

Sam started as hands closed over her shoulders. *So jumpy.* She'd probably been more adversely affected by this whole thing than Bobbie.

Patrick squeezed. "Sorry." His whisper was loud in the darkened room. "I didn't mean to scare you, but I wanted to say goodbye before I went home."

She turned in the chair and met his eyes. "Patrick, I'm so sorry. You've been my rock the last three days, and I've paid you back by ignoring you. I—"

He laid a finger across her lips. "I haven't been ignored. You and Bobbie needed some extra time together. I've enjoyed sitting back and watching the two girls I love take care of each other." Patrick paused. "You did notice Bobbie taking care of you, right?"

"Umm..."

Patrick squatted beside her and tucked a few strands of Sam's hair behind her ear. "I didn't think so. She sat in your lap when Seth wanted her to come play. She shared her snack with you, and after her bath, when you brushed the tangles from her hair, she spent time brushing yours. She sensed that you needed to keep her close for a while. The jerk who took her got one thing right. She's a great kid."

Samantha's lip twitched up. "She is that." She turned back to the bed and tears pricked the corners of her eyes. "Does it make sense when I say I've been given the greatest gift of my life a second time?"

"I completely get that." Patrick held out a hand. "Do you think she'll be OK if you leave her alone for a few minutes to walk me out?"

Sam took his hand and allowed him to lead her up the stairs. Her steps lingered an extra second in the doorway. She sighed in satisfaction and accented it with a silent prayer. *Thank You, Father.*

Patrick turned at the top, dropped her hand, and framed her face with his hands. His eyes were bright in the semi-dark as he leaned forward to brush a kiss across her forehead. "You know, now that Bobbie is home safe and sound, and the little matter of my salvation is cleared up, there's something I really need to ask you."

Samantha's indrawn breath echoed loudly into the quiet. *He's going to give me a second chance. He's going to ask me to marry him.* She knew her smile beamed. "So ask."

Patrick took a half step closer and leaned to bring his mouth teasingly close to hers. "Samantha Evans, can I please kiss you?"

It wasn't the question she'd expected, but she found it hard to be disappointed. She nodded, her "yes" a whisper against his lips.

Patrick lowered his head and wrapped her in his arms. Sam sank into the kiss, her heart doing its best to pound out of her chest. Their first kiss had been stolen in the dark of the porch a year ago, and she'd had to be firm about no more. Their second kiss had been one of frenzy as he offered her a proposal she couldn't accept. This...She managed to snuggle closer as his lips took full advantage of hers. This was their first kiss with no obstacles between them. Her arms snaked around his neck. As first kisses went, this one was pretty spectacular.

Louis hated orange, and he hated canvas tennis shoes. He stopped pacing to stare through the window at the guard sitting on the other side of the door. The cop lifted a cup and took a drink. And Louis hated not being able to get a freakin' cup of coffee.

The legs of the baggy orange jumpsuit swished when he resumed his pacing. Toilet to door and back. An amazing nine steps in either direction.

A groan issued from the top bunk across the room.

Springs squeaked as his burly cellmate propped himself up. "Man, will you just lay down? I'm trying to get some sleep."

Louis bristled. He added the sour smell of body odor to the list of things he hated. They obviously didn't offer showers on a regular basis in this place, either. "Shut your stupid face. I'm thinking, and I think better on my feet."

What he really hated, what chapped his butt more than all the rest, was Samantha and the kid. Every bit of this whole stinkin' thing could be laid at their feet. Louis kicked at the wall.

His roommate rolled over a second time. "I'm gonna rip your head off."

Louis rolled up onto the balls of his feet and motioned with his fingers. "Bring it."

The other man levered himself to the floor. He towered over Louis. "You got a death wish or something?"

Louis was too angry to care. He took a swing, and the bigger man grabbed his fist and squeezed. Louis's knees threatened to buckle under the painful pressure.

The door at the end of the hall whooshed open, admitting the guard. He strode down the hall and stopped in front of the cell. "Do we have a problem in here?"

The two men continued to stare at each other while the pressure on Louis's hand increased.

"If I have to open this door..."

The bigger man shoved Louis's fist aside and lumbered back to his bunk.

Louis took a step after him, coming to a stop at the cop's next words.

"Cantrell, you won't like it if I'm forced to restrain you."

Louis turned and forced a sarcastic smile to his face. "Just going to my bunk."

The guard crossed his arms. "Uh-huh." He pointed to a camera mounted above his head, then pointed into the cell. "You two better call it a draw and get some sleep. Breakfast comes early and you *will* be up to enjoy our fantastic cuisine."

Louis crawled into his bunk as the guard returned to his desk. "If I never see Sam or that kid again, it will be too soon."

Chick stood as the chaplain he'd requested entered the private interview room. The man held out his hand, and Chick took it in a hesitant grip. The old minister tucked a Bible under his arm and closed a second hand over his.

Chick found the contact oddly comforting. "Thanks for coming."

"No need for thanks."

Metal chairs scraped on the concrete floor as they took seats and faced each other from opposite sides of the table. The minister sat, placed his Bible on the table in front of him, and clasped his hands.

Chick's fingers beat out a nervous tattoo on the tabletop. *I need to talk to him, but what do I say? How do I start? I've been a really bad man.*

The older man leaned forward with a smile. "It's never easy, is it? I'll get us started, if that's OK with you."

Chick nodded.

"I'm Pastor Samuels, the on-call chaplain for the

Garfield Police Department. My given name is Ethan. I don't have a problem if you want to use it. You are...?"

"Chick Malone, You can call me Chick."

Ethan nodded. "Great. First names all around." He patted the table with his hands. "See, we're friends already. So, Chick, what can I do for you?"

"I'm in a lot of trouble."

"Is that why you had them call me?"

Chick swallowed. "No. I mean..." He stopped to motion to the room around them. "I guess you had that figured out from the get go." Heat seeped up his neck. This was his idea, why was it so hard? "I've done a lot of things I'm not very proud of."

"So have I."

"Yeah, well, but I've—"

Ethan raised a hand to stop him. "Chick, the Bible tells us that confession is good for the soul, but save that confession for God, not me." He patted the Bible. "It also says we've all sinned, and that Christ died to forgive those sins."

"All of them?"

He nodded. "Every last one. And you won't find a word in here that says murder is worse than a lie, not a single verse that claims adultery is a greater sin than...kidnapping."

Chick lowered his head at the minister's words.

"He died for all of them. No one's keeping a heavenly list, waiting for you to cross some line into unforgivable. If you're ready to ask for forgiveness, God's ready to forgive." He studied Chick. "Is that why you needed to see me?"

Chick tried to speak and failed. He cleared his throat and forced out a single word. "Yes."

Ethan stretched his hands across the table and took hold of Chick's. "Then let's pray."

An hour later, Chick sat on the side of his cot and fingered the Bible the chaplain had given him. The motion drew his eyes to his nails and the traces of ink lingering under them, in spite of numerous washings. Fingerprinted, photographed, stripped of his belongings, and treated to the worst meal he'd ever eaten, but Chick felt peace about his decision to own his mistakes.

He lowered his head to his hands. *How can that be?* "I'm looking at some serious jail time. And, if Carson ever decides jail isn't enough punishment for me, he can get someone in here to finish me."

I'll be with you.

Chick jerked his head up and looked around the ten-by-ten cell. No one lurked in the corners. He went back to his whispered introspection. "Even with good behavior, I'll be an old man when I get out." He thumped his forehead with the closed Bible. "I know I did the right thing, but I wish there'd been another way. I wish I'd been smarter."

No problem, pal. Once we get you settled, we're gonna study for that degree you were meant to have.

"What degree, I'm..." He stopped in mid-sentence. "I'm hearing things and talking to myself." Chick massaged his temples. "Whatever that kid has was contagious."

Chick, you're not crazy. What was the last thing Bobbie said to you?

Chick rubbed his arms as the hair there and on his neck stood to attention. He risked another look around as he tried to recall Bobbie's final words. He failed.

She said that you had an angel, too.

Christmas lights decorated the windows and lawns of almost every house Patrick passed between Sam's home and his. They reminded him that he hadn't purchased a single present. With the worry of the last couple of weeks and the stress of the last three days behind him, it was nice to have something relatively trivial to focus on. He mulled gift ideas as he drove.

Mom was easy: a gift card to the mall and the promise to go with her and buy lunch. He'd need gifts for his stepbrother and sister, Jeremy and Megan. And Sam.

A contented sigh filled the cab of the truck. Patrick could still taste their kiss on his lips. Her gifts would start with the ring she'd turned down last week. He didn't worry about being refused a second time. Bobbie would be the fun one to shop for. Christmas gift giving was more for the little ones, anyway. He'd have to get with Sam to make sure they didn't double up on something. Maybe they could go shopping together. It would be good practice for later, when they had kids of their own.

He braked at a stop sign. "Kids of our own?" Well, yeah. Down the road a ways, once Sam finished school. *I think I'd like at least two more.* Patrick put the thought into audible words. "A girl and maybe a boy to carry on the Wheeler name."

He accelerated and stared out the windshield as a light snow began to fall. His headlights lit the bits of ice like stars against the background of space, making him think of the sci-fi movies he liked so much. He shifted the truck into a higher gear. *Take us to warp six.*

"The Wheeler name?" Sam would take it when they married. Their children would have it by default, but Bobbie...? "I want Bobbie to be as much mine as they will be. I want her to share my name, be identified as my daughter. There's only one way that can happen."

Patrick pulled into the drive and killed the engine. An idea for the end-all and be-all of presents took shape in his mind. He could make it work. "But can I make it work between now and Christmas?"

CHAPTER TWENTY-NINE

Louis had sixty seconds, the time it took to walk from his cell to the interview room, to wonder who his visitor might be. He'd been in the Las Vegas County Jail for almost two weeks without a single friend coming to visit. The door opened. He took one step in and snarled. Samantha's loverboy sat in one of the two chairs at the small wooden table. His jeans and sweater were a stark contrast to Louis's uniform of the day...uniform of every dang day...the despised orange jumpsuit. Louis stopped just inside the door. "What are you doing here?"

The younger man looked up with a smile. "I came to ask you for a favor."

Louis snorted. "I'll bet. I've got nothing to give, wouldn't give it if I had it, so you're smooth out of luck." He turned to leave.

"Louis, I can help you."

The guard standing in the door frowned over his crossed arms. "Are you staying or not, Cantrell? I've got better things to do with my day."

Louis motioned him away. "Get lost. I'll talk to him."

The door clanked shut as Louis took the other chair. The men studied each other for several seconds. Louis sat back and crossed his arms. "Start talking. You can start with your name. We never got that far and, frankly, continuing to call you *loverboy* upsets my stomach."

"Loverboy?"

Louis shrugged.

The younger man stretched a hand across the table. "Patrick Wheeler."

The hand went ignored. "What do you want from me, Patrick Wheeler?"

Patrick pulled his hand back and slid a brown folder across the table. "Your signature on these documents."

"I left my reading glasses in my other shirt. Summarize it for me."

"Adoption papers. I plan to marry Samantha just as soon as she'll have me. I want Bobbie to be legally mine as well."

Louis scooted back from the table. "You're wasting your time. After the way they treated me. I wouldn't give either of them the sweat off my forehead if they were dying of thirst. Samantha and that kid can both go to—"

"I didn't come here empty handed."

Louis narrowed his eyes.

"You have a court date scheduled right after Christmas. Who's your lawyer?"

"Why, the best public defender money can buy, of course. Some little wet-behind-the-ears redhead out to save the world. She's three years younger than me." He leaned forward. "She's easy on the eyes, but not much of a lawyer. If it's possible to get life for grand larceny, she'll get it for me."

"How would you like to have a real lawyer in your corner?"

Louis stood up and patted the legs of the jumpsuit where pockets should have been. "Fresh out of dough, hero. What do you have in mind?"

Patrick tapped the folder. "You sign these papers for me, and in return, I've got a lawyer friend willing to call in some favors. He has a friend here, a seasoned criminal defense attorney willing to do some pro bono work. You're going to do time, Louis, but with him in your corner, you'll have a chance at a better deal." He offered a pen across the table. "Worth your signature?"

Samantha and Terri put the finishing touches on their Christmas Eve dinner table while Sam watched the clock. Kate was picking Patrick up from the airport and driving straight here.

"They should be here any time," Terri said.

Sam looked up with a grin. "That obvious?"

"Well, you've only looked at the clock five times in the last two minutes." The oven timer dinged, and Terri rushed back to the kitchen to pull a pan of fragrant yeast rolls out of the oven. "You still don't know where he went? Or why?"

"Nope. But it must have been important for him to travel on such short notice, in such nasty weather."

Terri wrapped a towel around the bowl to keep the rolls warm and handed it to Sam. She stopped to grab the salad out of the fridge. "I guess he'll tell us when—

"

The doorbell sounded, and Sam dropped the bowl onto the counter and raced for the front room. She opened the door and launched herself at Patrick. "I thought you'd never get here."

"I've only been gone two days."

"Felt longer." She grinned over his shoulder. "Hi, Kate."

Kate put her hand on Patrick's back and shoved the young couple out of the doorway. "In. You're letting out the heat."

Sam giggled as Patrick pulled her closer and sidestepped out of his mother's way. "Nice and warm here," she said, lifting her face for a proper hello kiss.

Kate shrugged out of her coat and tossed it over the nearest chair. She fanned imaginary heat from her face as she headed for the kitchen. "You two keep that up, we won't need the fireplace."

The family gathered around the table and the Christmas Eve feast. Samantha filled her plate. But instead of eating, she sat back for a moment of reflection. Dad and Terri murmured to each other as they prepared plates for Lilly and Seth. Iris looked across the table and winked at her. Sam winked back. Bringing Terri and their father together was one of the best things she and Iris had ever done. Kate helped with Bobbie as the four-year-old babbled about Santa's visit later that night.

Sam's eyes finally landed on Patrick, and her heart overflowed with gratitude. *Thank You, Father. You've answered so many prayers. I can't wait to see what happens next.*

Next came sooner than expected. Patrick stood up and cleared his throat to get everyone's attention. "I have some things I need to share." He pulled Sam up to stand next to him.

"First of all..." He stopped, pulled Samantha into his arms, and sent her senses reeling as he lowered his mouth to hers. When he ended the kiss, his eyes were as bright as she knew hers must be. He fumbled in his pocket and withdrew a small wrapped box. "I want you to open this now."

Sam took the box, too big to be the ring she expected, too small to be much of anything else. "What's this?"

"Just open it. While you do that, I'll explain where I was for the last two days."

Sam returned to her seat and began to unwrap the package.

"I flew out to Las Vegas to have a conversation with Louis Cantrell."

Her hands stilled and dropped to her lap. "Why would you do that? He's out of our life now, and good riddance."

Patrick dropped to one knee next to Sam's chair. "Go ahead and open your present. I promise, it's all good."

Sam studied his face and returned to her task.

Patrick continued his explanation. "Samantha, I want us to be a real family. You, me, and Bobbie. Maybe one or two more down the road, but there was only one real way to do that, and Louis had to agree."

The box finally came free of the wrapping and Sam lifted the top. She gasped. The ring was there, but there was a document rolled inside the sparkling silver band. She held it up. "Am I supposed to read this?"

Patrick took it from her and slipped off the ring. "In

a minute, but first things first." He focused his gaze on her face. "Samantha Evans, I love you. I thank God that you didn't give up on me. I want to build a life and a family with you. You turned me down a few weeks ago and said you hoped I'd ask again. I'm asking." He took her left hand in his. "Will you marry me?"

Samantha blinked tears from her eyes and nodded.

"Yes, Patrick. Nothing could make me happier than being Mrs. Patrick Wheeler."

Patrick slipped the ring on her finger to the sound of applause from the other family members gathered around the table. He leaned forward to brush her lips with his and handed her the rolled up document.

"Now you can read this."

Sam moved her plate out of the way and spread the document on the table. She read through the legalese, finally coming to the signatures at the bottom. Her gasp of surprise filled the room, and her hand covered her mouth. She raised her eyes. "Patrick?"

"Adoption papers, Sam. I went to see Louis to see if he'd sign his rights to Bobbie over to me. Once I offered him the proper incentive, he couldn't get his name on the paperwork fast enough. So, just as soon as we're married, we can start the process that will make the three of us a real family."

Samantha looked from her child to her fiancé. "Patrick, Samantha, and Bobbie Wheeler. Oh, I like the sound of that."

ABOUT THE AUTHOR

Sharon Srock went from science fiction to Christian fiction at slightly less than warp speed. Twenty five years ago, she cut her writer's teeth on Star Trek fiction. Today, she writes inspirational stories that focus on ordinary women and their extraordinary faith. Sharon lives in the middle of nowhere Oklahoma with her husband and three very large dogs. When she isn't writing you can find her cuddled up with a good book, baking something interesting in the kitchen, or exploring a beach on vacation. She hasn't quite figured out how to do all three at the same time.

Connect with her here:

Blog: http://www.sharonsrock.com

Facebook: http://www.facebook.com/SharonSrock#!/Sharon Srock

Goodreads: http://www.goodreads.com/author/show/64487 89.Sharon_Srock

Sign up for her quarterly newsletter from the blog or Facebook page.

CPSIA information can be obtained
at www.ICGtesting.com
Printed in the USA
LVOW12s0520110418
573050LV00002BA/216/P